FUNDED BY

PAL

PUTNAM ALACHUA LEVY
PUBLIC LIBRARY COOPERATIVE
NORTH CENTRAL FLORIDA

W9-CFQ-156

# THE
# CONFORMITY

# THE
# CONFORMITY

BOOK THREE IN THE TWELVE-FINGERED BOY TRILOGY

JOHN HORNOR JACOBS

Text copyright © 2015 by John Hornor Jacobs

Carolrhoda Lab™ is a trademark of Lerner Publishing Group, Inc.

All rights reserved. International copyright secured. No part of this book may be reproduced, stored in a retrieval system, or transmitted in any form or by any means—electronic, mechanical, photocopying, recording, or otherwise—without the prior written permission of Lerner Publishing Group, Inc., except for the inclusion of brief quotations in an acknowledged review.

Carolrhoda Lab™
An imprint of Carolrhoda Books
A division of Lerner Publishing Group, Inc.
241 First Avenue North
Minneapolis, MN 55401 U.S.A.

For reading levels and more information, look up this title at www.lernerbooks.com.

Cover design: © Lerner Publishing Group, Inc.
Illustrations of silhouettes: © iStockphoto.com/syntik.

Main body text set in Janson Text Lt Std 11/15.
Typeface provided by Linotype AG.

Library of Congress Cataloging-in-Publication Data

Jacobs, John Hornor.
The Conformity / by John Hornor Jacobs.
pages  cm. — (The Twelve-Fingered Boy trilogy)
Summary: "Shreve, along with Jack and his girlfriend Ember, travel to Maryland to solve the mystery behind "the elder," the ancient, malevolent force hidden near Baltimore, which has been sending psychic tremors out into the world causing mayhem, mass suicides, and the beginning of the end of civilization."
— Provided by publisher.
ISBN 978-0-7613-9009-1 (trade hard cover : alk. paper) —
ISBN 978-1-4677-6182-6 (EB pdf)
[1. Supernatural—Fiction.]  I. Title.
PZ7.J152427Co  2015
[Fic]—dc23                                                    2013028517

Manufactured in the United States of America
1 – BP – 12/31/14

FOR GEORGE PAUL

# PART ONE:
# FALLING APART, COMING TOGETHER

"A prison becomes a home when you have the key."

—George Sterling

"If one wishes to remain an individual in the midst of the teeming multitudes, one must make oneself grotesque."

—Salman Rushdie, *Midnight's Children*

## ONE

The sound, when it comes, is hard to take in all at once. It's too big for immediate comprehension. At first it's just the blaring sound of the Klaxons beating in the arteries of air, rising and falling in ear-rupturing waves, but then, layered above it, there's the moan that's more than a moan and more than a scream. It's the cacophonous groans of thousands of human mouths, straining. Agonized. It's the sound of misery. It affects me at a root level. I sit bolt upright in bed, shocked. My nuts draw up, my skin crawls, and my heart begins hammering in my chest like my rib cage is a penitentiary and it's gonna bust out, *incarcerado* no more, and start boogying down the highway.

The rib cage holds, but the heart keeps hammering.

Jack pops up from his bed—always the first to rise—with Tap right on his ass. They both rush over to the dorm window and peer out into the half-light of pre-sun morning.

"Holy shit," Jack says, and then immediately dashes over to grab his trousers. Somehow he tugs on boots as he's standing. I'm up and dressed and slipping on running shoes when Tap, still at the window, barks, "The Conformity! One of those walkers—" and yanks open the dormer window, letting a blast of frigid air into the room. He steps up onto the ledge and launches himself into the air. Jack, dressed, climbs up to stand on the wide stone casement.

Jack and I can't fly tandem yet, so I race to the dorm room door and yank it open. I feel more than see Jack lifting off into the air with a pulse. He arcs across the sky.

*Soldiers! They're in the valley!* he sends in a strange mental yawp to the Irregulars, exultant and fearful.

*On my way to the armory,* Danielle sends back, her mental voice cold and hard as steel.

*Casey? Where are you?* I ask.

*Heading up the trail toward the water tower.*

*Right,* I respond. *I'm coming.*

*I'm hustling, man-child,* Bernard sends. *I'm hustling. Here's a pick-me-up,* he says, and then there's a quick flurry of mental beats and staccato images and my body floods with energy, my muscles thrum, and I feel as though I could out-race the sun. The cold is pushed away. I'm warm now, like I've swallowed batteries and there's some unknown dynamo ripping a relentless rhythm in my belly.

*Wow,* Casey sends. *My hair's standing on end.*

*The crash, though, when it comes, is really gonna be a bitch,* Bernard adds.

I carom down the hall, past the surprised looks of other half-clad extranatural boys—most of us bugfuck non-flyers—down the stairs, and burst through the double doors and outside into the half-light of morning. The freezing air is now just an afterthought. Last week's snow is still clinging to the ground and piled in drifts along pathways, roads, campus sidewalks. My breath comes as vapor before my face.

I can't see it yet. The sirens are like a thin poison in the air, reminding me of the Helmholtz. It's hard to think with the rising and falling of the sound. But then it dies.

And the moaning, the screaming comes. Thousands upon thousands of mouths, groaning in agony. It's like an ambulatory circle of Hell.

There's a crack and then another, the hard sounds of timber shattering. The booms of trees falling. And moaning.

I run, arms pumping, across the valley. With Bernard's beat, the electric tempo running in my blood, I could outrun a leopard, leap over a bus. Eating the distance, feet pounding on pavement, on dirt.

A Jeep slews on the gravel path, carrying three Army soldiers, one of them Sergeant Davies. He spies me and double-takes, giving me an oh-shit-I-don't-want-to-fuck-with-this-kid-but-I'll-get-canned-if-I-don't look that the Army guys get now that they're pointing the guns outward, rather than inward *at* extranaturals. He motions for the driver to stop while the rear man hefts an M14 with grenade launcher and scans the skies. It's a tremendous weapon, but he doesn't look reassured because the sirens are screaming again and the cracks of falling trees split the air—like Godzilla himself is approaching.

"Don't you look excited, Li'l Devil," Davies says as I pull myself into the back of the Jeep.

"Bright-eyed and bushy-tailed. I need to get to the water tower."

He nods, looking grave. "That's close to Bunker H. We'll escort you there and then collect the Director."

I didn't know that's where Priest lurked at night, but it makes sense. He asks Jack and me to attend training briefings often nowadays—a bit of organization we never had from Quincrux—but we don't have a bridge club or play tiddlywinks or do whatever the hell they used to do for fun back when he was born, however many lifetimes ago. Biggest hobbies back then were crucifying Christians and toga parties, maybe. Who knows?

"And engineering?" I ask. "Any word? Without enough power, the Helmholtz won't have the juice to drop the soldier."

"None yet, but most of the power lines are underground so they won't be—" His radio squelches, and a string of muddy sounds comes from it, words only soldiers can understand, apparently. He squeezes the transmitter and says, "Roger that," then turns to me and says, "Teams are aloft," precisely at the moment when five red blurs cross the sky immediately above us. The Red Team, heavy with armament.

Davies shoves an oversized military walkie-talkie into my hand. "You'll need it."

"Letsgoletsgoletsgo," the driver says in the rapid-fire way I've come to expect more from war movies than from everyday life, but what can you do? World's gone to shit. We're just the pieces of corn making it more colorful before the end swirl down the toilet.

The Jeep surges to life, spinning wheels and tossing gravel into the trees behind us. When the water tower comes into view, they slow long enough for me to hop out. Normally I would have face-planted in the gravel, but Bernard's beat still thrums in my body and I only stumble a little, catching myself with a burst of speed up the rise and past the razor wire. A small silhouette waves at me from the top of the tower—Casey. She's already had time to climb or lift herself to the summit. She stands next to the fat antenna array of the souped-up Helmholtz field transmitter.

*Give me your hand,* she sends, *and I'll pull you up.*

*It's three hundred feet!*

*No, it's just like climbing on top of a van. Give me your hand, bucko.*

She's manipulating her perception to manipulate her talent. How long will it be until she can find a man's heart from a mile away and squeeze the life out of him? Would Quincrux have made her his assassin? I think that's very much what he would've done.

Casey's silhouette kneels—backlit by the sun now peeking over the eastern rim of mountains—and grabs hold of some metal framing with her single visible arm to steady herself. I reach up and feel her invisible hand clasping mine tightly. It's like stone covered in a thin layer of memory foam, and suddenly I find myself being pulled upward, alarmingly fast, up and up.

Casey grunts when I get right to the edge and leans back, hard, to get me over the metalwork railing at the top. There's more ice and snow up here, making footing treacherous. The wind is ungodly strong, pulling at my hair, my clothing.

When my body flops over, she falls backward onto her ass, breathing hard. Even with her magic arm, her body still feels the strain and stress of lifting. And that couldn't have been easy.

"You've got to lay off the lasagna, Shreve," she says, and I laugh because we both know I need to do just the opposite.

She rises, a strange movement almost akin to levitation. More and more, Casey's able to disassociate her phantom limb from her body. As long as she can think of different ways to perceive her arm, or distance, her power will keep growing.

From this vantage, the whole valley lies spread out before us—white and black and gray, wintery and stark—and we're looking straight down the bore of the mountains. The siren's wail falls away, and the Conformity soldier's polyphonic moans rise. Groaning. Creaking. Gibbering. Wailing.

More trees crack and pitch over, the crashes reverberating up the valley toward us.

The Conformity soldier hoves into view—a big-ass walker, not the round, flesh-star–like thing that formed in the air above Towson, but something it shat out mirroring the shape of humankind. The Conformity itself has grown too large, floating the skies like a swollen tick engorged with blood. It calves off parts of itself to roam the cities, sucking up humanity into its massive flesh. Two legs, two arms, a head, formed of countless subsumed people and going walkabout. A mockery, really, of the bifurcated man.

This one, the one that's bellowing and steaming into the Montana air, is twenty thousand bodies strong if it's a single one. A city on the hoof. Thousands of people stitched together by some massive and unknown telekinetic power, binding and fusing them so that they comprise the form of one gargantuan humanoid. As tall as this water tower, the monstrosity raises a leg slowly, steps forward, booming. Vapors pour from it. Even from this distance, I can tell it's warm—as warm as humans are, and churning with its own juices.

Another step, another soft *boom*. As it raises its leg once more, the bloody ruin of human bodies remains like a footprint behind it.

The walkie-talkie hisses and erupts with distorted talking. "—Team keeping position on target. Red Team keeping position." Blackwell's voice, deep, aggressive.

"Red Team, open fire. I repeat, open fire. By the numbers, if you please." It sounds like Tanzer, her curt, officious voice.

"Keep between it and the water tower and generators."

"Copy that."

The chatter and pop of gunfire echo up the valley, a small, tinny noise in comparison to the vast soundscapes of anguish the soldier makes across the frozen landscape.

Flyers are visible in the air now, two clusters of extranaturals making quick maneuvers past the lurching Conformity soldier.

*Jack, where are you?*

One of the flyers—a black dot in the sky—peels away and grows larger.

*Red Team's initiating delaying tactics, buzzing the damned thing to lead it to you. They're about to take out its legs and—holy shit, man!*

There's another tremendous sound echoing in the vault of heaven, and part of the mountain rumbles. Casey and I look away from the Conformity soldier toward the sound.

In the V made by the meeting of two mountains behind us stands another Conformity soldier.

## TWO

They say that if you overplan a bank heist and something goes wrong, not only are you going to lose the loot, somebody's going to die. The key is to plan just enough that everyone knows the process, but not so much that if something unexpected comes along everyone freezes, shocked into inaction while they try to figure out how to deal with the change.

We scripted the *fuck* out of a possible assault.

Here's the deal: a soldier comes in from either end of the valley, because of course a soldier would come in at the valley ends and not *over mountains*. That's the way a person would walk, right? And they look like people, don't they? So, according to plan, the monstrosity toddles upstream and the Green and Red teams delay it with armaments—M14s with grenade launchers, RPGs, the big-gun extranatural powers. They draw its attention away from the buildings and airfield long enough for all the noncombatant extranaturals to get in bunkers.

The soldier is distracted by the teams. Swatting at flies.

Once it's near enough to the water tower, we hit it with the Helmholtz. Some of the Nerd Turlingtons in R&D said they had a way to boost the field strength in a tight area so that we could isolate the Conformity soldier in the field but still have our combatants—namely the Green and Red Teams—outside of it, still flying and not falling to a messy death. It's just a matter of pointing the array at the soldier. Somehow, that job fell to Casey and me. Danielle, Tap, and Jack are assigned to team support and communications. Bernard reports to engineering.

All teams are redundant. All teams are autonomous. Everything goes according to plan, no worries. Everything goes horribly pear-shaped? Well, there'll be extra folks on hand to take care of bidness.

Why don't we just hit the Conformity soldier with missiles?

Because it's made of people. Like Soylent Green, except not as tasty.

But *made of people. Human beings.* Friends, maybe. *Family.* We'll have to do some damage to the Conformity, but we have to try to save the people caught up in the mass, the towering city of flesh.

They may be gone forever.

But we must try.

...

We first saw the soldiers in one of the planning sessions Priest held with Davies, Negata, Tanzer, Blackwell, Solomon (Green Team captain), and various other nerds and lab coats present in the big conference room in Admin. Priest—still wearing the body of Hiram Quincrux—passed a weary hand over his eyes and said, "The Conformity has awoken. It gathers strength, taking more and more of humanity unto itself. It demands worship. And sacrifice. Miss Tanzer, if you'd be so kind."

Tanzer placed the briefcase on the study desk and popped the latches. Inside was a laptop. Quincrux's computer. She opened it and jabbed at the keyboard, entering the passwords for access. A video began to play.

"This was taken yesterday over Annapolis," Tanzer said. On the screen, the Conformity hung in the sky like some gargantuan airborne parasite, dark and mottled. Its scale was hard to fathom, though the skyline gave some point of reference—it might have been a mile or more in diameter. "Our best guess is that it's subsumed at least half a million people."

Jack shivered. I felt like I was going to vomit.

"They're still alive?" Jack asked.

"As far as we can tell. Its temperature holds steady at 98.6 degrees."

My gorge rose.

"Here's the worst part," she said.

The Conformity distended, growing ovoid, lengthening. It pulsed.

"What's happening?" Blackwell asked.

"Watch."

A faint line of demarcation appeared on the surface of the hideous thing. It began to split.

"I've turned off the sound so you don't have to hear the—" She wiped her hands on her pants. "—screams. But it appears to be going through a form of cellular mitosis. It is dividing."

"Oh, God," Blackwell said, his words coming out choked. He stood by Solomon, all the color drained from his face. I vaguely remembered him wearing an Orioles T-shirt once in the dorms.

"Unfortunately," Priest said, "this is not all. Miss Tanzer, please show them the video of the 'Conformity soldier,' if you will."

She opened another file, and a new video filled the screen. "This was taken from a security cam in Philadelphia."

The view was of a long city street, lined with buildings. Something massive lurched across the screen, passed out of view. Then it lurched on-screen again.

Roughly of human shape, it towered over the nearest buildings.

"We're calling them soldiers. They operate independently of the Conformity, but they're definitely in communication with it."

"Telepathically?"

Priest looked at me sharply. "Yes."

It felt colder in there, just talking about the thing. For a moment, an image of millions of sightless eyes and soundlessly screaming mouths flashed in my mind. A melding of flesh and agony. Then it was gone.

A walking tower of flesh. Not as large as the Conformity itself, but huge. As it staggered down the street, windows broke outward, shattering glass in a wave front. Bodies of fresh humans floated toward it, caught up in some telekinetic field, adding to its mass.

"What's its area of effect?" Jack asked.

"For the two Conformities, many, many miles." A pained expression passed his features. "A large percent of the eastern seaboard is now under its sway. Due to what happened to the jet during Hiram's ill-advised mission, all air travel has been grounded except in the most dire circumstances."

I gnawed my lip. Ever since Booth's death, I couldn't think of much except finding Vig, dreaming of ways to bring him here, maybe. Keep him safe. For the moment Jack was good here; I needed to go back to my brother. In a weak moment, I'd given in to my urges and taken Vig's location from Tanzer's mind, and I didn't think she'd noticed. But Atlanta was four thousand miles away. Once again, I would need to steal a car.

As the session ended and the others filed out, Priest looked at Jack and me. "Please, you two, sit back down. I wanted to speak to you. I would like to apologize for all of the hardships you have endured."

"Why?" Jack asked. "It's not your fault."

"I'm afraid some of it is. Hiram was my student, and it seems it fell to you two to bear the brunt of some of his—" He searched for the word. "Enthusiasms."

"He was an enthusiastic sonofabitch," I said.

A small laugh escaped from Jack, and I wondered if Armstead Lucius Priest was well-versed enough in bitterness to hear it in that sound. Priest bobbed his head in understanding, but I wondered.

"In penance for some of my past sins, I offer to answer any questions you might have, in hopes of getting you to commit fully to our cause."

"Why?" It was strange—I kept expecting this man to cock his head, stare at me with dead eyes, Quincrux once more. Getting to know someone is just a set of expectations. His mannerisms, the ease of his smile, the way he held his body, the shadow of unshaven beard on his jaw told me this was not the man he once was.

"It is my wish that you remain here with us. I need you to be an active part of the planning. You have a special sensitivity to the Conformity. You have the abilities and strengths of Hiram Quincrux, but without the cruelty. I need you . . . how do they say it these days?" He smiled, sadly. "I need you on board. As if this endeavor were some sort of dinghy."

"What I'm concerned about is my brother," I said, standing and walking nearer to Priest. "I could take a Jeep. I need to get him, bring him here."

Priest's face grew still. He bowed his head, pursed his lips, thinking. "Shreve, this thing, this dark movement toward conformity that the entity possesses—it is my fault it is here." His voice sounded raw. I realized that, whoever this guy was, the body he wore had been thrown across the testing room and into a bank of plasma screens just a few days prior. He had to be sore all over.

"I was proud. Overconfident. I was the strongest mind of many generations, and I abandoned my body to fly to unknown planes and far-off etheric heights, only to return to discover myself unseated from my body." He trembled with real terror. His willingness to show his vulnerability was frightening in and of itself. On the inside, you show vulnerability, you're meat. "While I was out in my arrogant pursuits, I left the perfect vessel to be filled. The greater the mind, the greater the void when that mind is absent. And the void calls. The void wants to be filled."

"So, while you were slipping out, something else was slipping in."

He nodded. "You understand me."

"What does this have to do with my brother?"

Priest reached for the computer, opened another video file. The screen filled with light. A backyard, somewhere in America. A familiar backyard, wooden fence, trees showing over the top. I'd seen this one before, when I first came here to the Society of Extranaturals and Quincrux stuffed me in a hole in the ground and showed me videos of Vig being beaten. That video was the leash that kept this mongrel dog from jumping the fence and going feral once more.

"I'm so sorry, Shreve," Priest said.

Two boys stood in the yard, looking up into the sky. A shadow fell over them. One turned, a horrified look on his face, mouth opened in a scream of terror. The other thrashed, twisting, as some invisible hand took him in its grip and lifted them both from the ground.

A walking tower of human flesh appeared above the tree line. My brother and his foster brother rose into the air to join it.

Jack put his hand on my shoulder. I hadn't even known he was standing by me.

"So, Shreve," Priest said, very distinctly. "I need you to be present, here. To commit to us, without reservation."

I thought I knew desolation. I thought I knew grief. There was nothing for me then. Nothing except saving Vig. My heart throbbed in my chest. My tongue tasted of ashes and ruin.

It took a while before I could speak again.

"Answer a question for me," I said.

"Anything you wish, Shreve."

"When you were a Rider—" I said, wiping the tears from my eyes. I tapped my temple. "When you were riding around in people, you kept telling me to go to Maryland. I don't get why."

Priest's face stiffened, like someone had just pricked a long pigsticker into his belly.

"Certain minds are like beacons, Shreve," he said through bloodless lips. "You have seen them, have you not?"

I thought of all the people I've known, both in real life and in the twilight of the shibboleth. The match flames of minds. Some blazed bright. Some shone dull. But some incandesced beyond all imagining. "Yes."

"Of all the humans I've ever encountered, the brightest, the most luminescent, the most brilliant consciousness I've ever known was Hiram Quincrux." He raised his index finger. "Save one."

"One?"

He smiled again, but it was forced. The finger lowered and pointed directly at me.

"What are you saying?"

"You think Hiram gave you this terrible gift? He did not. He only awakened it."

I tried to digest that, but it was all too much. "That doesn't change anything," I said. "Why did you tell me to go to Maryland?"

In the fluorescent light of the Admin conference room, his face—once Quincrux's loathed visage—looked ashen and wan. "I thought you would draw it out," he said simply. "If not you, then Quincrux, who pursued you so closely."

Another bomb. The guy was just full of them.

I laughed. It was too funny. For a long while, I couldn't breathe I was laughing so hard. "I was bait! I knew you were too good to be true. You were going to use me as bait!"

"We are at war," Priest spat. He'd lost his composure at last. And there you go. I hadn't lost it. I could still get under the skin of the best of them. "I thought if I could draw the entity out by presenting it with something as bright and full of life as you, I could reseat myself in my own flesh and then contend with the monster."

"Bait," I said, shaking my head in wonder at it all. "Hey, Jack?"

"Yeah."

"Meet the new boss," I said. "Same as the old one."

"Shreve—" Priest rose, clutching his cane. He took two weak steps toward me.

"No. It's okay. I just like to know who I'm dealing with. And now I know."

Priest remained silent for a long while, thoughts churning at his features. "So you will stay? You will help me defeat this thing?"

Not for you, asshole. For my brother.

## THREE

The second Conformity soldier bellows with its multitude of mouths, a foghorn ululation that makes my skin prickle. It lumbers up and over the meeting of mountains, framed for an instant in a sky pink with the rising sun, and pounds down the slope, brushing trees away with mighty sweeps of its multi-formed arms.

*It's coming for us!* I send.

*We didn't plan for two soldiers!* Danielle says in my mind, and I get a visual flash she's projecting of the first Conformity soldier swinging its massive arm in a slow arc, the details of its "skin" coming into focus, hundreds upon thousands of people gripping each other tightly, running with the fluids and excrescence of humankind, straining against one another, mouths open in screams and moans, eyes wide in terror.

The stench of it assaults me through Danielle.

Then the sensation is gone.

Bernard sends, *I'm at the manual trigger down by the generator, man-child. Where's the Director at? Ain't he supposed to be here by now?*

I ignore that and lift the walkie-talkie Davies gave me before I ascended the tower.

"Uh, Red and Green Teams, we have a second soldier." I try to keep the terror from my voice. "And the bastard is right by the water tower. Split up the teams! Red Team, *intercept the soldier nearest the tower!*"

"Negative," the walkie-talkie burps. "Negative, we have orders from the Director to engage the soldier approaching from the south. I repeat, we have orders to engage the soldier approaching from the south."

"I could give a shit if you're following orders! We need help here! Soon!" I race over to the Helmholtz array and begin tugging at it to turn the focal lens thingamabob just like the R&D guys trained us. It squeals in protest.

*Here,* Casey sends, *let me help.* She doesn't move, but the array squeals louder, trailing the power cables that snake away from it and run down to the generators on the ground, so far below. It's taking far too long to turn the Helmholtz array. Far, far too long.

The radio squelches again. Hissing. And then, "This is Director Priest. I repeat, this is Director Priest. En route to water tower with reinforcements. Until that time, Shreve Cannon is in charge. Follow his orders until we're in situ. I repeat, follow Shreve's orders until we're in situ."

Hissing.

"Roger that," says Solomon, indifferent.

"Copy," says Blackwell. That isn't sitting well with him. The world's ending, and he's worried about his dick getting snipped a couple of inches.

"Red Team," I yell, pressing down the transmitter. "NOW! Move to intercept!"

The Conformity soldier slumps forward, a half mile away now, moving faster than you'd think a walking tower of naked screaming people could move. It doesn't even have feet, just flat bloody truncations that resemble an elephant's feet, but they get the job done. Each of its steps hits with a *boom*, and I can feel the percussive impact of the footfalls reverberating like shockwaves down the mountainside, up the metal struts of the water tower. The tower shakes and groans, almost in answer to the soldier's terrible call.

My stomach turns, my bowels begin to loosen I'm so scared. The thing grows.

I inhale the stench of it. The smell, like the noise of its thousands of mouths, is a multilayered thing, reeking of all the terrible fluids of mankind—blood, sweat, tears, shit, semen, pus. My nostrils burn and my eyes water. On the metal structure, I fall to my knees and a thin, sickly stream of yellow bile pours from my mouth.

*Shreve!* From Casey. *We need you, no time for partying!* I feel a massive hand steadying me, gentle but inexorable. I rise and stand. *Turn the array to face the soldier!*

The Conformity is almost upon us. We're looking up into its chest, and I can see with my own eyes the individual screaming faces of the subsumed, the nude torsos and arms straining, each one sheened in goo and grime. It's a window into Hell. And I'm no praying man.

*And I thought conformity was just a bunch of dicks dressing alike,* Tap sends. *Mean girls at school.*

*Shut up!* Danielle sends. There's a quick image of her whipping forward on currents of air, gun in hand. Then it's gone.

The torso fills our field of vision, tremendous and ever-expanding.

Thousands of people, many thousands coming toward us in a wall of flesh.

The arm rises.

I'm raising the walkie-talkie to my mouth to scream again for Red Team to get their asses over here when something streaks into my line of sight like a falling arrow, fast and deadly.

*I got you, **man,*** Jack sends. I get a distinct impression of him extending his hands, fingers splayed wide, and giving a massive burst.

The Conformity soldier's arm distends and expands in a widening shockwave of impact. The messy end of it—what we'd think of as a hand but really just a mad jumble of human bodies—shudders and falls away, the poor souls loosed from the hideous gravity that held them in mockery of the human form. Their bodies wheel and pitch overhead, falling.

Falling.

The Conformity soldier rears backward, and now I can hear the chatter of gunfire again. All of the people comprising the thing turn their faces, each individual head swiveling on a gimballed neck, and fix their countless gazes upon me. The multitude of mouths open.

*ONE WITH US.*

It's speaking. Such a heinous sound.

I feel a tugging in my guts, as if all gravity is gone and I'm falling, weightless. It's the telekinetic force of the soldier trying to draw me in, to subsume me within its captive population. I fight. I squirm. I flee my body, the shibboleth shimmering and wild within me, and I move into the ether to find some way to stop the monstrous thing.

In the ether, it appears as an incandescent tower of flame, each individual that makes up its form a burning mote, a human molecule, part of the greater whole. I move around the thing, probing with my shibboleth self, bodiless, a ravenous ghost, desperate.

It's a pillar of flame and pure force. It's incomprehensible, its power—the raw telekinetic power that holds so many humans in thrall, the telepathic power that controls each bit of it in turn. And there . . .

There!

I see a golden filament, beaten thin as ghostly wire, streaking off into the east. It's the puppet's string. It's the connection to the Conformity itself. Coming not from the "head" but from the crotch.

Figures.

I flee back to my body.

*WORSHIP US. SERVE US.*

It's hard to make out the words that the mouths chant. Other half-understood phrases are mixed in with the chthonic sounds, and I catch *servire* and *adorate*. My consciousness reels, and I feel like I did when the cacophony of minds at Casimir came crashing down in a collapsing event horizon. Right before they sent me to the nuthouse.

It's the sensation of incipient madness. The visage of this horrible thing, this walking monster, tries my sanity, and I feel all the languages of the world burning on my tongue once more like embers.

**Screw that noise,** Bernard sends. **That Helmholtz array in position, man-child?**

I steady myself. The metal squealing ceases, and the array points like a shotgun barrel right at the torso of the ungodly thing.

I yell into the walkie and send simultaneously, "Juice it, Bernard! Juice it!"

*Comin' up, my man!* Something begins to hum, and the ether begins to seethe and skitter.

The Conformity soldier erupts.

## FOUR

Whatever cohesion holds the thing together loosens at the area where we point the Helmholtz array—it is, after all, a field that negates telekinetic and telepathic powers—and the speed with which the mass of humanity begins to erode is terrifying. It's an avalanche of shrieking, falling people, plummeting to their deaths.

I catch a glimpse of one face, so near to me, a woman's face, skin smeared with reddish-brown, viscous fluid, her hair in a wild clotted mess, eyes wide in absolute terror, mouth open in the shape of a bell. Just a fleeting image burned into my retinas and then gone and others are falling, a demented jumble of whirling bodies and the spray of septic fluid now landing on us in fine droplets.

The water tower shudders and reverberates like a gong being struck as the bodies land near us with horrifying wet thumps. They slide away down the slope of the water tower surface, leaving bloody streaks.

*Shut it off! Bernard! Shut it off!*

The Conformity soldier teeters, sways.

"Shut off the juice, Bernard!" I bark into the microphone so that all the teams might hear.

The ether hiccups and begins boiling once more, then falters and dies.

The soldier groans and swings an arm out, drawing it back to swipe me, Casey, the Helmholtz array clear of the tower's summit.

There's a chatter of gunfire, and I whip my head around in time to see three red blurs arcing across my field of vision.

I can't be bothered with the walkie-talkie anymore. Half-divesting myself from my body, I go far enough into the ether to take in all the burning motes of light—the incendiary souls of extranaturals wheeling about the huge column of equally bright Conformity subsumed—and project with my mind, the shibboleth white-hot and burning inside me, *Aim for the shoulders! Aim for the feet! Drop the damned thing!*

*I've got the legs!* Jack sends.

*We've got your back,* someone responds, and suddenly I'm aware of the mental presence of Ember. *Red Team is with you.* There are crimson blurs in the sky, lancing downward.

Have I given this telepathy to everyone now, with my shout?

There's a hollow thud next to me as Tap lands, holding a massive automatic rifle. His nose streams crimson.

"Hold off on the fucking volume, would you, Shreve?" He chucks another round into the launcher and sights on the soldier, which now bringing its arm forward. He gives a quick glance at Casey, whose nose also pours blood.

Tap manhandles the weapon. *Thwup! Kachunk. Thwup!* The sound of grenades being launched. They make bloody craters in the conglomerated flesh of the soldier and explode with dull chuffs. Three members of the Red Team whiz by, blazingly fast, and I hear more chuffs of launchers, watch the wet, red impacts they make in the morass of walking flesh.

The soldier's arm stops its forward movement as the small city swinging toward us on the tower is severed from the main body of the beast. Hundreds of people, freed now from the telekinetic form, go flying, the momentum of their passage hurling them directly at us.

Thoughts flicker like lightning between us.

*Casey, I've got you!* Tap moves quicker than you'd think; two long steps and he's grabbing her around the waist and launching himself into the air.

*No!* she sends. *Shreve's on the tower—*

My mind is barraged with images coming from Jack—hands out, pulsing—quick glimpses of Ember, Blackwell, Galine, and the rest of the Red Team flying in formation, launching grenades, chucking rocks at the Conformity soldier's legs, using glamours and wardings to slow the teeming thing's approach, great heaving impacts that send groaning shudders through the creature.

I duck as the body of some poor soul wings its way past me in a fleshy smudge, spattering my face with something wet and distinctly human. The stench is horrific.

The soldier lurches forward, filling all the sky. It yawns over me, thousands of mouths screaming *JOIN US* in every language known to humankind. Its shadow falls over me and suddenly the tower shakes, lurches as the torso of the soldier crashes into it, human bodies spilling away from its central mass like some protoplasmic fluid, rushing toward me.

Things fall apart.

The tower falls.

I fall with it.

## FIVE

I've fallen before, and there's release with the plummet, like a kite with its string cut. Except that I never seem to fall up. Time congeals in freefall. Our monkey brain doesn't know how to deal with the reality of imminent death, so it enters into a stilled brain-time where events play out like film in extreme slow motion, the mind races so fast. There's a frisson between how fast consciousness moves and the seeming slowness of the world it perceives.

And I have time now, enough time for memory in the plummet. Jack cannot save me. Tap and Casey are gone with the rest of the Irregulars, locked in the lethargy of the real world. Beautiful Danielle, hair an inkstroke behind her. I'm beyond all of that now.

Now I have time to think of days gone by, of warm summers when all the world was new and two brothers sat together in a field, brilliant with light and teeming with dancing motes rising into the air. A field. Heat. The smack of a (stolen) baseball into a (secondhand) glove.

Time to remember the press of flesh, the warm mouth of love, sharp with sugar and cinnamon and fluoride as Coco's tongue finds mine (her father would kick my ass).

Time enough to flip lazily, suspended in thick opaline air, the truck out of control and tumbling, crunching, shattering. The truck I'd stolen earlier, a million beads of blood filling the air and slowing to a crawl in their bestilled trajectories.

Time to remember Booth, my friend, the smell of the man, the warmth of his smile and the humor of his enmity as he takes me in a bear hug.

There's all the time in the world.

Time enough for my monkey brain to give one last mortal spasm and cast the dice.

Time enough to leave my body and touch the minds of all those surrounding me. Time enough to know Jack once more, and Bernard—thrumming with rhythm. To feel the craggy contours of Tap's recalcitrant mind, the sharp steel of Danielle. The strength of Casey. Time enough to touch Ember and Blackwell and Solomon and Galine and Chakrabarti and Holden and everyone else.

Time enough to take their light to me, like some wheeling astronaut gathering up stars.

Time enough for the shibboleth to thrum within me.

And expand.

■■■

I rise.

Cruciform, I rise.

I've done this before, taking the power of others, their extranatural abilities. But it's different this time, I know. Something of it lives within me.

I am an arrow, stilled in flight.

I rise, and the clamor of their minds is a din I cannot put aside. Surprise, fear, hatred, disgust—all these emotions churn and roil in the ether like noxious vapors pouring off each mind.

I open my eyes.

···

It has all snapped back to speed and the water tower crashes to the ground below me with a cacophonous din, raw and thunderous and echoing, blotting out all other sensations for a moment. Sight dims, the feel of wind and cold, the smell of the dead and the still-living—all of it fades as the sound of the crashing water tower erupts and rises in a shock wave.

The Conformity soldier falls too—Jack and the Red Team have done their work, taking out its legs—so that when the blasted thing hits, it spreads like oil, bodies thick and greased and wet spilling out over the land in a bloody slick.

I inhabit two worlds now, the world of the flesh, the meatspace, and the world of ether, of incandescent light, souls like embers, souls like match flames.

The lights of thousands flicker and die.

The soldier is no more.

My eyes burn, sightless and unblinking. Tears hot and steady pour from me.

I can only sob with the darkness.

## SIX

*Shreve! The other soldier, it's coming!*

I tear my gaze away from the blood-grimed wreckage of the Conformity soldier. It's hard to bear, that amount of death.

Flight is new to me, and for a moment I wish for the monkey-brained slow-time imminent death had gifted me, so I could exult in the new sensations on my own terms.

Incarcerado no more.

But there's too much ruin to feel joy.

Blackwell, accompanied by Ember and Galine, come to hover near me, noses streaming blood. Seems I had the volume up to eleven.

They stare at me in wonder. Ember, wind altitude ruffling her hair, moves closer, reaches out to touch my shoulder, wide-eyed and unbelieving. "How can you—"

*I am you and you are me,* I send, and she starts. I have a near uncontrollable urge to giggle. *Though we always disagree.*

"How the hell can you do that? It's incredible!" Blackwell's shouting. I get the feeling he shouts a lot. He looks distracted, though. He touches the receiver in his ear. "Roger that." He grimaces, looking down at the remains of the Conformity soldier below us. "The Director says we're to fall back to Bunker H. All Society personnel are safe, blast doors locked. We fall back so we don't kill all the poor motherfuckers in that damned—"

He points. The first soldier, the one that set off the alarms and roused us all, slouches toward us, coming up the valley, sundering trees with great creaks and crashes and booms.

*Right. Enough people have died today,* I send.

Jack appears beside me, hands out, keeping aloft on a flurry of micro-bursts.

"Holy shit, man. Holy shit—"

"Right, bud. I'm flying."

"How'd you work that?"

"The shibboleth."

"What?"

Oh, I've never told him about it.

"It's the password, Jack. This thing we all share."

"This isn't a Starbucks. What the fuck, Shreve?"

Ember laughs but keeps her gaze locked on me.

"The devil got his angel wings," Galine says, her mouth twisted into an inscrutable sneer. It could be directed at me or directed at herself. I don't know. I do know she'll never forgive me for the first time I hijacked her extranatural ability.

Tap is with us now, making circles around us floaters because, like a shark, his talent doesn't tolerate stillness or rest. "Get your asses in gear. The Director—"

*Shreve.* His voice is cool, cold even. Armstead Lucius Priest speaks directly into my mind. *Please get them back to the bunker, posthaste. We shall not try to destroy the second soldier. I cannot countenance even more blood on my hands.*

I want to say, *We do what we have to do,* but instead I just say, *Yes.*

"Okay, Bunker H. Let's go. Fall back."

The Conformity soldier bellows, *SERVE US. WORSHIP US.* We fly.

## SEVEN

Landing is trickier than I thought it would be. In the air, it's hard to judge speed; the earth moves beneath you but doesn't rush up to meet you and smack you around. As I hit the ground, my ankles and knees crumple with the *momentum* and I'm able to pull myself into a forward roll.

***That's gonna smart, man-child,*** Bernard says as he trots over to help me up.

More extranaturals, members of the Red and Green Teams, land lightly around us, most of them staring at me openly, some in wonder, some with looks less wonder-ous. The word I'm looking for still ends in *-ous*, but it starts with *murder.*

I can't understand why they'd be jealous, but the more I know about people, the less I understand. Army troops and assorted team members—clad in merry green and red colors—make a ring around the bunker opening, weapons and armaments pointed at the source of the infernal noise, the crashing of trees, the moaning.

*SERVE US. WORSHIP US.*

For a moment I wonder, if we prostrated ourselves before the giant thing, would it let us be? Would it take a percentage of us and let the rest go?

The blast doors stand open, fourteen inches thick and made of dull gray metal, revealing Armstead Lucius Priest. He's had a bloody nose recently. Negata stands near him. No sign of blood on his face. I file this away for questioning later. When Negata's gaze meets mine, he gives me a small inclination of the head, which, for Negata, is like a high five and fist bump together.

Priest steps forward, limping, his face a cowl of distress. Concern, maybe. Fury? Though he's wearing Quincrux's meat-suit, I can't yet read his expressions.

"Come!" he says, voice raised. "We must get inside."

Every instinct I have is not to go back into that hole. Hiding in a hole doesn't sound to me like the optimum response to the Conformity soldier. But I don't want to have to kill all the poor souls caught up inside that monstrosity.

The reality of what I've done is beginning to become clear.

Twenty thousand people.

Something about Priest hardens, as if he can read my thoughts. "*Do not think upon it!*" he says. "If you brood on it, your mind will break. You have done what you should have to protect yourself, your friends. The future of our world. We are the last with the ability to fight it." He points at my chest with his cane. "*Come inside! It is almost upon us!*"

And at that moment there's a loud crash and boom. Some of the Army remnants and extranaturals respond with another chatter of gunfire, punctuated by the intermittent *thwup thwup* of grenades being launched. I can see Tap and Danielle empty-ing their weapons while Jack stands, arms out, hands splayed, ready to go explodey at a moment's notice. Beyond our small defensive circle guarding the blast doors, three boulders rise from the ground and one large log levitates, and I can feel in the ether the stress and strain of all the individual shibboleths.

Davies yells, "It's here! Letsgoletsgo—" and all my ability

to make a decision is taken as Bernard, Danielle, and Casey sweep me inside the blast doors and to the back of the motor pool garage, near the elevator. We turn, breathless, to face the closing steel doors, but they seem too slow, far too slow.

Framed beyond the doors, an angry spray of pines disintegrates into kindling as one massive leg swings into view. *JOIN US. WORSHIP US.* The hideous sewage smell of the soldier blasts into the confines of the bunker's garage. Bernard pitches over and vomits onto the concrete floor, and he's joined by Army guys and team members so that the stench of bile mixes with the awful miasma of the soldier.

The Conformity soldier bellows and moans with its thousands of mouths. It knows we're here, hiding in this hole like some frightened woodland creature.

Suddenly the view between the doors is of naked, straining, ichor-streaked bodies, each mouth screaming *JOIN US SERVE US WORSHIP US.*

Jack leaps to the opening, hands held out in front of him. The shock wave that erupts from him drives forward with the strength of his anger. By the time it hits the wall of flesh filling the bunker's door, it's moving at a thousand miles per hour. It rips through flesh, liquefying it, blasting everything—the abandoned Jeeps, shattered remnants of trees, the bodies of the subsumed, *everything*—out and away from the bunker and down the mountainside.

The soldier bellows and moans as the blast doors clang shut.

...

*BOOM. BOOM.*

We pant in the fluorescent-lit space of the bunker motor

pool. Ember goes to Jack, touches him lightly on his arm. Hugs him. But even in his embrace, she looks at me. Curious, maybe. I got my devil wings.

It's silent for a long while except for the booms of the soldier assaulting the door.

Once, when I was just a snot-nosed kid, a car plowed into the school bus I was on. Not too much damage, but a lot of kids banged heads or smacked their faces on the front seats. Afterward, waiting for the other school bus to come pick us up, we stood on the side of the road, all our lunchboxes in grubby little hands, backpacks on our backs, and stared at each other with hushed shock.

That's what this is like.

"Casualties?" Priest asks Davies, who, it seems, is now in command of the remains of the Army. I'd heard rumors about desertion—the US government has moved to NORAD, martial law declared—but now, looking at the ten or fifteen bedraggled soldiers remaining, I can see how far the military situation has eroded.

"Billings, McKee, Jeffries, Donaldson—we lost contact with them when the second Conformity soldier attacked the tower."

Priest nods, grave. "And teams? Losses?"

"Other than bloody noses and spanking bad headaches—courtesy of Li'l Devil—no. All accounted for," Blackwell says, glancing at me.

"And the Irregulars are all here," Tap says.

Priest bows his head, thinking.

*BOOM. BOOM.* The blows from the soldier shake the earth. Hard to countenance the fact that it's battering the door with human bodies. The reverberations travel up my legs from the floor. I can feel them in my teeth, my molars.

"Come, let's get the majority of you on a lower level," Priest says.

"It can huff and puff, but it won't get through those doors," Davies says, voice like gravel crunching under car wheels. He's a salty one—unshaven, craggy, missing only an unlit cigar in the corner of his mouth.

Priest stares at him, head inclined—for a moment I'm reminded of Quincrux—and then he nods. "Still, let us get some of them below. Captain Davies, Mr. Blackwell, Mr. Solomon, would you please devise a roster of watch for this level? Equal portions of extranatural and military, if you'd be so kind."

All three of them make sounds in the affirmative and trot off to put their heads together.

"A word, Shreve," Priest says, placing a pale, soft hand on my shoulder as I moved toward the elevator. "Just a moment."

When Jack joins us, Priest opens his mouth to protest until I say, "No, he's with me. We go together or not at all."

Maybe it's the fact that I'm making rules now. Maybe it's the dismay at our situation. Maybe his shattered leg—courtesy of Jack almost two years ago now—pains him. Maybe it's the weight of centuries pressing down on him. Armstead Lucius Priest sighs.

"Very well," he says, and he sits down on the bench next to the elevator door, crossing his hands on the head of his cane, to wait for the rest of the soldiers and extranaturals to descend into the bowels of the earth.

## EIGHT

The elevator car shudders and shimmies in the descent. Priest seems preoccupied with something I cannot discern, though I could probably suss it out if I dared dive into his brainmeats. I don't. I will not risk it. I fought the Witch. I struggled with Quincrux. I do not know Priest's strength, and I do not want to.

As we rock in the elevator carriage, faint *boom*s can be heard as the Conformity soldier throws itself at the mountainside.

"Mr. Cannon . . ." Priest frowns. Maybe he's accessing Quincrux's memory banks, maybe he's just unsure what to say. "Shreve. I am most pleased with your development. Indeed, with everyone's development. It is only in times of adversity that one discovers what one is capable of."

I really hate it when one uses the word *one* when one should just say *YOU*.

"One does what one can."

"You mock me."

"Only a little."

He smiles, and damn me if it doesn't look a little sad. It's an honest smile, at least, which is more than Quincrux ever gave me.

"Our lives are strange, are they not?"

"How do you mean?"

"We know many people who have occupied different bodies."

As he says it, I can't help but think of Moms. She's always been many people occupying just one body. I can't seem to hate her anymore.

"Yeah. Many into one. Like the Conformity."

"Yes. You and I, we contain multitudes."

"Legion."

"Yes. I am curious, though. How did you manage it?"

"Manage what?"

"Your ability to fly. Have you been hiding that ability?"

"No."

Priest rocks with the movement of the elevator. We're descending far, far into the earth. The air is cool and somewhat wet. If the lights went out, I would scream.

Weariness descends on me. Suddenly my legs feel weak and my head spins.

*Oh, man,* Jack sends. ***That's one helluva hangover.***

There's a bench at the back of the elevator. I sit there, waiting until my head stops spinning.

"You do not look so well, Shreve," Priest says, concern in his voice.

"It's the letdown. Bernard hit us with a shot of rhythm, and now—"

"Ah. The aftereffects have begun to set in." He shakes his head. "Extranatural abilities are wondrous—a higher rung in human development—but the ascent comes at a cost. As in all things."

I can only nod and cradle my head in my hands. Jack doesn't seem to be faring much better.

"Pardon my curiosity. But in all my long years—and I mean sheaves of years—I have never known any extranatural to develop *new* powers so late in life." He shakes his head. "It's one of the great fallacies of the old to believe that they have experienced it all. I am not immune. This revelation of your undiscovered talent came as a shock to me. And I do not relish shocks."

I look at Jack, and he's got this wary look on his face, like we're speaking gibberish to each other—which I guess we are. But I wanted him here, so I wink, and I can see him settle.

*Is this guy for real?* Jack sends.

*Yeah. He is.*

*I don't like him. He's too much like Quincrux,* Jack concludes.

*He is, but he isn't. I don't know. Maybe it's because some of Booth is in there too.*

*Well, if shit goes pervy, I'm blasting him,* Jack sends, matter-of-fact. And he will, I have no doubt. The force he released at the Conformity soldier was monumental, like the raw energies of the universe. The anger behind it was equally wild.

*Sssh. I don't know if he can overhear us.*

*Screw that,* Jack says.

During my exchange with Jack, Priest remains staring at me, hands crossed over his cane.

"So you want to know how I did it," I say to him.

He inclines his head slightly.

I gnaw my lip.

"I'm a thief." In my mind, when I thought of my response, it sounded cool, tough. But now that my mouth has made the words, it sounds terribly vulnerable stated so baldly. And I hate it about myself. I take and I take and I give nothing back.

"All you can think about is yourself, Shree," Moms said, so long ago. And she was right.

Priest purses his lips and lowers his head, thinking.

Jack and I are exchanging glances when he raises his head and says, "I think the reality of it is more complicated. Let me ask you a question."

"Okay. Shoot."

"Can you take my humor?"

"Humor?"

"A poor example. Can you take my personality?"

"No. But I can take your memories."

That troubles him; his face clouds. "This is, unfortunately, true. I cannot express to you how sorry I am that you ever were in a situation where that seemed your only option."

Damn it if a tear doesn't bead his eye. I don't know what to say to the man.

"You can take memories, but can you take my personality? Can you take my humor? Can you take my beliefs? My love of music? My abhorrence of poverty? And I don't mean remove it, I mean, *can you take it into yourself?* Graft it to who you are?"

"No."

"Then you are not a thief. And I am beginning to think you are the opposite of a thief."

"What's the opposite of a thief?" Jesus. This guy. He could give Jerry a run for his money, answering questions with questions.

"I don't know."

"It is one who gives."

"So, I'm a gift giver? Like Santa Claus?"

He smiles again, slowly. His lips tug downward, but his eyes crinkle. It's a sad smile.

I *hate* sad smiles. Quincrux never sad-smiled.

"No. It means you *are a gift*." He closes his eyes suddenly and half sings, half chants, *"Agnus Dei, qui tollis peccata mundi, miserere nobis."*

The elevator shudders to a stop, and the doors open.

Fuck me.

...

It's a lab, cluttered with the detritus of research and analysis, filled with large, white electrical machines of unknown use, at least to my eye (and I have the memories of quite a few medical practitioners rattling around in the noggin). There's an electron microscope. A bank of industrial refrigerators and freezers. There's a centrifuge. I have to assume the thing stenciled with the words *DELIVER TO GENOMICS* is some sort of DNA sequencer. There's something that looks like a clear vat of oil with wires and tubes swimming in its viscous depths. And racks upon endless racks of servers.

Priest limps through the laboratory, looking about with a dissatisfied air.

*Boom. Boom.* A flask rattles on a nearby worktable.

He gestures at the room. "I show you this because it is my greatest failure."

Jack looks puzzled. "How so?"

"Hiram. He was my student—indeed, my protégé—and I must atone for what he did. I bear the weight of his sins."

"He was a prick, that's for sure," I say. Then I think a little more. "A monster, really—a murderer, an abuser, a manipulator. But I don't understand how that was your fault."

He limps over to a stool and sits down. He looks tired. At this point, his psyche has settled in Quincrux's flesh like a tapeworm in a dog's heart. Now he's heir to all the excess and damage that Quincrux's meatsuit possesses. The shattered leg. The addiction to tobacco. Whatever other strange and demented predilections the man might have had. I've worn enough flesh to know, it's hard coming to grips with the physical wear and tear of another body. To take up residence has to be tiring.

"Pride. When I first came to know Hiram and understood his talents and desires, I thought I could control him, change him for good. And I did, I think, for many years. But when I—" A strange, dark expression settles over his features. For a moment the years fall away and he seems boyish, lost. Lonely. "When I was scattered among them, the people I rode, Hiram reverted to his old ways. His true nature."

"Still not seeing how that can be your fault," Jack says.

"We're all tied together, Mr. Graves, in ways that sometimes are hard to understand because humanity is in love with the idea of individuality."

"We're all snowflakes," I say, thinking back to Miss Roberts's kindergarten class.

Priest looks at me, cocking his head. "I haven't heard that before, but many years have passed since I have been aware of much more than the entity and keeping my consciousness whole." He nods, a brittle, slow movement. "The American mindset is that every man is a king, every person special, despite the weight of evidence against this perception. Most lives are dull, full of drudgery. The boredom of existence is made palatable only through the anodynes of media, entertainment, the surcease of pain found in alcohol and drugs. The platitudes of religion. The pleasures of the flesh. Is this not true?"

I can only nod in agreement.

"Few strive to be anything more than what their society, their community, their heritage expects of them. The inertia of their lives keeps them from striving for anything more than some artificial idea of normality." He scratches at his slightly whiskered cheek. It's been a day or two since our leader has shaved. "And so, the minutiae of daily life don't differ greatly from individual to individual. They are interchangeable components to the great experiment of humankind." He sighs. "The truth is that there was an ocean of mindless, animated flesh out there *before* the Conformity awoke."

"Right, so, back to why Quincrux's shittiness was your fault?" I prod.

He walks over to a freezer and opens it. The air condenses, and water vapor begins to fall from the opening like smoke. Row upon row of colored, indexed tubes stand revealed, each one capped by a strange-looking mechanical device.

Priest delicately withdraws one tube and hands it to me. It's freezing, and I have to shift it from hand to hand to keep my skin from fusing to it. "Hiram Quincrux was special. Unique. As are you, Shreve, and you, Mr. Graves."

Weird how he addresses me by my first name, but not Jack. An echo of Quincrux, maybe.

I look at the tube. It's full of a red liquid, thinner than blood. The top looks like a mechanical interface to a device. The glass of the tube has a frosty, opaque area for labeling. Someone has written there: *HOLLIS – Stasis.*

Priest's face turns grim. "But he *knew* the uniqueness of these poor souls. And he did this."

*Boom.*

"I am to blame," Priest says, "because I wasn't here to restrain him or temper his ambition. And so I must expiate that guilt." He looks at me. "I felt you abroad in the etheric heights as the soldier attacked. What did you learn?"

"The Conformity soldier is in communication with the Conformity itself. I saw the tether as a sort of golden filament. It's held together by a tremendously powerful telekinetic force and controlled by an equally powerful telepathic awareness."

"Where was the 'tether,' as you call it?"

"In the crotch."

Priest nods again, as if confirming something he already suspected. "That makes sense from a purely operational stand-point. The 'brain' is situated deep in the body so that it is more protected and signals have to travel shorter distances. Yes, it makes perfect sense." Priest stands. "Miss Tanzer has offered a theory on the soldiers, and I am agreeing with her more and more as new information becomes available. I would let her tell it to you herself, but she is occupied currently, preparing my plan."

"Your plan? You've got a plan?" I guess I'm amazed. I always make it up as I go along.

"Indeed I do."

"Can you both just shut the fuck up and get to the point?" Jack says.

I raise my eyebrow. "How can I shut the fuck up and get to the point? If I shut the fuck up then—"

"I will blast you, Shreve," Jack says, raising his hand.

Priest snaps his fingers, drawing attention back to himself. "Miss Tanzer was puzzled as to why the soldiers and the Conformity itself weren't subsuming everyone in its path. Just a percentage."

"Yeah, that is weird," I say.

"She believes that the Conformity is only subsuming people with extranatural abilities, either fully formed or latent."

"Wow," I say. It's a stunning idea.

"What about the worship?" asks Jack.

"Yeah, what's up with that?"

Priest looks grim. "Whatever the entity behind the Conformity, it's a dark and foreign thing. Bodiless and malevolent. It feeds on psychic energy and grows itself. Prayer and worship are its food, essentially."

"But it's just worship, right," Jack says, raising his hands, a great mass of fingers. "Worshipping something, *praying to something* . . . It's not actually *doing* anything. It's not *creating* anything."

Priest looks at Jack sadly. "Have you been listening, Mr. Graves?" He doesn't go so far as *tsk*ing but I get the impression he's thinking about it. "Everything is connected. We are— all of us—part of a great tissue that expands and contracts and breathes and shivers and thrums. We are a wave front. The human wave front. And what happens to one of us affects us all. Do you not understand this?"

Jack shakes his head. "It's bullshit. New-age crap. I do what I decide. I have free will. I'm not just part of the machine. Because if what you're saying was true—which it *isn't*—we're already part of a conformity."

"Precisely. And now that unity is being threatened."

*Boom. Boom-boom.*

I'm holding a freezing tube full of the essence of one of my friends while a walking tower of flesh is banging at the mountainside, wanting to either squish or subsume us. At a certain point, all the jibber-jabber becomes useless.

"This is all just dandy. But what's your plan?"

Priest limps around the worktable. He withdraws a set of keys, opens a steel storage compartment, and waves us to assist him. "That black box. Please remove it, Mr. Graves."

Jack picks it up with a grunt, and I see it's the same sort of matte-black box that the Orange Team implemented during the ill-fated attack on the Towson Veterans Hospital. Priest presses a button, and a compartment opens on its face. There's a mechanical interface inside it, including a suspiciously familiar-looking outlet.

"It is relatively simple. You place the weaponized genome here. It locks in and drains into the device. There's a synthetic organism in there that will, once you press this button, go into a frighteningly strong paroxysm of psychokinetic energy. It is, in essence, an extranatural bomb. Once triggered it will, in a matter of moments, bond with the weaponized genome and release its energy."

"So, this is the stasis bomb we kept hearing about?"

"It is and it isn't. It's whatever genome you place inside it. And it's good for only one burst."

"How many of these things do you have?" Jack asks, awed.

"Just the one." Priest gives a bitter laugh. "That box costs more money than it cost the United States to set mankind on the moon. Billions upon billions of dollars."

"One device? But how many genomes?" I ask.

"Many. Thirty or forty."

"So you're telling me Quincrux took that many kids and . . . what? Weaponized them? Killed them? Couldn't he just take their blood?"

He shakes his head. "Everything is connected. To weaponize an extranatural ability, it must be collected at the moment of genesis within the individual and harvested. The 'donor'—and I use that term loosely—does not survive." He waves a hand at the tank full of thin, transparent oil. "It is a frighteningly complicated process that I'm afraid, with my antiquated knowledge of science, I did not fully understand."

We're silent for a while, the only noise our breathing and an intermittent *boom* sounding in the subterranean laboratory. It's par for the course, really, that these avaricious men would harvest children for their own ends. What does it say about me that I'm not even surprised?

"So," I say, breaking the silence. "The plan."

"There are two more exits from this bunker. One on the other side of the mountain. Once again, I must ask you to be bait, Shreve."

I laugh. "Again? You didn't ask the first time."

His face colors, and I think for an instant that he's going to get angry with me. Because that's what adults do when confronted with my cunning repartee. But he doesn't. He looks ashamed, has trouble meeting my eyes.

"The soldiers are drawn to the brightest of extranaturals—"

"So you're saying they'll come after me?"

"Yes, they will follow you."

"What about the Liar? Cameron? Or that girl . . . the one with the sex-thing—"

"They will be evacuated. Both have been . . ." He thinks for a moment. "Both have been ill-used by Hiram. They are exceptionally strong, it's true. But they are nothing compared to you. You have expanded beyond all our knowledge of extranatural abilities. And neither of them has a connection to Quincrux, which means a connection to the entity, as you have."

Jack looks at me with worry corroding his face. "I'm going with him."

"Of course," Priest says. "And any others who wish to go with you. Your team of aptly named Irregulars."

"We'll take that bomb, too."

"That will preclude flight."

"You have a vehicle for us?"

"Yes, a troop transport. Captain Davies and Mr. Negata will accompany you. They have both volunteered." His face looks grave. "I will be honest. There's not much government left, as you might imagine. Our scientists at the Society have taken readings, and the general radioactive levels have risen around the globe, indicating there have been significant nuclear exchanges. Without people to tend them, many nuclear reactors have had critical failures. The fabric of society and civilization is torn. A Conformity hangs in the sky above Washington and almost every other major city on Earth. This has become an extinction-level event now. We've been in radio contact with the US Air Force, what's left of it. I have been able to get assurances from General Hodgson that an airplane will be waiting for you at the Bozeman airport in three hours. You will make for that."

"Should we lead the Conformity toward a population?"

He shakes his head sadly. "Bozeman is where the soldier came from."

"So that's it? We drive off, lead the soldier away? Catch a plane. And you'll be here?"

His pause is entirely too long. "Yes."

"Do we return here?"

"No. You'll go away from here. Far enough from the Conformity soldier to have time to regroup. To look for solutions. I will find you and come to where you are."

"That's the plan?" I ask, incredulous.

"That is the plan. You will lead the soldier away so that we might evacuate all of the other Society members, and the remaining Army and research fellows." He touches the matte-black surface of the bomb lightly.

"When do we go?"

"Immediately. I shudder to think of how many people die each time the Conformity soldier attacks the mountain. Cameras show it's sloughing off flesh"—it's easier to think of them as flesh than individuals—"at a great rate. Mr. Holden and the remaining scientists estimate the Conformity soldier has lost at least ten percent of its original body mass."

"So, thousands have died." The death toll is staggering. Mind-numbing. And I brought one down.

"Yes. And thousands more will. It is inevitable. We must try to preserve the subsumed, but we also must focus on the unincorporated. They must be safe." He limps a few steps forward, stops, and turns. "So you will lead the soldier away, to the east. Once the soldier is distant and the rest of the campus's population is loaded on transports and well out of the valley, I go into the ether and reveal myself to the creature. You will have to stay alive long enough for that."

"What? You're going to throw your life away?" I said.

"No. I will call the thing to me and see if I can wrest control of it away from the Conformity."

"Shit on a shingle, man, you're crazy."

"They say desperate times call for desperate measures. That saying was old even when I was young."

"And you think you can take control of it?"

"It will be a terrible struggle, I'm sure. I will burn bright as I may in the ether, to draw its attention to me. And should I succeed in this contest, we will have a way to take the fight to the Conformity itself."

"And if not, what then?" Jack asks.

"You will have to find another way."

"I should do it," I say.

"No."

"I am stronger than you."

"You are, this is true. But I am not inconsiderable. The entity knows me of old. Whatever amount of the Conformity's awareness is invested in the soldier, it will be drawn to me once I reveal myself."

"Damn. That's some Gandalf shit."

He looks at me, puzzled.

"Forget it. Modern cultural reference."

Silence again, and this time the awkwardness is dialed up a few notches. He doesn't say it, and I don't want to ask. But it's there. Those etheric heights. "When you do this, I'll need to be there, uh, at least in spirit," I said.

"Yes. Literally. Your astral self will need to bear witness," Priest responds.

"Shit. I hate that word. Astral," I say.

Jack snorts. "Asshole."

I laugh. Priest looks ineffably weary. "Alas, I forget that you are so young. So very young." He passes a hand over his eyes as if to sweep the fatigue away. "If we all survive this, I hope you will forgive me for burdening you with such responsibility."

Something in me gives, and I feel light and disconnected. I think about the years of raising Vig and my stupid betrayal of his trust—stealing that truck, getting shot, getting put in good ole Casimir Pulaski Juvenile Detention Center for Boys. I let my brother down. I forgot my responsibility.

I shake my head. "If I can bear it, I'll take it," I say, staring him straight in the eye.

He nods, places a hand on my shoulder.

"Thank you. This means more to humanity than you know."

"Oh, I have an inkling."

## NINE

I take the test tube with Hollis's weaponized genome and Jack hefts the extranatural bomb to his shoulder with a grunt. We follow Priest. He leads us through the maze of rooms and corridors under the mountain until we find a large storage area in which we can hear the mutters and shufflings of many people.

"Here I will leave you. I hope we will all be able to return here, eventually."

He extends his hand. I take it in mine—it's dry and soft and papery. We shake.

*We will not meet again in the flesh, I fear,* he says directly into my mind, and I realize this is true.

*It's a monster of a world, boss. But you never know.*

*A pleasure knowing you, Shreve. I shall look for you in the ether when I reveal myself.*

*I'll be there, bells on.*

His gaze searches my face, and I feel the faint scratching at the fabric of my mind, like he wants to get in and knock around, see what I'm thinking, hear my thoughts, but the scratching desists and he gives a rueful smile.

*Boom.*

"Good-bye, Shreve."

"Later."

I turn and walk into the storage area.

...

The Irregulars mill about in the corner of the storage area amid unmarked fifty-five-gallon blue plastic drums and crates of unknown origin and content. Goddamned Lost Ark is probably here.

The Red and Green Teams look like they want to throttle each other, while the nerds and lab coats and civilians just appear terrified. Muttering and moaning can be heard with each *boom*.

We crowd together. Our own little Conformity soldier.

Negata approaches, joining us.

"So, you know what's going on?" I say to him.

He nods. Davies approaches and says, "Is it just you, then, Li'l Devil?"

Jack moves to stand near me. "And me."

*What's this?* Danielle asks. *What's going on?*

Casey broadcasts a wordless, nervous interrogative. A quick image of a hand, opening as if during a conversation when a question is asked.

*I have to lead the thing away,* I respond.

*Why you, man-child? Why's it got to be you?*

*It's drawn to me, I guess. Bugfuck stuff.*

A concerned look crosses Danielle's features. *The second soldier did head straight for you.*

*Seems my noggin's like a big old lighthouse, and the soldier wants to snuff it out,* I say, trying to keep my nervousness out of the mental timbre.

I feel a secret warmth in the palm of my hand. Casey holds it with her own invisible one.

"I'm going with you," Tap says. "Not because you're all that, but because I can't stay in here anymore."

*He's got a point. It is getting a bit claustrophobic in here.*

Blackwell looks at me from across the storage hall and pushes his way over, Ember and the rest of his team in tow, like eddies swirling behind a particularly large walrus.

"What's all this? Something's about to happen?" he asks Davies.

Davies, sensing the alarm and fear rippling through the assembled extranaturals, raises his hands. "Listen up, people! Listen up!" The remaining Army guys straighten and come to attention. Lab coats rustle and shift their weight nervously. "Good news. There's a small service passage to Bunker G. In a moment, you're all going to get in single file, and we're going to take you over there. We'll assemble in the motor pool by the blast doors. Red Team, Green Team, you will be on hand to escort and defend the civilians. Understood?"

A soft tremor rolls through the assembled people. I can't tell if it's nervousness at the looseness of the plan or relief to be doing something. A bit of both, probably.

"Meanwhile, Shreve and his Irregulars will lead the soldier away while we evacuate the valley. Miss Tanzer and Mr. Holden have prepared a roster and will assign you to your evacuation duties once we're in Bunker G's motor pool."

"Hold up," Blackwell says. "Why are Shreve and his—" I've roughed him up in the past (and he me) so he stops himself before saying something stupid. "His little group leading the soldier away? Why not Solomon's team? Or mine?"

Captain Davies grinds his teeth. It's a terrible thing, really, grinding your teeth—it wears down the enamel and can cause all sorts of deleterious things to your choppers and your gums. But Davies is a freakin' natural at it. His jaw looks like steel girders stressing and groaning during an earthquake.

He does not like being questioned.

"Because, Mr. Blackwell, that is how the Director has designed the plan. And the damned thing has a hard-on for Cannon, or so the Director says." It comes out all smooth and measured. And then, "*Do you understand me, Blackwell?*" Spittle flies from his mouth. The force of his shout causes us all to take a step back.

"Yes, sir! Understood."

"You will escort the civilians and non-flyers. That is your job. You may start now." He turns, waves Holden and Tanzer over. "Let's start moving them to Bunker G."

*Man-child, I'm coming with you. Ain't going in them lifeboats.*

*You can't fly, Bernard. If you get caught in the transport—*

A quick eruption of angry drumbeats flashes in my mind, and Bernard says, "Neither can Davies or Casey. Or Negata here. And they're all going with."

"Your boy Iggy's lining up with the rest of them," Jack says, pointing to Bernard's paired telekinetic.

*Fuck that motherfucker. He's just some fool they assigned me. And you two have forgotten something.*

*What's that?* I send.

*I got the beat. You're gonna need me.*

"I'm going, too," Ember says. I didn't even notice her here. She looks at me with a defiant glint in her eye, as if daring me to naysay her.

"What about your team?" Jack asks.

"I'll write my resignation next time we're near a typewriter."

Jack looks stunned. Things are happening too fast. The Society—Jack's home for the past two years—is in shambles, and the world beyond its borders is in an even worse state. If there's one thing Jack likes, it's the fiber of daily routine.

"What, you don't want me to come with you?" Ember looks from me, cocking an eyebrow, to Jack.

"Of course I do! It's just, I've never heard of someone leaving one of the teams . . ."

"Learn something new every day, don'tcha?" She puts her arm around his waist and pulls him in tight. "Anyway, I wasn't going to let you run off with these Irregular girls."

Jack blushes. It's weird, but, when she says it, Ember's looking straight at me.

I know reindeer games, and this chick is playing them.

"Well, that's it, then. Where do we go?"

Davies says, "Back this way. It's a long walk to the warrens."

"The warrens?"

"You'll see."

• • •

He leads us back through another, smaller lab—this one full of equipment that would seem more appropriate on a space shuttle than beneath a mountain—and down a concrete stairwell that diminishes to a vanishing point both up and down and echoes strangely. A few floors below, he keys us into another door and through a weirdly mundane office complex full of fluorescent lights and cubicles, ferns and *Casual Friday!* fliers. Then we're out into another corridor, this one a rough-hewn hall cut from the living rock of the mountain.

I can feel the weight of stone above me.

At the end of this hall, Davies unlocks another keycard door to reveal a small armory. Tap's and Danielle's eyes light up as they spy rack upon rack of automatic weapons and smell the spiced fragrance of gunpowder and munitions oil.

"There's some clothing over there, I think," Davies says, pointing at a couple of crates. Bernard, Jack, and I toddle to the boxes and begin rifling through them. I set aside some flak vests. They don't look like they'd keep me warm, just not perforated. I don't think the forecast called for partly cloudy with a 75 percent chance of gunfire, but what the hell do I know? I'm a mind reader, not a psychic.

Bernard grunts at the discovery of black fatigues, and we all sort through them. Casey, pulling out a jacket, says, "Shreve, will you help me?"

I assist, pulling the jacket over her shoulder. The one sleeve hangs loose, empty, and she looks down at it with an unsatisfied expression. "This is going to get in the way." Her one visible hand trembles, and the resounding *booms* of the Conformity shudder through the mountain. My heart catches and begins to hammer in my chest.

Davies slaps a knife in my hand, and I tie the sleeve as close as possible to the shoulder, cutting away the rest, fast. With an almost imperceptible tremor in her voice, Casey says, "Shreve, promise me you won't do anything stupid." The rush is on me, and it takes a moment to discern that she doesn't mean the knife.

People have said that to me before. For a moment, I can only think of Booth, big-hearted Booth. My enemy. My friend. Whatever remnant of him will be left behind with Priest.

"I won't," I say. "Nothing more important to me than the integrity of my skin."

"I find that hard to believe." She doesn't smile, just looks more worried. "I've seen your scars."

I can only nod. She's close now, and I can feel the eyes of some of the others on us, and that makes me very nervous. It's one thing to be close to a girl, a beautiful girl, and another thing to be close to one in front of other people. I feel like I'm on a stage.

*Boom.*

With Casey's face so close to mine that I can see the delightful spray of freckles on her nose, I'm flooded with memories of all the lives I've known, each one bound in some sort of love. I've eaten those memories—sex with men and women, the fanatical whirlwind of ceaseless love, the mania of the bloodlust of war, the murderous pleasure in death and the causing of it.

She stirs things in me I'd rather keep tamped down.

Her lips are parted, moist, eminently kissable, but I move away because the cacophony of memory and emotion is almost too much to bear. And if I became swept away in it? What then? Could I burn out her mind? My own? Start speaking in other languages again?

No.

It's only after I move away—leaving her there, staring at me with an inscrutable look on her face—that I realize she never really needed my help at all. She's got her telekinetic arm that can do anything. It was just a pretense to be close.

Weird how my intelligence varies with proximity to girls. You can live a thousand lives, have countless memories of love and youth, but it never really prepares you for the real thing.

Davies gives us guns and heavy ballistic-nylon bags full of

armaments. I'm not real keen on toting all this crap around, but Tap looks like he's got a boner and Danielle looks like Santa just gave her a puppy, except this puppy fires one thousand rounds a second and has a grenade launcher.

I find some MREs—my best friends when all light is gone—and I dig into one with gusto. CHICKEN SPAGHETTI in a bag is the breakfast of champions.

Negata prowls the room, looking like a jaguar caged. He opens a door at the far side of the room, and I move to join him.

Beyond the door is blackness, absolute and, I will admit, terrifying. (You have someone stick you in a pitch-black hole for a week and see how you come out on the other side.)

When he walks forward, vanishing from sight, I reach out for him. He's swallowed by darkness. "Negata, don't—"

I hear a mechanical clank, and suddenly lights flash, flicker, and buzz. An electrical hum. The door swings shut behind us. We stand in a corridor much like the rough-hewn one we traveled before, twenty feet wide and equally tall, but this one stretches off into infinity, a straight passage through the heart of the mountain, flickering lights bursting into incandescence every fifty feet. The floor is smooth, like that of a garage. To my right I notice a pair of oversized golf carts near charging stations.

"So, we're taking those?"

"Yes."

Negata walks to one of the carts, unplugs it from the wall, and chucks his head at me, indicating I should take charge of the other one.

We pull the pair to the door to the armory. He stops me on the way back.

"As you lure the Conformity away from here, I want you to

think about the sensation of being noticed."

"I don't get it."

"The attention of the entity behind the Conformity will be upon you. I want you to become aware of the sensation."

"Why?"

He turns and opens the door to the armory. "Because you cannot become unnoticeable until you know what it is to be conspicuous." He holds the door for me. "Understood?"

"Okay."

"This is good."

Inside, everyone's geared up. We usher them into the corridor and load up the electric carts. Ammo, weapons, MREs. Nothing more. No personal items. No baggage. We're either refugees or nomads now. Or both. I can't decide.

I stop Davies before he slides behind the wheel of the cart. "I need to talk with you, just for a moment."

"What is it? Time is tight—"

"You've got walkie-talkies?"

"None in the armory. So no. We're just going to have to focus on planning."

"No." I point at the Irregulars. A motley group. "We're connected."

"What do you mean?" He looks puzzled, and that's to be expected. I've been in his head before. I know I can unlock the doors and putter around in his brainmeat, but it's important that this be voluntary.

"I can get in people's heads."

He nods, wary.

"We're connected," I say. "And they can speak to me and each other over distances."

Davies whistles.

"I can give this to you."

"No."

"It's a matter of survival, Captain. We need every advantage we can get."

"That mean you'll be able to read my thoughts?"

"I can already do that."

His hand involuntarily twitches. I imagine it's wanting to hold a gun or my throat.

I hold up my hands. "I'm not! But I can."

The muscles in his cheek are like steel bands. Mr. Toothgrindicus is here to stay. But there's a small shift to his shoulders, as if he's bearing some unseen weight.

"It'll just be like me flipping a switch—" Or so I hope. "And then we'll all be able to communicate. Well, except for Mr. Negata."

"Why not Negata?"

"He doesn't exist. In the ether."

"The ether?"

I wave away the question. "The telepathic world. He's a ghost. He can't be seen."

Davies stares hard at me, like he's evaluating something in me only he can see. "Give me your hand."

"What?"

"Give me your hand."

We shake, and then he says, "Okay. Do it."

I waste no time. I'm on him and moving in his consciousness like an arsonist. Blazing. His eyes widen and then no more.

He pats me on the shoulder and moves to the carts. Casey looks at me expectantly. Danielle, Bernard, and Tap watch as I clamber into the cart and Davies takes the wheel. Jack sits with

Negata, who simply stares down the corridor.

*I'd like you all to welcome Captain Davies to our little shindig. He's the newest member of the Irregulars,* I send. The ether thrums, the shibboleth stirs within me. I am a conduit, a switchboard.

The Irregulars send various jocular images and words of welcome to Davies, who looks gruff and slightly embarrassed. He grips the cart's steering wheel and mashes the accelerator.

The vehicles make small whirring sounds as we accelerate down the hall, and everyone remains silent. The tires buzz on the smooth concrete of the corridor floors. The reality of our situation settles, and I can sense small personal mental conversations flickering in the minds of my companions like heat lightning flashing on a far-off horizon.

Everything is hushed now, and expectant.

It's a strange feeling, riding on golf carts underneath a billion tons of rock, sliding almost soundlessly down an endless corridor to an unknown fate. But hey, that's why we get paid the big bucks, right?

After ten or fifteen minutes, Tap says, "Are we there yet?"

Davies, without missing a beat, says, "Don't make me stop this car, son."

The group laughs; there's an easing of tension. In the distance, a familiar-looking streaked-metal blast door appears and grows as we approach.

"Tanzer tells me this was originally a Cold War hidey-hole for high-level government officials and their families," Davies says. "God help the common man."

"It looks as if it *would* take a nuclear explosion to get through those doors," Jack says.

Davies stops the cart, climbs out, and approaches the keypad. He presses in an inordinately long string of digits, and then a grinding sound echoes down the stone passage. The blast doors begin to swing inward, opening, revealing another motor pool, similar to the one on the other side of the mountain we've just traveled underneath like some mutant species of dwarf.

A Jeep is up on blocks, wheels off, hood up, but a large troop transport—dull army green and marked with a white star on the door—looks ready for action.

"I'd suggest you get your shit in order, people, before we open those outer doors. I don't know how fast that thing will be on us, but our job is to lure it away. Bernard, Casey, Negata, and I will be in the transport. Shreve, Jack, help me to take off the tarpaulin covering the bed. There should be tools over there to remove these struts." He pats the bed framing.

Bernard trots over to the workbench by the Jeep. Tap begins pumping gasoline from an oversized drum into a smaller one to top off the transport's tank. Danielle and Casey rummage through a large mechanic's toolbox while Jack and I begin removing the canvas covering from the back of the vehicle.

I grab a wrench and begin removing the struts and ribbing of the transport bed as best I can.

"We need to move it, people," Davies barks. "It's now one p.m. The day is wearing on, and I do not want to do this in the dark."

This is a man used to giving orders. A natural at it. And I can see the calming effect that a firm hand has on everyone else. In the end, we're kids, and despite it all—the extra fingers, the flying, the exploding, the seriously fucked-up childhood-into-adolescences—having an adult in charge eases tensions and provides security.

*Check this out,* Danielle sends to the group. She wheels a large red box around the front of the derelict Jeep. *Plasma cutter. Back up, y'all. It's my show.*

*You know how to use that?* Tap sends, incredulous.

*My mom owns a construction company. I can do any job a man can do. Usually in half the time.*

*Dayum, girly-girl,* Bernard sends. *Beautiful and handy. Now that's a powerful combination.* Quick auditory impression of a drum fill ending in a rimshot.

*Shut it,* Danielle says. But she winks at him. And I don't even have to peep him to know that his gooey center just got gooey-er.

Danielle wheels the cutter into place, pulls on the protective mask, and goes to work, filling the motor pool with blue flashes of light and the mechanical stink of melted metal.

*Smells like a volcano in here,* Jack sends.

I help Jack and Tap remove the struts as Danielle cuts them away, while Casey and Bernard get the gear ready for loading. When it's all complete, we load the transport and stand there looking at one another, as if wondering what's next. But we all know what's next.

The Conformity soldier.

"Might as well get this show on the road," Davies says. He approaches the last keypad lock, taps numbers into its face, and returns to the transport as a yellow light begins to twirl and a buzzing alarm sounds, indicating that the doors are about to roll back. And they do.

Fresh air whips through the crack and sweeps the smoke of the plasma torch away. The mountainside is wreathed in pines, and a wide valley opens below us. Far wider than the narrow gully that's the home of the campus for the Society of Extranaturals, this valley stretches thirty, forty miles across.

There will be no place to hide out there.

There are times to acknowledge one's fears, to look them right in the face and claim them, and other times to push them away, deny they exist. The thing is, I wouldn't be so absolutely terrified if it was zombies, or an apocalypse of vampires, or nuclear war, or almost *anything* other than the loss of one's individuality into that giant, towering monstrosity.

Or worse, the loss of these people. People I care about.

There it is. Can't hide it. Can't push it away.

My bowels are watery and my legs weak. But Davies clambers into the cab of the transport, and Negata joins him. Casey and Bernard huddle in the bed—now our makeshift landing area. The ignition growls and the engine ratchets into gear, belching diesel fumes into the air.

*Let's go,* Davies sends. I'm amazed at how quickly he's taken to the telepathic communication, but the man is a veteran. I doubt much fazes him. *Shreve, now's the time to do your thing,* he says.

The transport takes off, out the double blast doors and down the gravel mountainside road, leaving Tap, Jack, Danielle, and me standing in the opening.

*You can do this, man?* Jack asks.

I just nod.

*Well, there's no time like the present,* Danielle says, and she chucks a grenade into the launcher of the M14 she holds and launches herself into the air.

*Come on, noob,* Tap says. *I can't wait to see you wallow about up here with the big boys.*

*Big girls!* Danielle sends. I get a quick image of Tap in drag.

Jack and Tap rise quickly, the speed of their passage making their clothes riffle. Soon they're little black smudges against the wispy cirrus clouds that streak the afternoon sky.

It's cold out here. I shiver.

Now it's up to me. I'm alone on the bosom of the mountain. The sky waits for me.

■■■

Before, it was a matter of desperation. Then that intractable part of me, the base part, would not give up life, and somehow it caused the shibboleth, this strange ability of ours, to shift and grow within me. Like the Grinch's heart growing five sizes too big.

I've become so much larger on the inside. And so much smaller on the outside. I feel like I'm shrinking.

*You'll need to do your best to cover your ears,* I say to them all.

*What? Ears?*

*Your mental ones, at least. It's about to get ugly.*

*What do you mean?*

I close my eyes, blotting out the queries and exclamations.

Darkness of my own making.

Something happens then that I do not expect. The shibboleth surges within me, as if it's a living thing and I am just its vessel. My eyes open.

When I go into the ether, it seems to lock to my body in relationship to everything else. Before, in the ether, there never seemed to be any logic to space and my location in it, but there's a twist now, and with my inner eye I can see the bright flames of the Irregulars in the troop transport rattling down the mountain, left and right and left and right, making the switchbacks on the craggy and winding road.

Above me I see the sparks of Danielle and Tap and Jack.

I turn, both my body and my shibboleth self, and stare westward, where we left the Conformity soldier battering the doors to Bunker H.

It's there, the towering accumulation of human flesh. Burning like a pillar in the mind of some demented god—and maybe that's what it truly is, the trials of some deity sent here for us to endure.

I will not have that.

Fuck *him*.

I reach out and touch Jack, Danielle, Tap. Lightly. I refamiliarize myself with them, their gifts, their strengths. Their loves and losses. They are the tethers that keep me whole. I am the conduit for their lifeforces. For their own burning embers.

In my mind, I rise above the mountain into the ether. And my body obeys. I see with two sights, that of the waking world and that translucent burning realm of the shibboleth.

The Conformity soldier stills. Wind fills me. The howl of wind and surge of blood are my companions, whispering *Shrrrreeeve Shreeeeve. Shreeve.*

Into the arteries of air. Into the sun I rise. I let all pretense fall away to nothing. I open my hands and let the pain and loss and desperation of all existence fill me and burn bright.

I incandesce as a star.

"*Come and get me, you son of a bitch!*" I yell, and the whole expanse of ether shakes with the force of my voice.

And the Conformity comes.

## TEN

It moves quicker than you'd think, that city on the hoof. There's a tremendous *boom* and the thing is clambering up and over the mountain like some ooey-gooey misshapen billy goat. In mere moments its torso peeks over the ridgeline, and the fucker bellows with a thousand mouths, *JOIN US. SERVE US.*

Jack and Danielle are by me now, hanging in the air like bits of flotsam in the crystal clear currents.

*That's one ugly mofo,* Tap sends as he sweeps forward in a tight, aggressive arc. Never stops, that one. *Where are you leading it?*

*Away from campus. Into the valley so we can maneuver.*

Jack gives a mental snort and says, *You gotta start thinking like a flyer. All you got to do is gain altitude and the playing field opens up.*

*I got that,* I say, *but I'm not here to punt a football. I'm here to lead that thing away. You gotta put the bait in the water.*

The Conformity soldier bellows again, an agonized multiform wail, vast soundscapes of pain and misery. It's standing on top of the ridge, and then it contorts, as if gravity is collapsing it upon itself. Contracting.

*Oh no,* Jack sends as the Conformity stretches its body out, lengthening and launching itself into the air.

The ether echoes and thrums with the telekinetic exertion

of the soldier. Jack and Danielle dash away like shooting stars. Tap arcs downward in a reckless and masterful trajectory over and through the trees and rocks of the mountain.

The Conformity fills the sky above me, descending. At the last possible moment, I jerk myself away from where I hang, particulate in the air. It's almost a mental exertion for me now, rather than a physical one, moving in space. I move myself in the ether like a dashing thought and my body, the vessel I inhabit in meatspace, moves in response.

The soldier lands with a thunderous crash on the ground, displacing air in a hurricane-force gale scented with the stench of shit, piss, blood, jizz. Like a cloying fog.

*WORSHIP US. JOIN US.*

The sound is so loud and so near. The vibrations of the impact shudder through my body, liquefy my innards. The Conformity soldier raises the dripping, steaming conglomerate arm—so amazingly fast—and swings at me. I spew hot bile into the air in an arc but move away, barely in time.

***Go, Shreve! Go! It's coming after you!*** Casey sends, urgent and intense. I can picture her face, drawn and worried. I send a quick reassuring image—a piece of cake, though hunger is the last thing I feel—and fly away, out over the valley, the soft rolling white hills and fields asleep beneath snow. It's cold now.

***You need a little spring to your step, Shreve,*** Bernard sends. A quick flurry of beats, images of hands, the wondrous jumble of sixteenth notes trilling up the scale and back down, and my heart spasms in my chest and the rhythm of haste fills me. I'm panting in the frozen Montana sky, my breath exploding from my mouth in skirls of vomit-reeking steam, ripped away by the wind.

You see Peter Pan and his Lost Boys floating about, hung like perfect ornaments on strings, and that's not what it's like at all, flying. It's a desperate submersion into fear and dizziness because the human body, crowned by that good ole monkey brain, has no frame of reference for the sensations pouring torrentially into your nervous system due to floating three hundred feet in the air. Falling without falling. Falling with no consequence. And maybe we are just like Peter Pan, immortal and ageless, and it's just living on the ground that kills us by degrees. I don't know. But flight is monumental fear without end, vertigo stretched into infinite configurations and permutations.

But I'm only hazarding my body, and it truly is a small thing, after all.

My tongue feels like a raccoon wiped its ass with it, but I don't let that delay me from moving away from the bellowing tower of meat. I dash east, fast as I can, swimming in the airstreams.

The Conformity soldier follows. *Boom boom. Boom.* Each step punctuated by the cracking of stone and the destruction of trees.

***Slow it down, Shreve,*** Davies sends. ***The damned thing is right on our ass!***

I had forgotten those in the transport. Looking toward the earth and the spray of trees wreathing the snowy mountain's foothills into the valley, I spy the green Army vehicle trundling down another series of switchbacks, taking them as quickly as possible, but still far too slowly. Snow and ice sit in clusters where the trees keep the roads in shadow for most of the day. It's treacherous driving. The soldier will be on top of them at any moment.

*JOIN US. SERVE US*, it moans, and now I feel the tug of its psychoactive ability. It's strong, so strong, like some ungodly tractor beam tugging at the meat of my body. The Conformity has sucked in thousands, hundreds of thousands—I've seen it myself—but now, now that its attention is focused on me, it's hard to bear the scrutiny. I am a morsel in its one-mind-from-many. I am a spark to be taken inside the inferno. I am desired, yet I am infinitesimal in its sight. Was this what Negata wanted me to feel? Was this what he wanted me to understand? That I'm nothing?

In the ether, the Conformity soldier's gravity is like a telepathic wind, a sinkhole where all the lights of humanity are drawn into a ball, become crushed by their own titanic mass, and turn inward, imploding into a black hole.

It wants us. It calls to us with its terrible powers. But we are nothing.

So strong.

As hard as I try to get away, I remain still in meatspace and the ether. I cannot move, and the soldier comes closer.

*Now's the time to use those guns, if you got them. Slow that bastard down,* Davies calls.

Ember responds, raising her weapon and firing, hair streaming behind her in a wild mess. But it is a struggle.

Yelps of outrage and fear come to me from the Irregulars' minds. Straining against the inexorable pull of the thing, language deserts us, and I have flickering glimpses out of their eyes, and I feel them looking out of mine. Frantic gesticulations and grunts and exclamations, but we are like ghosted images laid one on top of another. Jack whirling, falling, making countless explosions of anger to push himself away. Tap locked in an invisible stalemate. Danielle holding herself still in the air while still trying to raise her gun. Ember fires and chucks a grenade into the launcher's chamber and fires again, but the stress of holding herself away from the draw of it is agonizing. I can feel it. I'm in their minds, all of them, simultaneously.

I could make this whole yard of boys kill each other, Quincrux had said, so long ago. Gleefully.

We are becoming a collective, a linked entity in our own right, to fight the pull of the monstrous gravity of the soldier. Through Casey's eyes, I see Negata in the bed of the troop transport heft a RPG to his shoulder. He seems calm and unaffected with the struggle, the slight tug of his lip downward into a grimace the only indication he's doing something abhorrent—attempting murder.

Things slow. Bernard half falls toward the truck bed, alarm written in broad strokes across his normally genial face. Casey crouches on the wheel bed, grasping the edge with her phantom hand so hard the metal catches and dimples in a squeal. The explosion of smoke is just beginning to pour out of the back of the long tube that Negata holds, as the metal needle-nose of the rocket detaches and lances forward.

The Conformity's stomach explodes in a fireball. Charred remains of bodies fall from it like ash tumbling from an urn's mouth.

The fierce pull of the soldier ebbs, dies. For a moment we're loose from its terrible gravity. The edges of the creature become muddy, indistinct, as if the center no longer holds. It bellows, a rough indistinct sound. It staggers but does not fall.

*Go, go!* Bernard sends. ***I do not want that fugly mofo to fall on us.***

For a long moment the soldier simply remains still, as if collecting its wits.

The transport gains some distance, makes a turn onto a straightaway that looks as if it spans a mile, and I get a flashing image of whipping wind and trees whizzing by from Casey.

*Shreve, move away. Away from the transport, away from the campus. Over here!* Jack sends, and I spot him moving in a blur south, away from the truck's path.

*JOIN US. SERVE US*, the soldier gibbers, stepping forward, each step spanning a hundred yards. *Boom.*

*Here we go again,* Danielle says.

## ELEVEN

It becomes a clumsy, airborne dance. Me jabbing the soldier in the psychic testicles with a chopstick, waiting for it to get all pissy, and then fighting the suck of its telekinetic gravity long enough for one of the team to kick it in the gut with a grenade or RPG. Rinse and repeat.

Now it's just a waiting game. A war of attrition.

*If we kill the "brain" extranaturals in the thing's groin, it'll all come tumbling down,* Casey sends. *You said it's linking to the main Conformity back east there?*

*Hard to explain the connection to the Conformity. It's slaved to it, like a puppet,* I send. *But we don't want it to fall.*

Tap grimaces. I can feel his facial muscles tightening. It's almost as if we're all having each other's feelings, emotions.

*You want to kill it?* Jack asks.

*We're gonna run out of ammo eventually. And we're killing them, anyway. Each step, each blast it takes, people die. It's MADE OF PEOPLE, for chrissakes!* Ember says.

I shake my head. *No. We have to try to keep it whole until Priest is ready. He's going to try to take it over. To save who we can.*

Tap's got an angry set of shoulders. But his lips are blue, and he's shivering. Bernard's infectious biorhythms have ebbed, and now fatigue is setting in. I feel it in my bones and see it in all of their faces. Casey's face is taut, pale. Danielle's is a mask—she won't admit to exhaustion, even to herself. Jack hugs his long, narrow torso. But in Ember there's a fury building, and I can feel that invisible pressure like water in a hose, blood in a tick.

Flying takes concentration and effort. We can't take much more of this without deep-sea wetsuits, a good meal, and some fucking hot cocoa.

*Priest!* I send, broadcasting my words into the ether like a kid doing a cannonball into a placid pool. *We can't keep this up forever!*

Jack winces and Ember says, *Watch out there, trumpet boy. I don't need another bloody nose.*

I descend from the sky, toward the troop transport racing along a tree-wreathed, snowy road. Landing in the moving bed is harder than I thought—I have to gauge my forward movement with the truck's and hope it doesn't slew left or right as it hits a patch of snow or ice. I have a vertiginous moment when I think I'm going to overshoot the wooden slats of the bed and bounce off the cab's roof. I make it, but only barely, catching myself with my hands on the roof, keeping my body from slamming into the back of the cab.

No answer from Priest.

I send my awareness out into the ether, abandoning all conscious inhabitation of my body. I move across the mountain and miles back over the etheric darkling plain, where a trail of blazing soul-flames moves like a stream, trickling down a path. A few embers float above and around the stream, and I realize this must be the Red and Green Teams, escorting the evacuating population of the Society for Extranaturals campus. They're almost at the end of the valley at the paved access road, and then, with luck, it's a quick jaunt to Old Highway 10.

And there, on the slope of the mountain, is Priest.

It's hard to describe the sensation of being perceived in the ether. I have only felt it once before, from the entity that's causing the Conformity, when it slept. It's like the sensation of sunlight on skin, a real feeling, as if some sort of psychic particles radiate with Priest's attention.

Priest becomes aware of me, and I feel it.

*Is it time?* he asks.

*Yeah, boss. We can't keep this up forever. If you're gonna do something, it needs to get done.*

*While the rest of our Society members have evacuated I have been collecting myself. I sometimes feel . . . disjointed.*

If I had shoulders I would shrug, but it's just my burning shibboleth self. *Well, time for contemplating your navel is over. Let's light this candle.*

I get a flash of mirth from Priest, and then his flame, that burning bit of personal combustion that is naught but Priest, throbs and begins to grow.

*Shreve, it has been a pleasure coming to know you. You should remove yourself to the heights and watch as you can.*

Now it has come to this, he has to get all maudlin on me. *Yeah, boss, nice to meet you too. But the idea is to survive, right? That's the plan.*

He chuckles, which is impressive because he has no physical form right now. We are, in essence, just that: essence. And I don't mean spices. We are souls communicating as only bugfucks can. Mind to mind. But the mind holds dear to the idea of physical space and so landscapes of the mind are created.

*Remove yourself now, and bear witness.*

What he's doing deserves recognition, and I'm the only one here to give it.

*I will watch,* I send. *And I will remember. After all, you've got whatever's left of Booth knocking around in there.*

I can feel his sadness more than see it reflected in any aspect of his shibboleth form.

*Shreve, stay out of trouble, son,* he says, and I know it's Booth speaking. *You're as reckless as the day is long.*

He hugged me once, when I was hurt, and made much of my world brighter. I will not forget.

*Mr. Cannon,* he says now, with a different inflection, colder, more removed. *We are not so different, you and I. This has become apparent. But*—something twists in the ether and Quincrux is gone.

All the ghosts have said farewell.

*Remove yourself, Shreve, and I will begin,* Priest says.

With a thought I rise, up and away.

**...**

Imagine a stone tossed into a pool. Now imagine that stone detonating with the force of a hydrogen bomb. That's the intensity of Priest's telepathic yawp.

It goes up in a release of psychic energy so massive it's hard to keep conscious with the fierce pressure of it. I'm buffeted by the force. I find my mind spinning, careening out of control, and in the aftermath of the blast part of me in the ether shivers and feels like a tooth's nerve suddenly exposed to the cold. But then that sensation dies and, far off, in the distance—the pseudo-space of the ether that the bugfuck mind creates—I sense an awareness of what has occurred here.

I worry that he's expended so much power and effort with the challenge, he won't have the strength for the fight. But maybe that was his plan, after all. I don't know.

The Conformity soldier turns its attention toward Priest.

I dash back to my flesh, gasping, becoming aware of the physical world like a man taking the first desperate breath of air after too long under water. Blood bubbles and pops in my nostrils, thick and gummy.

The Conformity soldier stands immobile, knee-deep in Ponderosa pines, its body turning now toward the western mountains that we have just fled. The transport rocks and shudders on its shocks, picking up speed—putting more distance between us and the tower of flesh now arrested in movement.

It groans, desperate, and the timbre of the sound has changed. I hear simultaneously screaming and moaning and all the expulsatory sounds a human body can make. And then the soldier slowly sinks to the earth. It's not falling to its knees because it has no true knees. Instead the soldier's body loses shape and condenses in upon itself, forming a ball, a glomerulus of flesh.

Whatever psychic power controlled the Conformity soldier has been drawn by Priest's challenge. The entity is here now. The dragon from beyond the stars.

The full weight of its scrutiny bears down upon us. My head throbs, and my nose streams blood. It's like an alarm, the taste of blood, sending my body into overdrive.

What was once the soldier rises again from beyond the tree line, floating into the sky. And the sight of it, no longer shaped in mockery or emulation of human form, gives me an instant of pure, heart-stopping terror. It is a dripping, moaning star, coalesced of misery, despair, and the meat of the malleable human race. Just clay, we are, waiting for something strong enough to shape us into its mold, to suit its purpose. We are infinitesimal—I have always known it—but this piece-of-shit monster has to not only rub our faces in it, it has to wipe its ass with humanity. All of it, all of us, we are nothing to it.

It rises, and as I watch, the transport rocking beneath me, it begins to distend, become oblong.

*Shreve, I don't like this,* Casey says.

Bernard yelps, *Aw, naw. Naw, naw, naw. I've seen this movie.*

*It's splitting!* Ember yells.

Jack lands beside me on the transport bed. He quickly moves aside and is followed by Tap and Danielle. They look not only exhausted but hypothermic.

The Conformity shifts like an amoeba, and then there are two of them, two globules of flesh instead of one.

*Go faster,* I send, hoping my panic doesn't startle Davies into crashing. Everything is happening too fast now for reaction, and no amount of extranatural abilities can help us if we smash into a boulder or a brace of pine trees.

*A plane waits for you, Shreve,* Priest sends. *Go to Bozeman. I will contend with the—*

No more.

One of the spheres of flesh begins to rise, floating west, toward the campus and Armstead Lucius Priest. The other begins to move toward us.

*Faster!* Tap says. *It's not walking anymore!*

*Working on it,* Davies sends. *Hold tight.*

The transport clanks and rumbles, and the engine shifts to a higher gear and the speed increases. I sink down on my ass and throw my arm across the matte-black cover of the extranatural bomb. It's a rough ride even though we're not on a mountain road anymore but an old blacktop, clear of snow. Trees whizz by, blurry and indistinct. Wind tears through the transport bed, and I begin to shiver.

*It's too cold! I'm freezing!* Danielle sends, and Ember broadcasts a quick image of teeth clattering and pokey nipples.

The window at the rear of the cab slides open, and Bernard shoves out an overshirt and a military jacket. *Climb in if you can, young bucks,* he sends. *Ho-lee shit. Look at that.*

The Conformity has released the second globe to resume its chase. It reshapes itself into the rough, messy semblance of a man while still levitating in the sky. You can only feel horror and terror for so long. Then it's like watching a volcano erupt—yeah, it's tremendous, yeah, there's danger, but ho-hum, my nerves are about shot.

Is this what it means to be shell-shocked?

*We're twenty minutes from Bozeman,* Davies sends. *Let's see how much distance I can get between us and it.*

Danielle climbs through the transport window as we huddle down in the lee of the cab, where the bed meets chassis. Ember manages to climb through as well, but when Tap goes to push his torso through, they wave him away. Cab's full.

The newly reformed Conformity soldier lands with a deafening boom and the exhalation of thousands. It's now half the mass of the previous soldier—only two hundred feet tall rather than four hundred.

But the thing that amazes me is that monsters can continually reinvent themselves: the Conformity soldier has adopted a new form of locomotion, lunging jumps resembling the gait of an astronaut on the moon. Still steaming, still dripping. Still moaning, gibbering. But, its mass diminished, it's moving faster now than it was before.

Despite its vigor we begin pulling away, allowing the flyers outside the cab—Tap, Jack, and yours truly—a moment to catch our breath.

Tap pants, and Jack draws his knees up to his chest. I have something I must witness.

Into the ether.

...

Back to where I was, in the etheric heights, Priest stands like a naked flame burning in the night.

Everything old becomes new again. It feels like the first time I've looked at the awareness of the Conformity itself while in the ether, blazing and burning, like an electric current racing through to the inner eye. I witness the innumerable sparks of the souls it possesses, but beyond that, layered above it, is an emptiness, a void. A vacancy that allows the sparks to flame bright and then die.

The shimmering miasma approaches Priest, standing on the invisible mountainside. Priest's volume grows as the Conformity approaches, becoming an inferno.

The two are overlaid on top of each other, the towering flame of Priest and the fog of the Conformity, and I sense a great conflict of titanic energies coming together in contest.

And then only the Conformity remains.

## TWELVE

Much of Bozeman lies devastated. It's a flat, skillet-shaped valley ringed in majestic, snow-crowned mountains. Black smoke rises from multiple locations, and it looks like finger-of-God tornadoes did the jitterbug all around the town—leaving overturned cars and trucks, houses and business reduced to rubble, windows blown out, gouts of gas-main fires licking at the heavens, burning gas stations pluming oily-black columns of smoke into the sky. Sirens but no cops. No fire trucks.

And so very few people.

Most of those folks we see carry weapons. I think back to Priest telling me that this is where the Conformity soldiers gathered the mass they needed to assault the Society's campus.

These poor people. It's hard to bear that I—that *we*—killed thousands of families when the soldier by the water tower fell. They could have lived in these trailers, these little houses. Now they'll never return.

*It looks like a war zone out there,* Casey sends.

*It is a war zone, toots,* Tap sends. Always on the verge of being a tremendous prick, he's been pushed over the edge by exhaustion.

We make our way past trailer parks and pillbox houses. Down nice streets lined with trees. I notice some drapes being pulled aside, warily.

*The beginning of the end,* Bernard says, and his normal joviality—joviality even in the face of terror—is gone. He sounds tired and small and frightened.

Davies sends, *Priest said a plane will be waiting. The last card he had to play.*

*You think we should get on a plane? Remember what happened in Maryland? That fighter fell out of the air,* Danielle says.

*Most likely from pilot error,* Davies said. *The Conformity affects human flesh, right? Like bugfucks and jocks. It affects only us.*

That sounds right, but I don't know.

*Not all extranaturals are like that,* Ember sends. Of all of the Irregulars, she's been a member of the Society the longest. *Stonechuckers manipulate the physical world beyond just human bodies, right?*

*Yeah,* Jack responds grudgingly.

That does sound right.

*There was a girl once who was a tinkerer. She could do things to technology. Make it fizz out. Drain batteries of their charges. Make computers stop functioning.*

*What are you saying?* I ask.

*This thing eats humanity and takes its powers, right? It takes extranatural abilities and then uses them to take over more people.*

Bernard says, *I feel you. But I don't like what you're saying.*

*So, what's to say that it can't take the extranatural abilities of everyone it subsumes? Both overt talent and hidden?*

*Like some recessive-gene shit?* Tap sends.

*Maybe.*

*That's what Tanzer thought, too,* I say. *Priest said she thought every person inside the Conformity had some form of extranatural ability. Undeveloped, stunted maybe. But there. Otherwise, why doesn't it take everyone?*

Silence now. It's almost like I can hear the mental gears clanking and engaging. The Irregular collective chews on this information like masticating a particularly nasty piece of gristle.

*It hasn't stopped the transport,* Davies says.

*Maybe it's stupid. It fell for the misdirection,* Jack says. *The soldiers don't have good problem-solving abilities. But the Conformity itself?*

I remember Quincrux once saying, "I am old and know all the wiles of man." Not thinking, I let that image slip into that part of my consciousness that I share with these few Irregulars.

*That sounds about right, man-child.* Bernard's bonhomie seems forced, overly jovial in the light of this desperate situation. *The Conformity is a real bitch.*

*So we're cool to take the plane, right?* Danielle says.

The transport jumps a curb. The chassis rattles and the engine revs up, going into a higher gear. In the transport bed, Jack, Tap, and I slide on our asses as the vehicle wallows about. I'm thankful when it slides to a stop without tossing one of us from the bed.

I'm having a hard time feeling my hands. Pushing myself into a standing position is painful, and all my currently unincorporated flesh has become crotchety and stiff with the frigid temperature.

The transport is on a snowy, flat area in front of a double ring of razor-wired chain-link fencing—obviously a field kept clear due to security reasons. Beyond the fence I can see piles of dirty snow and the black of tarmac, rows of Quonset huts in the distance. There's a dull green plane—a C-130—sitting on the vast expanse of the runway.

The collective moaning of the Conformity soldier sounds above the rumbling of the truck and behind us, behind us in Bozeman, I hear the crash and crumble of buildings, the snapping of high-tension wires like guitar-strings. The thunder of explosions. It's coming. It's near.

*You might want to vacate the bed,* Davies says, *because I'm going right through that fence.*

Tap and Jack don't have to be told twice. They launch themselves into the sky like rockets. Once I dip my toes in the ether, out of the constant stress and din of the meatspace world, I rise up.

The transport grinds into gear and then barrels off toward the tarmac. It's moving fast when it hits the fencing, tearing through and bouncing down a drainage gulley and up the other side, slewing sideways in the snow.

Turning, I see the soldier is visible now. It has lost more mass—more people dead—as it wades through the trees and houses, gibbering and bellowing. A few people rise into the air to meet it. It's swelling its ranks again, adding to its mass. It screams, it wails.

*JOIN US. SERVE US. WORSHIP US.*

Time to stop dicking around. From above, everything below forms squares, rectangles of muted colors, browns, grays. It's a drab existence humans live when seen from a bird's-eye view. I fly away from the soldier, over the white earth, the gray rectangles of parking, the long brown building, the arrayed crosses of planes. The airport is strangely undamaged, but most air travel has been over for weeks.

I fly over the tarmac; it looks like a particularly evil skid-mark on the grimy underwear of the snow-gray runway area, scraped clean by plows. The ass-end of the C-130 is open, the transport parked nearby. Casey and the rest of the Irregulars spill out of the vehicle. Negata moves like a ghost, and I realize, because I haven't been in contact with him—he isn't part of the collective mind of our group—I had forgotten he was with us. And maybe that is his ability. Maybe that's what he wants me to learn. How to be forgettable.

The Conformity soldier bellows, moans. More cracking and snapping of wires. In the distance, past the snowy tracks of the transport, past the ruptured chain-link fence through which we came, beyond the fields, the tree line splits and the soldier thunders into view. It steams and drips.

*It's here,* I say to all concerned. ***Get on the plane.***

I land in the transport bed, next to the extranatural bomb.

***Come on,*** Jack cries. Casey, Danielle, Bernard, and the rest are inside the plane now, and its props begin buzzing, a thick, unbearably loud basso rumble, blotting out the soldier's weird ululations.

***Go!*** I send, broadcasting a quick image of the C-130 lifting off. *I have to trigger the bomb. We need the time.*

*We're not leaving without you,* Casey says.

*I can fly, remember? Just open the cargo doors once you're up.*

The Conformity soldier changes again. The thing loses shape, condensing back into the grotesque huge floating ball of flesh.

*Uh, it's flying now, man,* Bernard sends. *You best get your ass on board.*

I pop open the hatch to the bomb, make sure the genome is firmly in place and not damaged, and press the button. The pink fluid drains into the black box, and I can feel some sort of ozonic field, like the Helmholtz but more intense. Like feedback from radio, at first it's just static, white noise, but it grows.

*Come on, idiot!* Tap sends in the equivalent of a psychic shout.

I lift off the troop bed, glancing toward the Conformity. It's hovering over the fence now, thundering. For an instant I have the impression of thousands of grimacing mouths, thousands of eyes drawn into expressions of rage. The thing is pissed off, and now it's broadcasting it.

The plane is pulling away, moving fast, the screws of the props hauling it through the air, and I follow, not as fast. I'm numb, my body buffeted by wind so cold it's hard to breathe.

The plane screams as it ascends, and the Conformity swells and rises to meet it.

There's a great squelch of static in the ether, the detonation of the bomb. It's like an invisible grenade. It's the coagulation of ether into amber, a thick viscous impenetrable solution. And I am caught inside of it.

I know no more.

...

I can't tell if I'm dead yet.

My head's full of wind, a howling cacophonous torrent. I'm falling but not toward the ground. My clothes are ripped and ruffling violently. I'm hanging in the air, even though I've been unconscious.

*My God, Shreve, wake up! I can't hold on anymore!*

Casey. Above me, the ass end of the C-130 is open, the Irregulars huddled inside.

She's got me in the palm of her invisible hand. Her arm has grown long, indeed.

It hasn't been much time, a minute or two. Looking behind me, I can see the airport rapidly retreating from view, and the Conformity hanging in the air, motionless.

Thank you, Hollis. Thank you, my friend.

You are a hero. You saved us.

I go into the ether again, dangling on an invisible thread. There are strange echoes and vibrations there, in the space-not-space of the shibboleth world. I can only think that it's because of the detonation of the extranatural bomb, but there's something more.

I don't have time to investigate. The wind is brutal, we're traveling so fast, like swimming in a pressure-washer stream. I feel as though my face will be peeled away from my skull at any moment, leaving my skull slicked with blood, the flesh of my face and cranium flapping behind me like a grotesque hoodie. Until the moment I get inside the plane's cargo hold the sensation increases and then . . . cessation of wind.

I might be deaf now. I can hear nothing.

*It's moving again!* Danielle sends, urgent and terrified. *It's moving fast.*

*I'd spin the plane into a tizzy if it could hear my beats, Dani,* Bernard sends.

An idea prickles in the back of my mind.

*Can you spin a slow beat? Make the Conformity slow down?*

*Don't know,* he says in my mind, very slowly. From where

87

we stand at the back of the cargo hold, the mesh webbing ruffling with the suck of our passage and the howl and buzz of the propellers, it's easier for us all to go into our shared headspace—to blot out the overwhelming sensations from the real world. *I need some contact with it. Eye contact, you know, always worked before. But that was with people. Real folks, not that—*

He stops. The plane is really ascending, at thirty-five, forty-degrees, and it feels like we're going straight up in the air because the back cargo door shows no view of sky, no hint of blue. All we see is a bird's eye view of the snow-covered mountaintops and dark green forested ravines of the Rocky Mountains.

We hit a spot of turbulence, and I'm nearly thrown from the plane. I scuttle over to the nylon webbing where Ember, Jack, and the rest of the Irregulars have latched on, white-knuckled. Casey stands free, no doubt holding on to a bulkhead with her invisible arm.

*I can help you, Bernard. I can get its attention.*

Radio silence.

*Eventually,* he sends. *Don't know if I want that damned thing peeping me, you know?*

I'm about to argue, but the plane levels out and the cargo hold begins to close. I don't want to lose sight of the Conformity, but when the hatch shuts all the way, the cessation of noise other than the muted thrumming of the props is like a balm. I'm beginning to be able to think again.

"Why'd the pilot shut the door?" I ask, using my real voice. In the still air of the cabin, I'm beginning to realize how cold I am. My hands are almost blue, and my teeth begin chattering uncontrollably. Shivers rack my body.

"You look like frozen cat shit, Shreve," Tap says, and he

takes off his jacket and throws it at me. It's so warm to the touch, it almost scalds me. I pull it over me, half lying on the mesh and curvature of the airplane's bulkhead. Exhaustion washes over me.

"We're picking up speed," Davies says, and I realize that must be true, now that the cargo hold door is shut. "I'll go talk with the pilot, see what's up."

I close my eyes.

■ ■ ■

I must have passed out, because when I wake, I feel warm all over. Jackets cover me and there's an arm thrown over my chest and someone delightfully soft fully pressed along the side of my body.

*Don't get any ideas, Shreve,* Casey says in my mind.

*About what?*

She ignores that. *You were freezing. We worried that you were going into hypothermia. We had to heat you up somehow and body heat was the best bet. We drew straws and Bernard lost.*

*So Bernard and I spooned, and I wasn't awake to enjoy it?*

I get a mental snort of mirth from her. *He refused, and you looked like you were going to die.*

*So ...*

*So, I saved your ass again, boy-o.*

*Thanks.* A thought occurs to me. I start, halfway sitting up. She pulls me back.

*The Conformity?*

"Still coming," Ember says, and I notice she's standing by us. I can't help but wonder if she's been eavesdropping on our conversation. The walls are breaking down, and sometimes, when I close my eyes, I find myself dislocated for just an instant, looking out from someone else's eyes.

Jack clears his throat. "It's following, but with the hatch door closed, we're outpacing it for the time being."

*We can get to Oregon, maybe, before the fuel runs out. The pilot is pushing the plane as hard as he can,* Davies says, and I get a long look at the cockpit through his eyes. The pilot, a lean, pockmarked little man with oversized hands and bright green eyes, sits near him, wearing a flight suit. He's talking, flipping switches and tapping gauges. Then the image is gone and I'm back among the Irregulars. And Negata. He's sitting quietly by the bulkhead door, buckled in, eyes closed. He seems perfectly at rest, unfazed by everything that's occurred.

"How long was I out?" I ask.

"Twenty, thirty minutes," Tap says. "Napping on the job."

"Nice. Thanks for the jacket," I say, and I mean it. I don't really like Tap, and he doesn't really like me. And that's fine. Not every meal has to be delicious. Not every person has to be my friend. But I respect him.

There's something happening here, and I need time to figure it out. All I want to do is lie here, bask in Casey's warmth, away from wind and cold. But I have to look. On the etheric heights we fly when I open myself up to the shibboleth world overlaid upon ours. And there, the darkness is pinpricked with thousands of clustered lights, following, over the dark fields and spaces.

*JOIN US,* it says in one voice. *ALL IS ONE. WE/I WILL BE WORSHIPPED AND SET IN THE HEAVENS AS A STAR.*

The force of its scrutiny is like a tether drawing me to it. All of its telepathic power is focused on me, and I can feel the vast expanses of its experience, its malevolence, its disregard for life or love or light yawning before me like the abyss. And that is what it is—the apotheosis of nothingness, the essence of oblivion.

I can only meet it with defiance. I'll not submit. I'll not join. I'll never join it.

With all the mental volume I can muster I scream into the ether.

**Fuck you, buddy!**

It's not elegant, I know. But the entity doesn't deserve anything more.

If I had a hand, I'd shoot it the bird.

**Fuck you!**

Something in me swells, the shibboleth thrums and expands again, and then I feel pinioned by light, linked in an electric daisy chain. Casey is with me here in the ether. And Bernard and Tap and Jack and Danielle and Davies.

All of us are one.

To defy the Conformity, we've become one.

Our minds have merged; our thoughts have dissolved into a seething boil.

All is one. One is all.

I am you and you are me.

There's a rhythm now, to the ether, a beat. We swell with the phantom percussions.

**Watch me now. Eyes right here,** we say. Mirth and light. It seems our Bernard aspect is still in business. *Doom. Boom doom. Doom. Boom doom.*

It's a lethargic beat, a dribble of molasses. The Conformity congeals, slows.

*Doom, boom. Doom, boom, baby,* we say in the ether.

We feel a surging elation now as the slow, driving beat begins to sink into the Conformity and it drifts away. Slowing. Slowing.

*Doom.*

The sensation of multi-awarenesses merged is almost overpowering. The walls have crumbled; the notion of I is gone altogether. We are protoplasm; we are unified.

*Boom.*

And then the one part of us, the hard part, gives another terrible ethereal shout, ***Fuck you!*** And an invisible shockwave of pain and anger and hurt and regret blasts away from us with tsunamic force.

The Conformity is gone.

■■■

Disentangling ourselves is confusing and not a little painful. It seems I am the controlling awareness, so as I release each aspect of me—Jack, Ember, Casey—it's as if I'm cutting away a bit of my soul.

And maybe I am.

***That's seriously fucked-up, Shreve,*** Jack says. At the end, he blasted the Conformity so that it couldn't follow us. Bernard's aspect slowed it, but Jack's dealt the final blow. It's hard to compartmentalize, each of our personalities and abilities suffusing the others. It's not simple now, if it ever was to begin with. There's a film, a residue of each of the Irregulars' personalities, remaining with me. And the after-echoes of their personalities.

"Yeah, I guess it is."

"I feel dirty," Jack says.

"It's only dirty if you do it right," Ember says, winking.

We've reverted to normal speech. All of us, for that short time, were so close, so much more intimate than any sex, any marriage, any confession; by speaking instead of communicating telepathically, we're trying to set the walls back up for our own protection. Maybe for our own sanity.

In my junkie days of eating memories—devouring the emotional content of the bright, ringing moments of the unwary—I experienced every kind of pleasure, but this is different. Then, I'd invaded and consumed. With Ilsa Moteff, the Witch, I ate her and took all of that evil into myself. But now? The sensations weren't secondhand; we experienced the defiance of the Conformity together, joined.

Everyone remains quiet, and I realize that Casey is still pressed against me. I can feel the warmth of her hand on my stomach, her small breasts flattened against my side. I marvel at the walls of our bodies and the pressure of her hands. For a moment, the plane drones through the air, we sway back and forth in the cargo hold, and everyone remains silent, lost in their own impregnable thoughts, individuals once more.

Everything is quiet.

But the ether thrums in a way that's hard to describe—it's as though a great hammer has fallen on a bell and the note that rings out hangs forever in the pregnant air, a permanent vibration. There's no pain, no discomfort with the ethereal sound, but it rings forth and I look to my companions' faces to see if they hear it. Ember stares at me, wide-eyed and alert.

*What is that?* she sends.

Before I can answer, the plane's props stop roaring, and the axis of the world shifts, tilting, and my stomach lightens and rises in my body cavity. Looks of alarm and mental exclamations follow, like an eruption of radio chatter.

The plane is falling out of the air.

Falling again. Always falling.

Time congeals, and I reach out again to the minds there, now parts of me. The Davies awareness in the cockpit reveals a dead instrument panel and a frantic pilot.

We must get out.

I'm not expansive enough to control everyone and everything that must be done, so I release my friends from the collective mind. Thoughts flicker in braintime, faster than light, and we know what to do.

Falling. The wind howls outside with the speed of our descent.

It all happens at once. Davies bursts through the cabin door, dragging the thrashing pilot with him. I whip the jackets away from myself and launch across the cabin toward Negata, screaming *"Unbuckle!"* Negata and the pilot are the only souls on the plane not part of our mental union.

Tap, pushing himself away from the cabin wall, grabs Casey while Danielle snatches Bernard into a great hug. Ember moves toward Davies.

Jack, near floating now, raises his hands, splaying his fingers. He gives me a wild look and sets his shoulders. He screams when the blast rips from him, tearing out the rear of the plane.

We're sucked out into the air, along with crates and jackets and trash and weapons. There's a million particles of blood like a spray of stars whirling out into the gunmetal-gray sky, cold as stone, and I realize the blood is coming from me. Bodies pinwheel in the roaring air currents. We're buffeted like leaves in a tornado. Minds scrabble at my consciousness, and I let them in and we become one, our own union, and the shibboleth seeps into us all and we begin to slow in the mad, deadly descent toward the earth rushing up at us.

But then the ground is there and everything goes dark.

# PART TWO:
# SEATED IN THE FLESH

"Strange to say, the luminous world is the invisible world; the luminous world is that which we do not see. Our eyes of flesh see only night."

—Victor Hugo

"Consciousness is much more than the thorn, it is the dagger in the flesh."

—E.M. Cioran

—asleep in his nest of laundry, Bugs Bunny in drag on the television, singing opera, volume low, and his chest so small rising and falling as the box fan hums and the close air of the trailer smells of cigarette smoke and burning plastic like a whiff of the end of everything, or just a trailer fire. Vig stirs when I move him, lifting him up and onto his bed, his little hand whacking me on the neck and then flopping over. He chuffs air through his open mouth and says something that sounds like "momma, momma, don't" but he quiets as I get him under the covers and I take his place in the nest of dirty laundry on the floor, like a dog sleeping at his master's feet. I lay there wishing I could find unconsciousness, that I could close my eyes and sink into the oblivion of nothingness instead of this life where we're abandoned but Moms doesn't have the courtesy to properly leave. There's some of Moms's vodka left. For an instant I think of going to the kitchenette, taking out the bottle and drinking until I dissolve into nothing. But the loathing I feel at the idea, I could never get beyond that. Never. Vig stirs in the bed, I can feel him as he shifts, the floor is so thin and the trailer so flimsy. No sound from Moms. She passed out hours ago but the trailer still stinks of smoke, will always stink of smoke. I watch Bugs riding on the fat horse, singing, the sound of the television low, so low, the electric ratcheting of the VHS nearly blanketed by the fan's white noise, and laying in dirty clothes wishing for sleep, dying for sleep—

# CASEY

We fall like angels cast from heaven. There's screaming and shouts and snow and weeping, but all I can really focus on is his face.

He's not handsome in any definable way. He's got this wolfish, intense face, like he's always hungry. And his eyes are too alert, really, like he sees every part of you, even those that you don't want anyone to see.

And bad things happen around him.

It's both pleasant and a little abhorrent when we bond as a group. Like fucking—there's the loss of self when he enters me (or am I entering him?) and begins to move, but there's the warmth and the pleasure and, I hope, the love there too. Not that I've fucked any of the Irregulars.

I look at Shreve lying there in the snow, remembering when the collective mind shattered. Negata kneels over him, touching Shreve with light hands, his breath billowing out in front of him. Shreve's head is swollen and smeared in blood. His breath comes in stitches.

Ember screams and screams and all I can do is wish that she'd shut the hell up but she keeps screaming, *"They're dead! They're dead!"* and scrabbling about on all fours.

Eventually, I stop looking at Shreve's face and stand to go look at the bodies.

■■■

I don't know if something in me broke when our minds shattered or if it's breaking now, looking at Bernard's and Danielle's remains. We can't find Davies and the pilot at all. It's hard to come to grips with how torn and distorted their bodies have become: it's almost impossible to recognize where Danielle ends and Bernard begins. They're a great bloody smear on the roadside.

...

We're on the side of a road on a mountainside. The western slope. Not in Montana anymore, I don't think. The air and terrain seem different. I don't know how I know, but I do. Maybe Idaho. Oregon?

Off to our right, in a snarled wreckage of trees, blooms an orange flame pouring black oily smoke into the darkening sky. The fuming carcass of the plane. It's so cold, I imagine trudging through the drifts and warming myself at the fuel and plastic fire.

Jack grabs Ember, pulling her into a tight hug and whispering something in her ear, and she quiets down. When she stops making noise, it's like a blessing. Negata looks at me and says, "Shreve is alive. I cannot tell whether he is in danger, but we all need to get inside."

Negata speaks! That recognition is like a single firecracker set off in an auditorium. A very small pop in a wide space that in any other situation might be quite interesting.

Tap says, "There's a sign over there. Looks like a big building." He tromps off in the hissing, falling snow.

Jack and Ember huddle together, and I must have drifted off because the next thing I know is that Negata has his hand on my shoulder, tugging me back to Shreve, saying, "I need your help."

I never knew what to make of Negata. He was present during my testing, like Ruark's shadow.

"You have a radio? A phone?"

He shakes his head, a quick, precise gesture.

"Davies did, but—"

"Davies is dead. And Shreve will be too if we don't get him somewhere warmer." He takes off his jacket—more black military-issue—and lays it over Shreve. "Give me a moment."

He moves like a big cat into the trees by the road, away from the plane crash. The way he moves is almost ballet-like.

The smell of the fire is noxious—like burning tires—but some of the trees around it have caught, tingeing the odor with the slightly more wholesome stink of burning pine. One of the trees, totally incinerated, cracks and falls over into a drift, half extinguishing the flames.

"The drive's cordoned off, but there's some sort of lodge up here," Tap says. There's something about Tap that's a little skeevy. Not like he's a panty-sniffer or anything—and we've shared minds, so that's a little weird—but he's like a big, intemperate dog that only wants to eat and shit and fuck. He's not stupid, but base. Trish used to talk about all the ways she was going to sex him—God, she talked too much—because he is good-looking in a brutish sort of way.

Negata emerges from the trees dragging two long branches. When he gets to where I kneel by Shreve, he removes the jacket we've draped over him and feeds the thick branches through the sleeves of the jacket.

"It will have to do." He spreads the jacket, now framed by the wood, on the ground. "Help me move Shreve onto it."

I stand. They say you should never move the injured in case of neck injuries. And Shreve's head is sure to roll about when we lift, so I wave Negata back. He looks at me strangely but does as I instruct.

I flex the *ghosthand*. It's kind of weird that I've started thinking of it like that, naming it and all. It's sort of like guys naming their dicks. But all guys have dicks, and only I have the ghosthand so I guess that makes it okay. It's better than when they wanted to call me Handjob.

Shreve called it the *shibboleth*, and I don't really know what that means. To me it's the ghosthand and my imagination. Pretty simple, really. So I imagine it swelling and flattening and growing large enough to scoop all of Shreve up in its palm and then I lean forward and lift, slowly. If you were only watching, as Negata is, it would appear that Shreve just levitated off the ground two feet, floated over a couple of feet more.

I set him down on the travois as gently as possible.

Afterward, my skin sheens in sweat and a wave of fatigue passes over me. I can do a lot with my ghosthand, but if I lift a big weight, it still has a direct effect on my body, as though I picked up Shreve and put him on my shoulders. Which, seeing how freakin' skinny he is, I probably could.

Negata doesn't smile or do much of anything except give a small, tight nod. I don't think his mother breastfed him enough, maybe. But he moves to a branch, grips it like a handle, and chucks his head, indicating he wants me to help him.

I look around. I feel like we should do something for Danielle's and Bernard's corpses, but there's not much we can do. They're not going to get any deader.

I take up the branch in my ghosthand, and we drag Shreve up the snow-covered mountain road toward where Tap waves to us.

■■■

I try to unlock the door, but it's deadlocked, and while I can easily picture my fingers as itsy-bitsy little lock-picking nubbins, I don't know how locks work well enough to pick the thing. Eventually, Jack has to blast the front door in so we can enter.

It's a massive old hunting lodge, made from thick timbers and stone. From what I can see in the dim light it looks like it housed park rangers at some point. I don't know why I think that, maybe because there's no flat-panel televisions, or computers, or stereos, which doesn't make sense because whoever owns this place has to have a lot of money. It's a big freakin' lodge.

It's dark and silent in the main hall of the lodge, smelling slightly of mothballs and ashes. To the left of the entrance there's a fireplace you could cook an ox in. The heavy drapes are pulled back, and the weird half-light you get from snowfall casts a pallor over the rough stonework. The sounds of our footfalls echo, and the scraping of the stretcher's branches sounds overloud in the dead air.

"Let's find some lights," Jack says. He walks over to a shadowed area and feels around for a switch. Ember joins the hunt while Negata and I, with Tap's help, drag Shreve toward the fireplace, standing in a pool of weak and watery light from a drape-less window.

"I'll go find some firewood, if there's any. Does anyone have a light?" Jack asks.

Ember gropes for her phone, finds it, and then says, "That's weird. It was fully charged back when we were in the Jeep."

"So, no lights," Jack says. "And the electricity must be off, too." Clicking sounds. Jack must be fiddling with the light switch. Negata watches implacably.

Tap says, "Screw it," and walks over to a larger dark shape, picks something up—I realize it's a wooden chair—and smashes it on the floor, once, twice, three times, and then brings the pieces over to us, where we've laid Shreve down. He tosses them in the fireplace and begins tearing at the cushion with thick, blunt fingers, ripping out the white stuffing. "Lighter? Matches?" Ember saunters over, lights a cigarette she pulls from her jacket, and then slaps the lighter in Tap's palm.

In moments, Tap's got the cushion's innards burning—it smells terrible, like plastic—and the wooden chair begins to smolder. Smoke fills the room until I unlatch the flue. Silly boys, they'd all suffocate if I wasn't here to rescue them.

The fire is very small in the large fireplace. The orangish-yellow light reveals a sooty wooden box with a small amount of old newspaper and kindling. Tap goes to work.

Jack and Ember shut and brace the massive wooden front door, and for a little while we all stand around, peering into the dim, wide room, watching the breath come visibly from our open mouths. It's hard to stay still with Danielle and Bernard and Davies out there somewhere, dead in the dark. I should be feeling more now, I guess. Danielle was my closest friend and Bernard was just . . . Bernard. Everyone loved him. But I feel nothing.

I check Shreve's pulse. It's there, but thready.

"You think the Conformity will find us here?" Ember asks.

Negata shakes his head, slowly. "I do not know. But the Conformity is drawn to telepaths of Shreve's and Priest's intensity. With all due respect to Ember, I do not think it will be drawn here as long as Shreve is unconscious. And maybe not after, if the boy can remain . . . how do you say? Inconspicuous."

"So we're rooting for Shreve to be in a coma?" I ask. Negata blinks in the flickering light of the fire. It's like the cold doesn't even affect him, standing there in only his shirt. I'm shivering, and I still have my jacket.

"No. I do not know how, but everything has become focused on this boy." He looks down at Shreve, who's pale now, very pale. Negata's face is grim.

If Bernard were here, he'd say something light to ease the tension and then Danielle would tell him to shut up.

"We should check the joint, man-children," I say. "Let's look for some eats and sleeps."

They look at me like I'm crazy, and maybe I am, some.

Then Jack says, "Shut up, Bernard."

For a moment, it's like they're here with us, in the room. Ember smiles, wan and tired. It's been a tremendous bitch of a day, on the real. Tap says nothing, and I can't read Negata. But Jack looks at me strangely, cocking his head. And he must feel it too.

■■■

We trudge through the lodge. Tap's found the woodpile at the back of the building, and he stokes the fire after some help loading frigid, snow-encrusted logs in. Jack and Ember play grab-ass and suck-face in the kitchen until I begin poking them from across the room with my ghosthand. Our friends are dead and the world is ending, and all they can do is rub their junk all over each other and swap saliva.

The kitchen's a small affair with a large dry pantry full of industrial-size cans of cheap tomato sauce and tinned vegetables. They manage to get the gas oven on—though Jack nearly burns his eyebrows off lighting it. We stand over the hissing thing for a while, holding our hands in the warming gap.

It's getting dark, real dark, no more of this phantasmic reflected blue light. Ember discovers a couple of candles and a flashlight and a new pack of batteries all in a utility drawer. More matches and many packets of votive candles. Whoever used this old lodge, they were prepared for long periods without electricity.

"Finally, some real light," Jack says, tearing into the new packet of batteries. He loads the flashlight and then thumbs the blister-button. It only clicks. No light.

"Batteries must be dead."

We all take up candles and walk down a long, wood-paneled wall, shielding the candle flames with our hands. Like we're pioneers instead of the extranatural badasses that we are.

"Any of you mutants know how to glow or something?" I ask.

"Is that you or Bernard talking?"

"All me. Well, almost all of me. We buried my arm in the backyard."

"What?"

"Yeah, Mom worked at the hospital, you know? Small town. Once I was stable and healing, they let us take it home. We had a funeral for it and everything. All my friends came."

"Trippy," Ember says. Ember and I have never bonded, really. Not much in common, and she's a bugfuck, so you never know when they're sniffing around upstairs.

Also, a man-eater. Since I've been with the Society she's gone through three, four guys. All much younger. She likes to play matron to their randy student. I'm sure she fucks them into submission.

We find lots of individual bedrooms, most of them with stripped and graying mattresses on the beds. The ones with any blankets or covers, we take as much of the linen as we can carry. Most are coarse, military-grade wool blankets. But warm.

I'm having a hard time keeping the layout of the place straight in my mind, most likely due to the general gloom and darkness; it all seems just dull stonework and massive knotty timbers and bland, unadorned rooms. But at the end of the main hallway that runs the length of the building we find a larger room with bunk beds and its own fireplace. A couple of big, wooden trunks reveal more moth-bitten blankets.

We all drape ourselves in scratchy wool and wander about like kids under sheets playing ghosts. Jack and Ember disappear. Negata stays downstairs, seated near the fire but with the drapes pulled aside, watching the snowfall and the darkness. Tap and I rummage around in the kitchen, which has warmed considerably. We find a large tin of soup and manage to open it, heat it over the gas stove. It's salty, but satisfying.

When we're done, we rejoin Negata and watch the night with him.

There's not much to do except wait for Shreve to come around, show some signs of life. The other teams from the Society . . . we have to assume they're dead or have been taken into the Conformity.

When we're quiet and still, the absence of Danielle and Bernard seems all the louder. And Shreve lies between us, breathing shallowly.

"Fuck," Tap says. I'd think it was apropos of nothing except I was thinking the same thing.

"It's a bad deal." For a moment I'm angry. Angry at myself

because that's all I can think of to say. Angry at the world for sinking to this level of shittiness. "Fuck," I say.

Negata doesn't glance at us, but occasionally he looks at Shreve.

"You looked like you thought of something earlier," I say.

Negata remains silent, but Tap perks up.

"When Ember's phone didn't work."

"Where are Ember and Jack?" Negata asks.

Tap snorts.

"One of the bedrooms, maybe," I say. "Maybe upstairs, looking around. The lodge is seriously dark."

Negata simply nods in acknowledgment.

"Where are we, anyway?" I ask.

"Idaho," Tap says. "Near Oregon." He lifts a wad of papers he's clutching in a meaty fist. "This is a workhouse for the Game and Fish Commission and the Devil's Throne Park Rangers."

"The middle of nowhere, then."

"Pretty much."

Negata seems to be thinking. "In answer to your question, Miss Klein, I did have a thought."

"Love to hear it."

"It is complicated. And not fully formed." Negata pauses before and after each word. Nothing about the man is hasty or unconsidered. His English accent is almost perfect when he speaks slowly.

"That's okay, I can live with uncertainty."

He turns his head toward me, considering. "This is an admirable trait. Many people cannot."

"So what's this idea?"

"Why did the plane fail?"

That's a good question. A very good question.

"The insomnia? There was that earlier plane crash. Maybe a maintenance guy hadn't been getting enough sleep and didn't put oil in the right place." It sounds good coming out of my mouth, but I don't know if I believe it.

"Why is the electricity out?"

Tap says, "Because the Conformity has taken all the population! No one to work the plants, no one to make sure if a line goes down it gets put back up. You know, *infrastructure*. Roads and power lines and telephone lines and shit."

"Why did Ember's phone fail?"

"What's with this? What are you hinting at?" I ask.

He raises a hand. A flat, blunt hand, square and deadly. "It may be as you say, Miss Klein. And most likely is."

"But you don't think so."

"No."

"What do you think?"

He looks back to the window. The white's coming down in big, thick flakes, so heavy you can almost hear it. The fire in the plane will have been extinguished now. Danielle's and Bernard's bodies will be tucked in under a blanket to sleep. For a moment I picture them, lying faceup and eyes open, as crystalline snowflakes land on their milky white eyeballs and cover their blue-gray lips.

"I think that the entity has changed the reality of our universe. On a subatomic level. A quantum level."

"What do you mean? I don't understand," Tap says.

"The Conformity draws extranaturals to itself. It uses this power to fly, to create soldiers. With each person it absorbs, it gains their energy and also their ability. It is harvesting mankind."

"Well, that's just about the worst thing I've ever heard," I say.

Tap glances at me, alarm written all over his blunt, dim features. If he's picking up on this, it's got to be bad.

"I think—" Negata says, very slowly. "No, I fear that the universal phenomenon that allows us to manipulate electricity doesn't work anymore. Maybe the entity has eliminated the matter of the universe's ability to retain an electrical charge, positive or negative."

Tap's face scrunches up with what seems like intellectual pain. Like he's lifting weights or something.

"So, you're saying—" Tap says, rubbing his temples. "That bastard has killed electricity?"

Negata stares at us, unblinking. "Yes."

I clear my throat. "Hey, you two geniuses don't need to strain yourselves. If the Conformity changed the nature of physics to not allow positive and negative charges, we'd be dead as doornails. There's electrical crap going on everywhere in your body."

Negata nods—obviously, he's realizing the truth of it—and Tap just stands there mouth-breathing and looking about for somewhere to drag his knuckles.

"It is possible, Miss Klein, that the Conformity has negated electricity in some other manner."

"Sure, but those are all the little questions. The *hows* of it all. The big questions are what have me worried. The *whys*."

"So, what are you suggesting, Miss Klein?" Negata asks.

"The one thing we know about the Conformity is that we're no good to it dead. It might not give a shit about injuring itself, but we're raw material for it."

"I'm following," Tap says. "It needs us for the juice."

"And it can think, yeah? The Conformity has adapted to us. Instead of being totally led away when the old man lit the candle, it split in two and sent one after us and one after Priest, right?" When they say nothing, I go on. "I was on top of that water tower with Shreve when we turned the Helmholtz field on it. The soldier—" I scrunch my eyes closed and think back. The thousands of mouths opening, bellowing, screaming, moaning. "It was surprised when we hit it with the Helmholtz. We alarmed it."

"Fuck yeah, we did, the bastard," Tap says. "But so what? We killed that one."

I shake my head. "Don't you get it? It's all connected. Obviously, the soldiers are autonomous at times, but they're part of the greater fabric . . . flesh . . . of the whole."

Tap looks at me blankly.

It takes a lot of effort not to roll my eyes. "We hit it with the Helmholtz—an electrical field—so as we were escaping, it hit us with an *anti-Helmholtz* field. Right? One that negates all electricity."

"But how, I might ask." Negata remains still, eyes like black pools, watching me closely.

"It doesn't really matter. Look at what Shreve can do. Look at us. Any one of us extranaturals can do lots of damage. Imagine the kind of telekinetic power it takes to keep a Conformity soldier, or the Conformity itself, together. *Levitating!* It's incredible."

Tap nods, slowly. "It has the power to blanket large areas with fields. Maybe, at this point, the whole earth."

I turn back to look at Shreve. At times I think he's going

to shift, open his eyes, and smile. Say my name. But he hasn't yet.

"That's the *why* I'm trying to puzzle out," I say. "Why is it doing this?"

"And do you have any theories?" Negata asks.

"It's reshaping the world to suit it. And it's moving toward that end."

"What end?" Tap says, his voice going up an octave.

—no food for two days except the meat sludge served me at school and she's there with fat Billy Cather watching TV on the couch when I come in, she's drunk, her lips and chin red and raw from sucking face with Cather's fat stubbled mug. Moms checks her shirt, making sure the buttons are in line or maybe checking for cum stains and negligently waves her hand when I ask after Vig. "Out in the woods," she says. When I turn to go find him, she says, "Get me a pack of Kools, hon, willya?" and when I hold out my hand for the money, she turns to Cather expectantly. It only takes him a moment to pull out a grubby five and put it in my hand. I wish she'd get more from him, because right now she's screwed him only for a pack of smokes and whatever booze he brought over. Leaving, I head straight to Cather's trailer and climb through the bathroom window—his trailer's almost as messy as ours—and clean out his kitchen cabinets, dumping cans of Dinty Moore and refried beans and fruit salad in a plastic bag I find under the sink. In his filthy bedroom at the back of the trailer, I scrounge all his change before going to find Vig who's somewhere in the woods, behind the house, near dark. I'm so very angry, furious, and it feels like a fever that's on me, this anger, yelling for my brother in the dark, carrying stolen food. He's half feral when I find him and he pops the lid off the fruit salad and drinks the syrup like Moms with her vodka and then dips his fingers into the can, his filthy grubby fingers, and all I can think is "someday we'll live somewhere clean, someday we'll live someplace clean" as I take his sticky hand and we walk to the Git-N-Go to get Moms Kools and go—

# TAP

If I could do damn near anything I wanted, I'd be chugging beer on a beach with big-breasted supermodels with Eastern European names and minimal English. I would not be freezing my balls off with a Japanese guy and a one-armed chick who talks too much, a comatose dickhead, and two lovebirds in some abandoned government sweat lodge.

But there you have it. Everything is ending thanks to the super-blob sucking up all the people and, if what Negata says is true, sending us down a path to destruction. The universe unraveling like a moth-eaten Christmas sweater.

The end of the world always sounded fun when Megadeth screamed about it. I didn't think it would be so fucking boring. And cold. I'd strangle a puppy if I could wash my nuts in warm water.

But whatevs.

Shreve continues to be useless, conveniently in a coma, and the rest of them, as usual, need someone to take care of business when they're too weak to do what has to be done.

Two days now since the plane fell and we fell with it. No electricity, no news. No Conformity or soldiers either (so that's a plus) but the woodpile's shrinking. We started with a cord of wood, but this is a big-ass building and the logs are well-weathered, burning like bastards. And there's no ax in this whole dump.

I find Negata and Casey with Shreve by the main fireplace.

"Not long before we start freezing our asses off. I need an ax," I tell them. I can't get a handle on Negata. His face is like a mask. That, or the Japanese pack all their facial expressions into the fine art of blinking. "You know, a little chop-socky on the woodpile?"

Casey's been in my brain, and I've been in hers—all thanks to Dillweed here, lying on the floor. They've made him all comfy and cozy for his nap. With my foot, I nudge his leg.

"Don't do that, Tap."

"Anything from him? Or is he out of action like—"

"Like Bernard? Or Danielle?" She looks at me like she's just sucked a lemon. "No, he's not dead."

I nudge him again with my foot just to be sure.

Her mentioning Kicks and Dani makes me nervous, and for reasons that are strange to me, yeah? I mean, not just because they're dead. But because there's some retarded shit going on.

Like last night, I was coming in from the woodpile— only me and Jack are willing to tote wood—to get the bunk room warm enough so that our toes and noses and nipples don't freeze right off in the night. It had been cloudy, but the snow had stopped, you know, and without the reflected glow of electric lights nighttime is now absolutely pitch-black dark, so I had to get the logs almost by feel. As I turned back to the lodge, clouds opened up and the moon and starlight swept through the clearing making everything stand out, sharp, you know, like a video with the contrast cranked to the crushing point.

So as I stood there breathing into the night, my neck hairs began bristling. Something was watching me. There might be bear around here, or worse, mountain lions, hungry as fuck in this bitch of a winter. So I stood as still as I could and peered at the forest.

Two shapes became clear. One bulky, one somewhat lithe, standing near each other. Other shapes in the trees. Dark fir trees, darkness upon darkness, gray and brown and green blending into black. Familiar faces I could almost make out in the dark. Behind them a taller silhouette.

I did not wait around to see what they were. I'm sick of this watery, salty, canned soup, and I've got the runs now and don't ever intend on giving the squirts to some bear or mountain lion. Those bastards can eat rabbit or squirrel and fuck right off. God, I hope they haven't sniffed out Danielle's and Davies's and Bernard's corpses.

But I'm getting cabin fever. And we can't stay here forever, so I need to see where we are. Find some other food. Some pasta or canned meat or something. I seriously can't take any more ketchup and chicken noodle.

I nudge Shreve's foot again. "I'm gonna make a scouting run. Look." I hold up a brochure for Devil's Throne I found in one of the rooms. "To the southeast is a town called McCall. I fly down there, check it out. Maybe grab some food—canned veggies and shit—and pop back."

They look like they're going to argue. But they don't.

"Find a doctor," Negata says. "Or a nurse. Shreve needs some professional attention."

"Right. Gimme your jacket. And those gloves."

Negata hands me his jacket and gloves and says, "Take Jack with you."

"Nah, I'll work better alone."

Casey frowns. "You'll take Jack with you. What if you run into a soldier, or one of the Conformity itself? Don't be stupid enough to think you could handle any of that alone. All you can do is fly."

She must have lost her sense of humor with her arm in that car wreck.

"I'm a pretty good shot."

"Not good enough. Jack's going with you."

We've all been avoiding speaking mind-to-mind since Shreve collected us into our own little mini-Conformity, but now Casey sends, *Jack, Ember, get your asses down here.*

There's a few flashes of alarm and the dregs of sexual energy and a quick flash of ruffling clothing. Jesus H. Christ, they're upstairs fucking in one of the rooms, and that pisses me off because it leaves only this one-armed bitch for me and everyone knows anyway that she's all doe-eyed and dewy-thighed for the Li'l Devil.

Fuck my life.

When they finally join us, looking sheepish, Jack and I gear up and do what we can to prepare for the cold. Thank god it's stopped snowing and the air is still. Flying in winter, in a hard wind, is like saying I want to have my dick fall off from frostbite.

"I'm going too," Ember says.

Casey looks furious and then tugs Ember out into the hall for an estro-con. When they return, both look angry. But it doesn't look like Ember is going to come with us after all.

Casey says aloud, for Negata's sake, "It's gonna be hard to find us again. We're in BFE."

"I have an uncanny sense of direction."

Abruptly, I feel a hand on my chest. Working around my back. Feeling every inch of exposed skin. It's Casey.

"If you're not back soon, I think now I can close my eyes and find you in the dark."

"Did you just feel me up?"

She gives me a withering look. "Puh-lease." With her

one good hand, she holds up her pinkie. "I don't think so."

Ember snorts.

"So not true," I say. "And you know it." She will seriously regret saying that. "Who put you in charge?" I ask.

Negata stands and takes a step toward me and then stops, his feet apart, his hands free. "I did, Mr. Tappan."

I think I can take him. But it looks like Dillweed is going to die if we don't do something, and I'm seriously getting cabin fever. So, I'm not going to put the beatdown on him today, you know? And fine, I didn't want to be the ringleader, anyway. I'm a lone wolf. Yeah?

"Okay. Don't get all feelings about it," I say, and I head toward the door.

I don't even look to see if they follow.

I've got to get out of here.

# FIFTEEN

—it's just a look, that's all, it is a glance. Mrs. Stevens's eyes crinkle at the edges like she's in pain when she sees me, as we walk past her trailer, me holding Vig's little hand, taking him to where the school bus will pick him up. It's cold this morning, and our breath is visible in the air, and I'm in short sleeves, hugging myself and trying to keep my teeth from chattering like some cartoon character embedded in an ice cube and Vig swaddled in my only coat, a denim one and thin at that. Mrs. Stevens calls for us to wait, waving a soft, fat hand and waddles inside her trailer and returns with a stained box. Questioning, I open the top and see it's full of clothes, boys' clothes in Walmart styles that seem like they were popular a decade ago. But they're clean and don't stink of cigarette smoke. And the woman is smiling. Her jowls wobble as she smiles her look-at-how-kind-I-am-giving-these-poor-kids-my-table-scraps smile. And all I can think of is slapping her fat face and the surprise that will blossom on it as her cheek reddens after the impact. I stare at her thinking about it, how wonderful it would be to bitch-slap her fifteen minutes into the future. And maybe my stillness broadcasts to her, because her do-gooder smile withers and dies. I say "Thank you," and she says "God bless," and neither of us means it and I think about how I'm going to break into her car tonight—

# EMBER

It's like everything is a chorus, the fading strains of a song, repeating over and over again, the afterflash of Kick's rhythms in my head.

They lodge in you, these earworms, these aural phrases—the shibboleths—and they repeat and repeat again.

When I was a girl, my Gram told me about the Mississippi River—*em eye crooked letter crooked letter eye crooked letter crooked letter eye humpback humpback eye*—and that there were eddies and currents in that great flow that never stopped circling. A body trapped in one, under the surface, would circle and circle again in the eddies.

...

Bury ourselves in the flesh to keep from thinking, bury ourselves in our crotches to keep from thought. Our hands, our spit. So much death and devastation.

All I want, all I want, all I want—get in bed and pull the covers over my head and sleep for the rest of the year. But Jack's in bed with me too now and it's easier to forget when he's pressed against me, his mouth on mine.

Feel a little guilty—guilty when she talks—when Casey sends, *Jack, Ember, get your asses down here.*

Too cold to dress out in the naked air of the room—we don't sleep in the bunkhouse near the fireplace because . . . *awkward.* Snatch up my clothes that are huddled under the blankets at the foot of the bed and we dress, a jangled, disjointed mess, under the covers. We take the still-warm woolen blankets with us, draped over our shoulders like cloaks, soldiers hunting for the bones of the tsar.

Down in the great room, down into the room so great, Tap sulks and pads about like a caged bear at the zoo. Casey explains the mission to us and then glares at me when we don't hop to it immediately.

Sometimes when I close my eyes, I can see that horrendous *thing* coming for us. That hellish, stinking tower. The weird emanations pouring from it. I'm no halogen bulb, like Shreve, but I can feel it when something stirs up the arteries of air.

Haunts me, o fearful me, it haunts me, la de *da*, la de *de*. Their faces, the misery twisting their features. It's like a circle of Hell took form and began walking the earth. How Grandma would have loved it. Thank whatever gods there are that she's rotting in her sanctimonious grave.

But when I'm with Jack (and—I don't like to think about this too closely—with Shreve) I don't feel as terrified. We can lose ourselves in the flesh.

Casey tugs my arm, pulling me into the frozen hall, away from the others. Her breath smells terrible. But I imagine mine does too. None of us thought to bring toothpaste with us when we fled the campus.

"What the hell is wrong with you? We're trying to figure out how to survive, and you're upstairs with Jack?"

I don't think I'm blushing. If I am, I shouldn't be. The anger and outrage and worry pour off her like a miasma.

"So? Better than stewing down here, pining for Sleeping Beauty," I say. The throttled rage crossing her features is, honestly, terrifying. I realize, of all of us, she is probably the most dangerous. Her invisible arm recognizes no wall or boundary or flesh.

I shiver.

"I've seen how you look at him. You've got Jack now, but you burn through them, don't you?"

Now it's my turn to get angry. "Listen, Casey. I don't know what this is all about, but you need to mind your own—"

"If you say 'business' right now I'm going to fucking kill you," she says, very quietly. *"Staying alive is my business,"* she hisses. "And it should be yours too. All of ours."

Shitty thing about being called on the carpet is when they're right. I've been hiding from the situation we're in. Orgasms just helped me forget it all. But I'll be primped like a pig if I'll let her see that. She's obviously wanting to piss in a circle around Shreve. Territorial markings are so insecure.

Allow myself to nod, as slowly as possible. Can tell by the way the energy pouring off of her has changed that she finds this acceptable. Her furrowed brow relaxes, some at least.

"Tap's stir-crazy, and Shreve needs some sort of medical attention."

"I'm not staying behind, Casey."

"Yes, you are."

Put my face right close to hers, so my breath brushes her hair from her cheek. "You can go fuck yourself. You might think girls have to stay nice and safe at home, but *I* don't."

Casey laughs. "God, I've always known you were self-centered, but this beats all. I don't want you to stay here because I think you can't keep up with those idiots! I need you here!"

"What?"

"You're the only bugfuck we've got now. Shreve's seriously hurt. I need you to try to connect with him, mind-to-mind." She shakes her head as if clearing her thoughts, and for a moment I can see the panic and worry hiding behind her abrasive facade. She's scared he'll die. And even though she's terrified of me taking him from her, she'd rather risk it than let his state go on like this.

"Oh, Casey," I say, but I've never been good at sympathy. "You're in love with—"

Something takes my breath, stopping the words from leaving my mouth. Casey's invisible arm.

"Shut your mouth. All of human existence is on a knife's edge, and you're fucking and blathering on about love." She calms herself and allows the wind to reenter my lungs. "He's in a coma, maybe. He could be in there, trying to get out, to say something. You've got to *try*, Ember. You can't hide away from it."

Don't want her to see she's won so easily. Don't want her to see that I want to do it. It's the Li'l Devil. Of course I want to poke around in his head. He deserves that. He's poked around in mine.

And in some way, he's been inside me—*yeah you wanna know me, yeah you wanna know me*—far more than Jack ever has. Than Jack ever could.

There's that to think about.

"Okay."

"That's it? Just 'okay'?" She sounds exasperated.

"Yeah. What do you want me to say? No?"

She looks like she wants to say twenty different things then, but she manages to get out, "Oh, just shut up. Shut up."

We return to Jack, Tap, and Negata. Jack's sitting by Shreve, looking at him, his face grim and grave. They've been through a lot together, and I know how Shreve tugs at him. He's the only family Jack has.

The boys have suited up, putting on as many jackets as they can find. Tap's stoked the fire and now fiddles with his rifle. I hope the armaments will keep him warm.

"Well," I say, taking Jack's hand and pulling him up. "If you're gonna go fly off like superheroes, you're gonna need your capes." I pick up Jack's blanket from where he let it fall to the floor and draw it around his neck. Thick wool is rough to the touch and heavy but I'm always prepared, and I punch a hole in the fabric with my pocketknife and use a bit of nylon rope to fasten the blanket around his neck.

He seems surprised and then bemused by it all.

"Be careful, you," I say.

"You're not going?"

"No." I glance at Casey, who watches us avidly. "I'm going to stay here and try to contact Shreve, mind-to-mind."

Jack's eyes widen, dawning comprehension showing on his face. "Yes! That makes sense." Then he looks like he wants to say something to me, or to Shreve through me, but he just opens his mouth. Shuts it. Opens it again. Looks foolish.

He'll stand there all day if I don't do anything. I kiss him.

Goes on for probably longer than it should, and with people watching to boot. Negata gives a slight, quiet cough.

Casey's flushed and furious when we're done, and Tap looks like he could strangle a chicken. Negata's face remains blank.

"Hey, where's my cape?" Tap asks, killing the mood. "And my kiss?"

## SIXTEEN

—at the bus stop, the big one with the nicer clothes, new sneakers, rolls up on me with a kind of expectant grin, hands nervous, and says, "So you're the bastard." The word comes out like it's a bike and he's taking it out for the first time. So maybe that's why it doesn't really register on me and I say "What?" and he says, more confident this time, "A bastard, dude. You don't know what a bastard is? It's a kid without a dad" and I stand there blinking, blood rushing in my ears because of-fucking-course I know what a bastard is and then I'm reaching out with my finger to touch him on the nose—no, not my finger, my fist. How did that get there? But he's big, like his balls have already dropped, and he moves sideways at the exact moment my fist should be touching his face and he's not there and I'm turning my head and there's his fist. It closes my eye, and then I'm falling and he's on top of me and the blows to my face stop hurting after the first five or six and then it's just the laughter of the boy and his friends that are killing me and then it's nothing at all except the throb of my swollen face and tightening of my skin as my cheeks fill with purple blood—

# JACK

Soaring.

Ground wreathed in snow and fog and the trees standing like forgotten sentinels in some invisible war. Whipping overhead, the wind tears my face. Tears stream from my eyes.

Flight.

Gliding over the dark-blanketed forests, skimming my head in the low clouds. Tap racing along beside me and for a moment we are horses, neck and neck. We are salmon leaping upstream.

Cold.

I can't feel my fingers. I hold them out before me, like Superman as he flies, not to pose, but to funnel the icy wind away from my face.

Land passes beneath us and for an instant, when the wind changes direction under the gunmetal-gray skies, everything stills and quiets: the howling wind, the throbbing rush of my blood in my veins, my pounding temples. The world stands still. Or maybe I am still and the world continues to move, driven by inertia.

But the wind changes again and the howling fills my ears and racks my body once more.

I watch the earth, trying to remember.

•••

A patchwork quilt from above, the little town. A white empty space to the north. A frozen lake.

My anger is like waves in me, swelling and receding, the pain and the heat that anger brings. I worry what that means now, for myself. For Shreve and the rest of the world. Sometimes I feel like if I let my true rage come out, the whole world would go up in flames, those I love, those I hate. The innocent and guilty alike.

Those I love.

I'm freezing now, I've never been so cold before. I don't think I'll ever be warm again. Even thinking about Ember doesn't warm me up. Not the memory of her hands and mouth on me, not the thought of when I took her clothes off the first time. I have only fear and anger. I want to crow! I want to cry. It's so dangerous. So scary.

*We need to set down out of sight,* I say.

*What the hell for?* Tap says.

*You think we should just fly into the town square?*

*Why not?*

*We'll get shot, that's why!* I send. Dense as a steer. *As far as I remember, most people don't fly.*

*We do.*

*Yeah, we do. But what's to keep them from thinking that we're part of the Conformity?*

*Because we don't smell like shit and piss and walk around like Godzilla, that's why,* Tap sends.

*How the hell will they know that? We can fly. That's enough to blow their minds.*

He's quiet for a long while. *Fine,* he sends, eventually.

We land on what must be a highway leading into town. Hard to tell because the snow is high and hasn't been packed down by any vehicles. I do see some tracks, possibly human. Other tracks of creatures that run on four legs make braids and tangles in the white powder.

So cold, parts of me feel like they're not mine anymore. My feet, my hands, they're numb, like big, blood-filled sacks of flesh. I'm beyond myself. Tap, bulky and thick in the extra jacket, tucks his head down into his chest. There's smoke coming from up ahead on the left.

*We should stop there and get a read on this shitburg.*

It's the first time Tap has contacted me, mind-to-mind, since we merged in the plummet from the sky. Necessary, that merging, so that we could fly, so that Casey and Negata could live. But we lost Danielle and Bernard and Davies and the pilot anyway.

But the worst was when I was inside Bernard's mind, and he was inside mine, when he died. A static-filled fuzziness, like all your consciousness is just an Alka-Seltzer tablet dissolving its way toward oblivion. Scrabbling, full of desperation. And then darkness. It's hellish and beatific all at once.

Bernard. Danielle.

Sometimes they're with me. Danielle's sharp wit and sharp tongue, Bernard's beats, the music of him, his rhythm, his love of life. Scent on a shirt your friend has worn. Or your girlfriend. Slip it over your head and then your head is full, for a moment, with that unknown-but-familiar scent. The essence of someone else filling your nostrils, foreign, a little unpleasant. But *them*. When I was ten I tried to get the Arkansas foster care agency to find my parents' effects, but they were gone. I just wanted to smell them, to see if I could tell something about them from smelling their clothes. But they'd all been sold.

I have that moment from time to time. My nose is filled with them.

"You smell that?"

"No," Tap says, bullish and gruff. I don't know if he's just saying that because he's a stubborn bastard or because it's the truth.

"For a second I thought—"

"You thought what?"

"Nothing."

He mutters something, but Tap is always muttering something.

Up and over the rise, following the white memory of road, pushing snow in front of us until we have to start high-stepping where it gets deep in drifts. On the air I smell woodsmoke, and off in the distance a dog barks, a lonely sound, so small in the wide expanse of world around us. The land itself could be Montana except for the fog-wreathed mountains. Not as raw, maybe, and the forests are lusher, dense with evergreens. Dark, impenetrable.

Stillness. Everything around us is hushed. The low-lying gray clouds. No wind.

Our breath comes heavy as we walk.

Eventually, we reach a place near where the smoke rises. In the distance I can see the gray pillars that signal more fires. From the air, I didn't see any of the scarred countryside that comes from Conformity soldier attacks. But I didn't do a close pass.

*Careful now,* I send to Tap. *Only communicate mind-to-mind.*

*I'm always careful,* Tap says.

Of course. Nobody can tell you anything. But I don't send that. *We should let Casey and Ember know we're about to make contact.*

Tap snorts, disgusted. Caution isn't his style. Like Shreve.

*Approaching a house,* I send, thinking of Ember, the feel of her mind. Shreve has talked about how distance affects talents and how it has something to do with what he calls the ether. Before, with all of our conversations, we were close. We had no problem speaking telepathically. But now? So many miles between us, and Shreve's not here to boost the signal.

Tap stops, breathing heavy, billowing steam from his mouth and nose. He looks at me, waiting. If there were grass, he'd eat it.

Faintly, very faintly, comes, ***Be careful, Jack. And you need to hurry.*** It's like an echo coming from far painted hills.

Tap shrugs and starts trudging forward again. I follow.

**...**

It's a small house, and it looks like any house in any neighborhood in any city I've been in. But this one is surrounded by dense woods, and as we approach, I can hear the tinkling blue of a small stream nearby under ice. Two white mounds stand in the space before the building itself—a sedan and a truck, I'd guess. Smoke dribbles skyward from the chimney, and the idea of warmth makes me that much colder.

Tap takes the steps up onto porch, and in the silence of the day, I can hear someone grunt. The drapes near the front window are whisked back before we can knock. A dark, bearded face with one wild eye peers at us and then the drapes close again before I can take in any more details.

"What do you want?" The man's voice is gruff and hoarse.

"Please, sir. Our friend is hurt and we need a nurse or a doctor," I say.

There's a long pause. Tap holds up a fist like he wants to punch someone.

"There's no doctor or nurse here."

"I realize that, sir. But seeing as we're walking, we hoped you might be able to tell us something about the town, and where we can find a doctor."

Another long silence.

"It's freakin' cold out here," Tap says, angry.

*Shut up, idiot. Yelling at him won't help.*

*It'll make me feel better.*

*Yeah, think it'll make you any warmer?*

He's got nothing to say to that.

Behind the door, I hear the unmistakable sound of a shotgun being pumped. My stomach drops.

"I'm sorry we bothered you!" Tap and I make a hasty retreat from the house, back into the snow-covered yard.

As we pass the cars, I hear the door opening and stop, tense. Ready to launch myself into the air.

"Wait." The man comes onto the porch, holding the shotgun pointed, if not at us, then in our general direction. The black hole of the shotgun's bore makes my legs weak. I can't fly faster than a bullet. I'm so much weaker than a speeding train. My fifteenth birthday is next week, and I'm scared.

The man looks us over, eyes narrowed. He's older, gray-whiskered and washed-out, standing in overalls with a heavy sweater and Coke-bottle-thick glasses. "Follow the road into town," he says, gesturing with the gun's barrel. "You'll pass a strip mall on the left, a grocery store. You'll need to take a right at the first light—they're not working anymore, just like our cars and TVs and—" He stops. Searches for the words. "First the goddamned insomnia, and now this."

"When did it all stop?" I ask.

He sucks his teeth, making his white-stubbled cheeks look cadaverous. "Few days back. But the world went to hell long before that."

I nod. It's true.

"Take the right. Go fast. I don't suggest getting near the church."

"The church? Why not?"

"Just take my word, son. Any building with an eyeball painted on it . . . you'll want to avoid."

"An eyeball?"

"That's right. An eyeball. Ain't gonna say any more." He shakes his head, purses his lips, and spits into the snow. "Keep going. You'll see the clinic right past the library."

"Can we come in? I can't feel my feet," Tap asks. The way he says it, even I wouldn't let him in. He's a sour one.

"They'll warm up the faster you move them," the man said, gesturing again with shotgun barrel.

"Thanks for the info, mister," I say. And we truck out of there.

···

It's maybe a mile more to the town. We pass shuttered and dim houses on the left and right of the highway. What windows are visible show no faces. Drapes remain still. No birds flying, no dogs barking now. Few signs of life anywhere.

Tap mutters and gripes about the walk, but any thoughts of flying the rest of the way into town evaporate when we see the first house with an eyeball painted on the front door. It's not the flying that's problematic (other than the cold). It's that we're not bulletproof.

Tap approaches the house. I want to tell him to stop, but fear, in others, is something Tap enjoys more than anything. You'd think a front door painted with a symbol would look weird, but it doesn't. I can imagine a real sign painter doing the job. There's a word underneath it.

"What's that say?" Both Tap and I jump at the sound of his voice.

*Can't tell, really. "Panoply"? No. It's "Panopticon,"* I send. "Panopticon?"

*Shut up, man. We're not here to draw attention to ourselves. Just to find a doctor.*

*What the hell does* panopticon *mean?*

*No idea,* I send.

We keep moving. Snow, light, making a soft hissing sound that blankets all other noise. We've been out in the cold for hours now, and we need to get out of the elements soon if we want to keep all our toes and fingers from frostbite.

More houses now and there, ahead of us, bundled tightly in thick, down-filled winter clothes, is a figure, trudging through the white. I want to call to him (or her), but the wildness of the man who first gave us directions gives me pause. And the strange paintings on the door. Looking around, I see more of them on the fronts of houses. Small, modest homes. Some with smoke coming from chimneys, yet dim and unlit. With eyes on the doors.

Tap raises his hand to hail the figure, but I stop him. The eye and the word *panopticon* and the silence all around make me wary.

*Let's not contact anyone until we find the clinic. That's the job. That's why we're here,* I send.

*I'm freezing, Jack. We've got to get there soon. Let's fly the rest of the way, since we know where it is now, generally.*

I gesture off to the left of the road we're walking. Drapes fall quickly as Tap turns to look. Up ahead, the down-clad figure has stopped and turns in our direction. *They've spotted us, Tap. Flying now would be especially bad.*

*Explain to me why again,* Tap says. Of all of us Irregulars, Tap's probably the best at expressing tone and feeling mind-to-mind. Almost like Shreve. The problem with Tap is that it's usually only one tone and one feeling.

*Come on,* I respond.

We make the intersection—the figure scurries off, head down and hustling—and trudge down the white-blanketed street, among the whisper of evergreen needles and the shushing of our feet through the snow. I feel watched. Like an old fairy tale, children lost in the woods. And maybe we are.

A grocery with its big front plate-glass windows boarded up with plywood and decorated with one large eye. Black streaks rise on the cinder blocks above the windows and doors—it looks like there's been a fire. Ahead of us, a thin dribble of oily black smoke rises skyward from the remains of a convenience store, its building husked and the gas pumps a twisted mess of petroleum-stinking black metal. Gas explosion.

And the panopticon eye is scratched into the char on the hood of a blackened car.

*Well, that's seriously fucked up. Looks like the apocalypse happened while we've been playing house,* Tap says. *That eye creeps me the fuck out.*

*What could've happened here?* A picture is forming. The world's been sleepless, and now there's the Conformity. Shreve said that New York was disintegrating before the entity rose. I can't help but think it's gotten worse and the infection has spread to these smaller towns.

"The center cannot hold," Shreve would say. If he says anything ever again

*Let's hurry,* I say, and Tap nods vigorously.

There's an open lot, and the snow has drifted on the roadside as we trot forward. We pass a low-slung dark log building with a Payette Library sign in front of it and on our left—between the marina, condo, and boat rental signs—the glimmer of a wide, white expanse that must be the lake. The wind now comes off the lake in gusts. Cuts through the jackets and numbs my already frozen arms, hands, legs. I see a small strip mall. Fir trees along the front walk, with a small sign that reads *D. Willamette, MD*, along with some other names with strings of letters after them. A dentist. A veterinarian. Bingo: a medical center.

A woman's voice interrupts our beeline to the door with Willamette's name. "That's far enough."

Only now that she's moving can we see her. She's draped in some sort of white camouflage, perfect for the snow, and holds a hunting rifle in her hands. She'd been sitting on a bench. She must have been watching us for a long while.

"You with *them*?" she asks.

"The eye people? No," I respond.

She looks at me. It's hard to tell her age; she's heavily dressed in winter gear, and the camouflage she's got draped around her makes her seem a white blob against the snow and the off-white of the building's painted walls. The rifle's black bore points directly at my chest. Does not waver.

"Well, move along. Nothing for you here. No drugs. No booze. There's a liquor store if you keep going the way you were headed. And a pharmacy past that."

"We don't want drugs. We need help. Our friend's hurt. In a coma. Are you a doctor?"

She's silent for a long while.

"Veterinarian. And a coma's bad news."

"Is there a people-doctor in town?" Tap asks.

"No. This new church . . ." Her face sours. "They don't like people who go their own way. Like doctors. Or police. You're either with them or against them. Once the crazies started marking houses and holding their prayer sessions, those who had cabins or places to go lit out."

"Why didn't you go?"

"This is all I've got." She gestures at the building behind her.

She shifts her weight and pulls away the camouflage and the cowl of her heavy coat, revealing her face. Mid-fifties, with a lot of laugh lines at the corners of her eyes. Smart blue eyes. Lips tight with unhappiness.

"And that's why you're sitting out here with a rifle," Tap says.

She looks at Tap and nods slowly, as if reluctant to admit it. She's proud, it's easy to see. And rugged. Protecting what's hers. Like a frontier woman.

"Can we come inside and warm up?" I ask, tugging my blanket—no, cape—around my shoulders.

"No." Zero hesitation.

Tap turns to me as if she's not even there. "So, this old broad is a dead end. Where to next? Do we go back?"

"Shreve will die if we don't get help."

"What's wrong with your friend?" the woman asks.

"He fell. A long way. He's got some internal injuries, we

think. And a huge knock on the head," I say.

"What'd he fall from?"

"A plane." I probably should lie, but something makes me think she'd know it.

She laughs. "Okay. Stop wasting my time and move along. If they haven't got wind of you yet, the crazies will be sniffing around here soon enough."

"I'm not lying. The plane we were in crashed near Devil's Throne."

"Then how did you get here? That's twenty miles away, as the crow flies."

I say nothing and look at Tap, shaking my head.

*We should tell her. Show her,* Tap sends.

*She's got a gun. She's already freaked out as it is. What if she just blasts us?*

*Screw it.*

"Like this," Tap says, twisting his body into the air and holding it aloft, five feet from the ground, hands out.

Her eyes bug out and she raises the rifle, pointing it at Tap. I raise my hand and show her my palm. Ready for the worst.

"You're part of that . . . that—"

"No, we're not," I say, trying to make my voice sound firmer than it feels.

"That *thing*. We saw it on the news, before the power went out. You're part of it. You've come to take us over. *Get out of here.*"

She sights on Tap, still hovering there.

"We're not part of the Conformity. We're not! We're just trying to help our injured friend. Please—"

"Go. I should kill you before you can hurt anyone. *Get out of here before I shoot!*"

"Ma'am, you're making a terrible mistake." For the second time today, I back away with my hands up. She holds the gun on us, unwavering. Tap settles back on the earth. He backs away, not turning, hands up. Twenty yards away, beyond the cars, we turn and trudge back the way we came.

*So, that's it? That's all we get?* Can't tell if Tap's angry with her response at his show of extranatural ability or if he's pissed because we're still out in the snow.

*No. Let's go to the library. There's no one there. Get warm. And then figure something out. It's getting dark anyway, so we're not going to be able to make it back to the lodge tonight, not unless they've got a bonfire blazing outside.*

*We could force the old lady,* Tap sends. It's a mental message that's empty of tone. It's an idea, and Tap doesn't really know how to feel about it.

*Kidnapping? Really? I'm not ready to lose all my self-respect,* I say.

*Suit yourself. It's just Shreve we're talking about. No big whoop.*

*We can wait until after full dark and break into the medical office and take some drugs,* I offer. I hate giving in. Becoming looters. Part of the chaos. Too much of my life's been lived without order. I want it. Tap can say whatever he wants about Shreve and our little band, but Shreve was always pressing some kind of schedule on me, little rituals. On the run from Quincrux, our practice sessions, cooked dinners wherever we squatted, the same shows on television. The same tired jokes. All of Shreve's energy was spent in keeping the chaos at bay in small ways. I think deep down he was as desperate for that as I was—like a little boy still. And Tap couldn't care less. And now I have to become the disorder in order to keep it at bay. To save Shreve.

Tap nods, grinding his teeth. Lots of anger in him and not all of it due to the hand he was dealt in life. He must have been born angry. There are folks like that. Shreve's kinda like that. Maybe I am too. But I don't want to be that way forever.

...

The inside of the Payette Library has been wrecked. Hard to tell if that's from kids looting, or the crazy eye-church people, or what. Shelves knocked over, books everywhere. Near the circulation desk there's a stain on the floor. Dried blood, maybe. Even inside, I can see our breath pluming in the dim light, but it's marginally better than being outside. At least there's no wind. Or painted eyes. Or people pointing rifles at us.

"Let's make a fire," Tap says, his voice loud in the empty building. "I brought matches."

"Where? With what?"

He looks at me. I guess it is a silly question, but burning books just seems wrong to me. When I was growing up—a year ago? Two at the most—I moved from foster home to foster home, and the only thing that kept me sane was books. The libraries—always welcoming and warm and orderly. And now Tap's proposing to burn one to stay warm. Goddamn. There's so much we give up to keep ourselves going.

"Doesn't look like anyone's gonna give a shit. Look at this mess."

"Let's start with periodicals, at least. Newspapers."

In a far corner of the library, near the large-print paperbacks, Tap grabs an old-school metal trash can, his blanket-cape hanging limp and wet from his shoulders, and plops it down unceremoniously. He begins wadding newspaper up and tearing paperbacks in half. He lights a match (and I can't help but notice the unsteadiness of his hands; shivers rack his body), making the shadows loom and flicker for a moment before lighting the newspaper. The paper catches. The room turns yellow. I can feel the heat on my face. For a long while we feed the licking flames newspaper and cheap romance and crime novels while we huddle over the trash can. More like cavemen than hobos. Turning our hands over and over and putting our boots right on the burning metal of the can. The smoke is whisked out the broken window into the gathering dark.

I can't tell how much time has passed, but it must be a long while of us just watching the flames and heating our hands before Tap stands up, walks out of the circle of light, and returns with a huge book. Well-worn spine, easily eight inches thick. *Oxford American Dictionary*. Tap and vocabulary don't usually go together, but I can guess the word he's looking up.

He tears through pages, holding the book down and away so that the light of the trash-can fire shows the words. I feed more paperbacks into the flames.

Tap reads, "Panopticon. Noun. A building, as a prison, hospital, library, or the like, so arranged that all parts of the interior are visible from a single point."

"What does that mean?"

"Fuck if I know."

I stand myself and walk back toward where I think the reference area is. After a few moments of squinting in the dark, I return with a brown leather book embossed with a P. The *Encyclopaedia Britannica*.

A little sinking sensation in the pit of my stomach. Tap must see my expression because he says, "What, man? You're killing me."

"Panopticon. The architectural form for a prison, the drawings for which were published by Jeremy Bentham in 1791. It consisted of a circular, glass-roofed, tanklike structure with cells along the external wall facing toward a central rotunda. Guards stationed in the rotunda could keep all the inmates in the surrounding cells under constant surveillance. *Pan* means 'many,' I guess. *Opticon* means 'seeing.' So a prison where the captors see everything."

"Fuck me with a rake," Tap says. A new one to me, even after all my time with Shreve. Hard to picture. "It's crazy. So these people are what? The captors? The prisoners?"

"Who knows? We won't be around here long enough to have to worry about it."

Tap nods, drops the dictionary, and shoves it away. "It's dark now. We should see if there's anything left here." He jerks his head toward the rear of the library where there are a few doors to offices and administration.

It's a small library. It's a small town. There's not much to explore.

Tap tromps off and I follow him, trying not to slip on any loose books lying on the floor. The light from the trash-can fire gives us enough illumination to see, but it's very dark now. We both walk with our hands out.

One of the doors to the offices has been kicked in or otherwise forced open, hanging crazily on one hinge. In the offices, we rummage about long enough to find the lost and found box—full of brightly colored knit caps and wool mittens and musty-smelling scarves. We're able to beef up our poor winter wear with some of the kids' castoffs. In a desk we find a couple of scented candles and some saltine crackers. An empty thermos that smells of chicken noodle soup. I light a candle—its perfume tickles my nose—and take the thermos to the restroom to rinse it out in the sink. Thank goodness the water here still works.

Tap keeps rummaging. Finds a knitted shawl—the kind a grandmother might wear—that he tosses over his shoulders on top of his blanket/cape and wraps around his torso. As he does, he looks at me and says, "Not a word, dude."

"My lips are sealed, Gamgam."

He snorts and moves to open another drawer in a desk. He pulls out a canned weight-loss shake, tosses it to me, and withdraws another for himself.

We drink the shakes, standing in the near-dark. In a shitburg town twenty miles away from where my best friend lies dying. We're almost finished with them when the sound of the library door opening echoes like a gunshot. Torchlight whites out our candles.

A heavy male voice: "Come out of there and into the light of the All-Seeing."

—they call me thief, they call me trailer trash, but that kid called me titty baby and all the C-wing goons laughed and watched me with lidded eyes, appraising, scanning for any weakness. So I follow him down out of B wing on a Saturday morning for breakfast when everyone else is in Commons. He's older than me, seventeen, but thin with long arms and a malicious grin that tells me he'll be hell on earth when he gets out of here, this stint in Casimir is just another notch on his belt, a little more clout in his street cred. But I could give a shit. I've been here longer and know the ropes. I follow him, hanging back, and we pass Sloe-Eyed Norman and pass through the howling boys of Commons on the way to the mess hall and in the crook of hallway with the disabled camera, Ox waits. It's expensive, what he wanted from me to be there, but I can afford it. But just barely. What I can't afford is not doing anything after this cock-munch dissed me in front of C wing. We settle things here, however we can. When the bitch sees Ox, he stops and backs up and then sees me and the malicious grin dies on his face and all that's left there is a wounded look, the look of someone that's been abandoned, or hurt, terribly hurt by someone he trusts. It's an of-course-this-is-happening-because-the-world-is-a-sewer look and for a moment I feel a sinking inside because I'm the one making his world a little shittier. But it's only for a moment and then Ox wades in, big fist falling, and the boy doesn't have any time for reflection on the harshness or shittiness of the world—

# CASEY

It's too easy to forget what's going on out there. But sometimes when I close my eyes, even at the strangest of times, I see the towering walls of people, melded together, staggering through the world and pouring steam and waves of stench. Sometimes, even when all of the lodge is silent and the snow hisses outside, I catch my breath in a panic, race to the window, waiting for the silhouette of the merged form of thousands of souls to appear, lumbering, bellowing. Moaning.

Jack and Tap haven't returned, and it's dark now, though the day never lightened to more than a gray gloom. Negata hasn't said anything for hours, and his inscrutable face makes me wonder, sometimes, if he's not sleeping with his eyes open. The man possesses a stillness that I've never seen in anyone, neither priests, nor monks, nor statues.

Ember's disappeared in the lodge—she said to get some more blankets, because the temperature has dropped drastically since nightfall. I've asked Negata to get more firewood.

For the moment I'm alone except for Shreve, lying beside me. His hair is tousled and his skin pale, but the swelling on his head has gone down and his chest rises and falls with more strength than when we pulled him from the snow. He seems stronger. Yet he's still not awake.

I reach into the fire with the ghosthand and turn the logs and pile the coals so that when Negata returns the fire will be perfect for whatever logs are left to us.

I touch Shreve's cheek, stand, and, taking a candle, turn to go find Ember.

...

It's a big building, two stories and there might be an attic, but we haven't been able to find access to it in the dim light. Everything's hushed except for the occasional *crack* of a falling branch weighted with snow outside. I hold the votive candle high overhead so that to an observer it would seem to be floating. At first I feel a strain keeping it there, three or four feet above my head, but after a while it becomes normal.

There are three stairwells, the one in the atrium and one at either end of the lodge, which is shaped in a rough U so that the valley—whenever it's not so overcast—can be seen through the big front windows. It was built in another time, when materials were rugged and the scale of everything was larger, so that the rooms are tall and airy (and hard to heat) and the hallways are quite wide. The floating candle makes everything seem darker at the edges.

I take the atrium stairs, a grand affair of heavy wooden planks. The only sounds are the soft padding of my shoes on the steps. The air is hushed, expectant.

Upstairs, I send the candle floating down the left hall. "Ember?"

Someone is there, I think. Just out of reach of the candlelight.

I walk forward. "Ember. Don't—"

The shadow moves to the right, through a door and to the back of the building. I follow, sending the candle floating after it. In the doorway, I stop. It's a bedroom, with a stripped bed, a small dresser, and a bedside table. The heavy drapes are pulled aside and the window, rimed in frost, is lit from beyond with a bluish light. As I look at it, a face appears in the pane, dark. Girlish, long dark hair. Eye sockets dark. Mouth open in a bell. Blinking, I rub my eyes. Not been getting enough sleep, watching over Shreve.

And it's almost too cold to sleep anyway. When I look again, the face is gone. Then, slowly, the cold radiator begins to tick, as if it was heating up. But the room remains so cold. The ticks resolve themselves into a rhythm, slow. Somewhere down the hall there's a bump. A slide like someone dragging something. A tick.

*Bump. Slide. Tick tick.*

*Bump. Slide. Tick. Tick.*

Then it stops.

I get the hell out of there.

■■■

I find Ember back with Negata. She's begun piling blankets on the floor.

"I was looking for you."

"Here I am," she says, making a pallet from a particularly moth-eaten wool blanket. "Saw something weird and went to check it out."

"Was it a face at the window?"

"No, someone standing in the hall. And a noise. I might have just imagined it."

"So now we're being haunted." I can't help but think of Bernard and Danielle sleeping out underneath the snow, bloody smears.

Ember's expression clouds, and she must be thinking the same thing. But she shakes her head and moves on. "We're so low on wood, I think this is the only room we can heat for now. Might have enough for a day or two."

I move to sit down by Shreve. Negata watches me, silent.

"That's a good idea. No more keeping two rooms heated. We'll have to all sleep here." I glance at Ember, but she doesn't seem to notice.

"I've shut every door I could. We need to shut those two that lead to the front hall. Pull the drapes. Less draft. Less air to heat."

Negata nods.

"Makes sense," I say. I wait a few moments. "When are you going to do it?"

"Do what?" she says, like an idiot.

But I shake my head and say nothing. Why get into it with her? She knows what I'm talking about.

She fishes in her jacket pocket and withdraws a cigarette. She holds it out to me, and I shake my head. "Got a light?" she asks. "Don't want to waste matches."

I grab a small cherry coal from the fire with the ghosthand and hold it out to her. She touches the end of the cigarette to it and draws long enough for it to glow. I replace the coal and Ember stares at it, fascinated, as it floats back to the fire. The smell of the burning tobacco mixes with the hardwood smoke of the fire. It's not altogether unpleasant.

She smokes in silence for a long while, and when she's done, she flicks the butt into the fireplace and sighs.

"Okay. I guess I'm going in."

"Tell Shreve . . ."

She looks at me sharply. "Tell him what?"

"Tell him it's time to wake up."

She nods, the muscles in her cheek standing out. She crosses her legs on the pallet she's made and stares into the fire.

"Might be he can't. Swelling brain or something," she says. She glances at me and then at Shreve's face, giving nothing up. "But we'll see. And away we go."

## EIGHTEEN

—she's gone when Vig and I get back to the trailer. I cook him Hamburger Helper, putter about, ignoring my homework. It's not until the next morning that I even notice she's still not there, it's not rare for her to stay out after her lunch and evening shifts at the Waffle Hut. I don't realize she's not sleeping it off until Vig says, "Where's Momma, Shree?" and I pad back to her little bedroom at the end of the trailer. Walking back there, part of me hopes she's done us all a favor and suffocated in her own vomit, but the room is empty. The next day he asks, "Where's Momma, Shree, where's Momma?" over and over and over again and I finally break down and call the police who come by and remove us from the trailer and place us into child services and we spend the night with prayer people, always asking for blessings from the bearded god on a fluffy white cloud before we can eat Spaghetti-Os or Spam sandwiches. It's two more days before she comes back to get us. In the car she smokes and says nothing and it's only after Vig's in bed does she come and stand in front of me, an intense and unreadable look on her face. She slaps me, hard, bringing tears to my eyes. When my vision clears and she comes back into focus, there's a pensive look on her face like she's deliberating something and then she's decided. She slaps me again, a big open-handed slap that knocks me sideways and into the trailer wall. She says nothing. She doesn't even look at me. She goes to the kitchenette and takes the vodka bottle there and walks stiffly back to her room and shuts the door—

# EMBER

Used to emotions, picking up strong feelings and the most obvious of thoughts—lust, rage, love, jealously. Only once have I ever had direct mind-to-mind contact with anyone else, and that was with the Li'l Devil here.

Think about how he felt, his presence. The scent of him, way he held himself, that ridiculous shit-eating grin. The smell lingers, that slight essence of him that you don't really notice until it's disassociated from the body. It seems stronger then.

That's what I focus on. The scent of his mind.

Bernard said he thought he'd taste of chocolate. But he didn't. He tasted of yeast and bread. Danielle had the scent of cinnamon and ozone.

Shreve? He smelled of everything and nothing at all. Of alcohol and water and unnamed spices. But there was a pressure there, to his mind. He's more than a scent.

I think of his face, the intense, wolfish gaze. His eyes are blue, but in my mind's eye I see them as gray and that's okay. Messy hair. Narrow, bony chest. The sound of his voice, whip-crack intense. His ferocity in speech. In action.

He's there. I feel him.

Not so much popping a bubble but merging with him. For a moment I'm surrounded by a tempest of scents and smells and sounds, all ineffably Shreve, and then I'm in.

I'm in.

■■■

A shithole of a trailer park. Washed in gray light so that everything seems desaturated, like they've sucked the color from a television signal. The grounds are littered with moldering baby carriages, grimy refrigerators, bent bike frames, and dented, overfull trash cans. Trucks up on cinder blocks.

Every window is barred.

Hear crying children and televisions blaring and the barking of dogs, but there's no movement and I see no one as I walk through the park. I pass a scaling sign that says *Holly Pines Trailer Park, Inquire at #1 for leasing information*. That people don't even own these shitty house-trailers is appalling.

There's one trailer, and I don't know how I know but Shreve is there, inside. I know. Of all the trailers, his is the shittiest. It looks like a Conformity soldier has half hammered in the roof, and it sits crooked on blocks. Nearby a radio blares Lynyrd Skynyrd. I can hear a man coughing. Hacking. Bringing up sputum and phlegm. Spitting.

Hear the rhythms. A thrumming beat of a heart or a bass drum, and I'm lost because it's Shreve maybe but Bernard too.

I approach the trailer, scared at what I might find inside. There's a weathered black mailbox hanging beside the door with adhesive letters spelling AN ON.

I open the door. It gives a metallic squeal.

Inside, a television, tuned to some reality TV show, blasts noise in the close confines. I feel like the room is shrinking, like my head is brushing the ceiling. There's fast-food wrappers and piles of empty vodka bottles and oversized ashtrays brimming with cigarette butts and the whole place stinks of fire and bacon grease and stale cigarette smoke.

"Shreve?"

Move into the trailer and on the one clean bit of counter I find a piece of paper. At the top it reads *Child Protective Services* and below that *Vigor Ferrous Cannon*. As I look up from the paper I find I'm not in the trailer anymore.

Gray cement walls and a metal door with a small, wire-crosshatched window. Turn back and there's a shabby metal bunk bed with Shreve lying on the top bunk, whispering into a vent. I can't make out his words but his voice is desperate, raw.

"Shreve."

He starts, surprised. He looks at me strangely and then swings his legs over the side of the bunk.

"You can't be here. Booth's gonna be pissed," he says. He blinks and says, "I never hurt you."

"I'm here anyway. But you're not."

Conversation's slipping away from me, now that it's happening. I don't have control over what I'm saying, or at least what I want to say comes out wrong.

"I'm not?" Shreve's wearing an orange jumpsuit. "It's prison, Ember. You never really get out."

"Then how do you know me?" I'm still holding the piece of paper in my hand, and Shreve's gaze goes to it and his brow furrows.

I hand it to him. He doesn't look like he wants it, but he takes it anyway. Looks at it. Pain crosses his features, and he crumples the paper and throws it across the room. It bounces off a wall and rolls out the open cell door.

Before I can stop myself, I follow it. Shreve says, "No. I don't want you to see."

But I keep going. I hear him jump down from the upper bunk and follow me out.

It's a cellblock, and Shreve's cell is on a metal walkway lined with doors, each one standing open. In each open door, a person stands. In the nearest, a little boy, looking very much like a younger version of Shreve. A thin, almost anorexic girl with huge eyes, staring silently. A big, beefy guy in a cowboy hat and sparkly belt buckle. An old man with white curly hair and kind eyes.

There's that strange guy, Norman, in a doorway but his expression isn't the glowering one I remember from the Red Team; he's smiling now. There's Priest, too. And Hollis.

All staring at Shreve, who's come to stand beside me.

I hear a jangling, metallic step and turn to see a man coming up the stairs to the walkway. He's wearing a neat warden's outfit. He stops near us and looks at Shreve.

"There's more in C Wing and D Wing, Shreve. Waiting to see you."

Confusion crosses Shreve's face, and he looks hurt. "I'm sorry, Booth. I'm sorry."

Booth says nothing. Shreve walks forward to join him.

It's like a fog, this dream. Clouds my judgment and moves along with an interior logic all its own.

"Wait, Shreve. Who are all these people?"

Shreve doesn't look at me when he says, "They're people I've hurt. People I've let down."

The man Shreve calls Booth says, "Danielle and Bernard are waiting, Shreve."

I'm cold again and the lights dim and flicker. Danielle, Bernard, and Davies stand below us in a pool of ghostly blue light, their faces upturned toward us, white, so white, with graying lips and milky eyes. Snow-covered eyes.

A great rhythmic booming echoes through the building, *boom booom boooom*. The sound of a Conformity soldier hammering to get in.

Shreve shakes, racked with sobs. Want to grab him, fold him in my arms to get him to stop, but something in this interior landscape keeps me from touching him. Maybe it's my own reluctance to open myself to him; maybe it's his natural defenses. We're in the cellblock of his mind, and he calls the shots.

Bernard, his skin so pale, raises an arm and slowly extends his finger, pointing. Like the needle of the compass, he swings around until he's pointing behind him toward the shadows down the length of the cellblock, which now stretches into infinity.

The shadows move, shambling forward.

Thousands of people, moving forward out of the shadows. All staring at Shreve.

*Boom boom boom.*

The dead from the attack on the campus. The Conformity soldier's dead.

Damn. This kid is drowning in a sea of guilt and remorse. How he can even get up in the morning, I don't know.

But that's why I'm here. I'm here to wake him up.

Shudder and break through the invisible bonds that hold me. The invisible trolley track that has kept me, inside Shreve's mind, from doing what I would. Takes all my effort to raise my arm and touch his shoulder.

"You've got to wake up, Shreve. These people aren't your responsibility."

"No. No . . . I don't deserve to be free. I don't deserve it . . ."

"It's not your fault! You don't have to—"

He turns, face contorted with fury. "You don't know *shit*," he says, and he raises his hand, fingers splayed.

I'm surprised to see that, in his mind, Shreve has six fingers to a hand. But it's all I can take in before the percussive blast sends me flying away from him, in the empty air over the floor of the cellblock, falling.

And then I'm out and opening my eyes.

## NINETEEN

—I am you and you are me and should we ever disagree one and one and one makes three—

# CASEY

I'm thinking about what's waiting for us when it all changes.

Shreve twitches and moans once while Ember sits with her eyes closed. After a long while, she opens them and then digs in her pockets for another cigarette.

I wait. She likes playing out the tension.

Eventually she says, "That kid's seriously fucked up."

"So, he's alive in there? His mind's awake?"

"Sort of. Like he's stuck in some sort of prison."

Negata says softly, "He was incarcerated once. With Jack."

Ember shrugs. "Still is, in his mind. He said you never get out."

"I imagine he's right," I say, looking at his face. With his eyes closed, his expression is soft in sleep. He almost looks at ease. Like a boy his age should. With them open, he looks feral. Always hungry. "My mom always said, 'A hundred and eighty degrees from sick is still sick.'"

"I don't even know what that means." Ember holds up her cigarette to me like I'm some trained monkey. I ignore her. She continues. "Head's filled with people he feels he's let down.

Never seen anyone so buried in guilt. Thousands of people. The nameless from the Conformity soldier he brought down." She pauses. "Bernard and Danielle."

That's alarming. While she was out, I could have sworn I saw a shadow coalesce in the corner that looked like Danielle. And the lodge began to settle in rhythmic creaks and pops.

"So, these ghosts, you think Shreve's causing them?" I ask. "Like he's dreaming them and they infect us, or something?"

It's obvious from Ember's expression that she hadn't thought of that. In her defense, she's only been awake for a few moments.

"Shit, anything's possible with Shreve. He could be broadcasting." Her eyes narrow, and she looks at Negata. "Have you seen anything?"

He slowly shakes his head and says, "No, but I am ... difficult to affect. Shreve might have the strength to make me see things, but he would need to bring all his attention to bear upon me. And in his current condition—"

"Okay," I say. "Let's just assume it is Shreve causing these—"

"Ghosts?" Ember says.

"Yeah, ghosts. And get on with our lives."

Negata stands, moves to the window, and pulls aside the drapes, staring out into the night. "It's easy to discount what you might have seen because reason and the supernatural are usually mutually exclusive," he says. "But from what I understand about your situation, you've all shared minds. Is this correct? Even Captain Davies?"

Reluctantly, Ember says, "Yeeesssss," drawing out the word.

"And you were in mental contact at the time of the crash? Sharing your powers?"

I nod.

Negata bows his head. "Then I suggest that it might not be Shreve broadcasting images. You might still be in contact with them. Some part of their consciousness—their spirit—lives on in you."

"What? You're saying—"

He smiles at us sadly. It's an expression so foreign to his features, it's frightening when the skin tightens around his mouth, the corner of his mouth tugging down.

"You're not delusional or being affected by Shreve. You're really seeing ghosts."

## TWENTY

—I am you and you are me and should we ever disagree, one and one and one make three. I'm crying, I'm crying, I'm crying, I'm crying.—

# JACK

"Come out of there and into the light of the All-Seeing," repeats the heavy male voice.

I've got my hands up, ready to blast them if they come through the door. Tap whips out a pistol I didn't even know he had and works the chamber, feeding a round into the pipe, just like they taught us back on campus.

"No, I don't think we will, man," Tap yells. "Why don't you come back here if you want to talk."

There's a metallic clatter and then a gasoline can sloshes into the office area, rolling, slinging liquid all over the tile floor in a spreading pool. The torchlight from outside the room grows stronger.

A thick voice, a woman's, calls out, "You two. Come to us, and we will speak of your situation. No one can hide from the sight of the Panopticon. If you don't, you'll be given to the fire."

Tap looks at me. *Can you knock down a wall or something? We can fly the hell out of here.*

*I can try,* I say, waving him back, away from the gasoline. Near the back of the office there's a bank of windows.

"Do not try to escape. You cannot avoid the all-seeing gaze. We know you now. *You are marked,*" the thick female voice says, and I feel a touch upon my mind, like those times when Shreve or Ember wanted to worm inside.

***Bugfuck,*** I send to Tap. ***This is very, very bad.*** I think I don't let him know how scared I am, how I just want to run and run and run and find Ember, find Shreve. They could handle it, I know, they could deal with it. Both of them, they're never scared of anything. But I'm about to piss my pants.

***Let's go,*** he says once in my mind, but it seems to repeat over and over. I throw out my hands, releasing the angry pressure building inside me. The bank of windows explodes outward, away from us, in a rush of powdered brickwork and glass shards.

I jump through the opening, giving an upward blast, and clear the remains of the wall. I hover there, turning to see Tap still standing, locked midstride toward the hole I just came through. Beyond him, a figure appears in the door. A big man, holding a torch, dressed in heavy winter wear. He waves the torch inside the office, not to ignite the gasoline on the floor but to illuminate the space. Holy shit, a real-to-God medieval torch like we were vampires or something.

But Tap is just stuck there, a blank, vacant look on his face, nose pouring blood. Fucking bugfuck.

I duck my head, hovering low, the force of my pulses throwing debris and knocking over chairs and desks. As quickly as I can, I'm inside the wrecked library, grabbing Tap to lift him out of there. It's risky because the bulky man could toss the torch at any moment, but I can't leave Tap behind. We don't do that.

When I've got Tap in my grip, my left arm hooked around

his rib cage, my right hand free to direct pulses, I lift him off the floor and we're caroming out into the night and it's only then I see the torch-bearing man lift his other hand and there's the dark shape of a gun in it.

*Boom.*

The sound is massive in the small space of the library. Something hits my face, burning like fire, and I slam into the broken frame of the window. I sense more than see Tap wheeling into the snow outside.

I am blind. Something hits me, all my wind is gone, and it's cold when my body comes to rest.

Voices. Hands.

Darkness.

—agnus dei, qui tollis peccata mundi, miserere nobis—

## EMBER

*Jack, Jack . . . can you hear me? Jack?*
Nothing.
Starting to get worried.

■■■

Jack and Tap haven't returned by morning. Casey wants me to go back inside Shreve and rattle him about. She's being very bossy about the whole thing.

After drinking the instant coffee that Negata boiled to bitterness in the wood fire, I make another run at Shreve, just to get Casey off my back. His mind has the consistency of a wall of soft, porous rock. It crumbles as I try to get through, but it's still not letting me in.

Awake in there now, I think. He's doing something, and he might not be altogether at home. But I can't tell why or what.

■■■

Frontiersland. From what I can tell from our CPR class and the limited medical training they gave us back at the campus, Shreve looks like he's doing much better. His pulse is strong; his breathing is deep and steady. His color is good. His eyes, when you peel back the lids, respond as they should to light—though I have to be careful not to drip any wax on his corneas.

Negata left this morning to scout the area. The cloud cover has passed. The snow has stopped, and now it's a brilliant white outside. The temperature inside the lodge has risen marginally, and we've thrown back the shades to let all the light we can inside the great hall where we've bunked down.

Casey tends the fire, sweeping up ash. Collecting bowls and tins of old soup that we heated near the flames to keep from having to go to the kitchen and let in the colder air from other parts of the lodge. She fetches snow and melts it in a big bucket she's taken from some pantry. We've become pioneer women, cooking by the fire, tending house. And that really pisses me off for some reason.

Pissed off. But not pissed on. The *thing*, the walking city of people, there's no sign of it. Any moment I'm gonna hear a foghorn or something and it'll come through the firs, trees cracking.

The waiting is the hardest part.

One smoke left, and I'm saving it.

When Negata returns, he looks cold and exhausted. But he's carrying an ax.

"I have found a supply hut a half mile down the road with a sledge. Some cross-country skis. I will eat some food and then go down the mountain as far as I may. I think I saw a chimney there, through the trees, and will see if I can find any medical supplies." He looks at Shreve. "But I do not think now that this is an ailment of the body."

"Look for transportation," Casey says.

I snort. "Like a horse?"

"Exactly," she says, nodding.

"So, is this what it was like back in the eighteen hundreds? Seems like so much effort just to stay warm and catch a ride."

Negata purses his lips. A very small gesture. "All of life is a struggle. Most people spend the lion's share of their energy trying to deny the fact that we live in a hard world."

"Didn't seem that way until just a few days ago," I say.

He looks at me, face blank. "Truly? I would think you'd feel otherwise with your obvious . . . differences."

"I'm talking physical hardships."

"It amazes me that we continue to separate the physical world from the mental and spiritual," Negata says.

"Bugfucks and jocks, dude," I respond.

"Exactly. Yet Shreve and you are more than this. You are both."

He's got a point. Casey's face sours. She doesn't like Shreve's and my names spoken in the same sentence. It prickles me some that I'm grouped with him, but in some ways, it's a mark of honor. Li'l Devil is feared, and I don't mind some of that rubbing off on me. "Why don't you just go find a horse or something?" I say.

"Yes, and while I do that, you will need to go see if you can locate Jack and Tap," he says. "I know it has not yet been twenty-four hours, however . . ."

"They've been out overnight. Right," I say.

"Ember needs to try to communicate with Shreve again, not go running off after Jack and Tap. We decided, did we not—" Casey says with a little prim and proper adjustment of her torso, like an English schoolteacher settling into a couch for a cup of tea. "That she would remain here as the only other flyer in the group?"

"Have you attempted to contact them telepathically?" Negata asks.

"Of course," Casey says sharply. "I've even *felt* for them with my arm. But I'm too far away. There are proximity issues." Imagination fails once the distance is too great. Our minds can only ignore physical separation so much before the mental construct or spiritual tether snaps.

Negata inclines his head slowly. "Then I think it would be best if we stick with the original plan, at least for today. If Jack and Tap haven't returned by tomorrow . . ."

A cloud passes over the face of the sun and the light in the great room dies, the room becoming darker than seems normal for morning. Shadows gather.

Casey gasps and asks, "What's happening?"

Beyond the pallet where Shreve lies, Bernard and Danielle stand. They're whole, not bloody messes. But they're there and not there all at once. It's like the possibility of them plays out in my mind, bypassing all retinal brain activity, but superimposed in real space. They are near. They are far. They are bodiless. They are possibilities.

"We have come," Danielle says. Her mouth moves haltingly, like she's trying to remember how to speak.

"From far . . ." Bernard says. Behind him, another shadow flickers into existence. Davies, his cheeks hollow. He'd been in contact with us too. A member of the collective, if only for a while.

"Not far," Danielle says. She looks troubled; her skin becomes mottled with more shadows. It ripples from pink to gray to blue. Her lips are ghastly. Her eyes covered in snow. Then she's pink and normal again. "No distance..." She pauses, rippling again, and now I see the same thing happening to Bernard and Davies.

Maybe it's just us, and not the visual manifestation of our dead friends, that's causing the rippling, changing appearance of them. They're broadcasting from inside our own minds and projecting themselves onto the real world. But...doesn't this make "their" world more real now and ours, well, a little less real? Or just different.

"Can you see them?" I ask Negata.

He looks at me, puzzled. "No. You are seeing what?"

"Danielle. Bernard." I point to where they stand.

Danielle shakes her head, and her hair swirls around her as if she was immersed in water, a slow liquid movement. "We have come with..."

"With a message," Bernard says, the words falling like wet stones dropped from a statue's mouth. "A message."

"A message? From who?" Casey asks, her eyes growing wide and her face gaining this eager, almost hungry look.

"From Shreve," Davies says, finally joining the ghostly conversation.

"What?" Casey says. "What's the message?"

The trio looks at me. I remember all the horror movies I've seen where the ghosts look upon the living in that one moment when their needs and desires remain unfathomable and indistinct and then...freaky ugly ghost face. But Bernard, Danielle, and Davies just stare, their faces rippling cycles of corpse gray, frozen snow-rimed, and pink and healthy. Thank whatever gods above that we're not getting the bloody smear effect.

Negata says, "Girls, you might want to—" He raises a hand and points to Casey's nose. It's pouring blood.

Ooof. My head throbs, like hammers and hydraulic pressure and some demented factory worker ratcheting up the gears. I can taste blood. I wipe at my nose and the back of my hand has a long, crimson streak on it.

"Ember," Danielle says, "you must find the Liar."

"The Liar? That kid, Reese Cameron?"

"Yes. He is needed."

"That's it?"

"Yes. We must go. It is . . ." Danielle shimmers and ripples again. "It is hard."

"To return," Bernard says.

"Wait!" Casey's voice is raw. "Did Shreve leave a message for me? Will he wake up? Did he say anything?"

But they're already becoming shadows once more, slipping into the veil of normal optical stimuli and out of the world of possibility.

"Wait! Did he—"

They're gone. We remain silent for a long while, letting Casey compose herself. Might have been a tear there, at the corner of her eye—for the three ghosts or for Shreve sending me a message and neglecting her, who knows?

So that settles that.

Go find the Liar.

But not before I find Jack.

## TWENTY-TWO

—Dies iræ! Dies illa
Solvet sæclum in favilla—

## TAP

When I come to, the crick in my neck and the gag and ropes make me seriously want to kick someone in the vagina. The crazy woman with the bruiser. She's talking now, but all I can see is that we're in some sort of office—nice office, lots of books and a thick oriental rug and a big desk—but they've got us tied fast to these chairs and facing each other. The ropes are crazy tight. I can't feel my toes and fingers.

Jack's face looks like shit. It's bright red and beading with little pinpricks of blood and tears; snot runs down his face and chin. Blasted with rock salt, looks like, right in the puss. And, holy shit, does he seem pissed. But he's looking at someone behind me so I turn my head to get a look. It's dark in here, and they've got what looks like a massive church candelabra standing on the mantle above the (sadly) cold fireplace. It'd feel like we'd gone back in time five hundred years if it wasn't for our wardrobes.

The eye of the shotgun isn't the best thing I've seen all day. He's got it up nice and close to my face so that there'll be no funny business. I don't know if Jack can use his powers tied up—maybe he can, maybe he can't, but he has always been very handsy when flying and attacking. From outside the room I can hear the murmurings of people and the voice of the lady. The crazy one. She's got a thick, fruity voice that reminds me a little bit of Bernard's, but the shit she's spewing is the worst sort of mindfuck Bible talk.

"For when I brought your ancestors out of Egypt and spoke to them, I did not just give them commands to burn offerings and make sacrifices, but I gave them this command: Obey me, and I will be your God and you will be my people. Walk in obedience to all I command you, that it may go well with you. But they did not listen or pay attention; instead, they followed the stubborn inclinations of their evil hearts. They went backward and not forward."

There's a mutter of agreements and the shuffling of feet. Sounds like a regular tent revival in there. The bruiser, keeping the shotgun trained on me, backs away and steps out of my range of vision. But I've got to assume he's letting her know that I'm awake.

"Know ye not, that to whom ye yield yourselves servants to obey, his servants ye are to whom ye obey; whether of sin unto death, or of obedience unto righteousness?" she says, her voice strong and vibrating, like she's ending on a high note. "This is the word. This is the word of the All-Seeing God. The Panopticon. All things are possible within his vision, and he has come among the sheep to gather our flesh to his and our wills within his greater will. We are born into the end times, and now we call to us the Rapture."

She's a damned natural, that's for sure. With each word her voice thrums and resonates with just the right quiver of emotion. Judging from the murmurs and shuffling feet, she's got the crowd now and she's working it.

*Can you blast loose?* I ask Jack silently.

He gives a single shake of his head, so small I'd miss it if I wasn't sitting facing him.

*Have you tried contacting Ember? Casey?*

*Of course, idiot. That's the first thing I did. They're out of range. Or we're not strong enough without Shreve as a signal booster.*

*Don't have to get shitty about it,* I say. *So, you can't blast loose?*

*I can blast out of here, sure, but the man said if I do anything he's gonna shoot you. And it won't be rock salt.*

*Yeah, your face is totally fucked up, man.*

*I should let him shoot you,* he says. Jack's kind of a trip: he's one of those kids you meet who's totally chill, just a regular dude hanging out, but there's that light switch inside of him and if it gets flipped he goes red-hot. Like habanero-up-the-ass red-hot. When he was blasting the Conformity soldier. And when he knocked out the back of the plane, it was . . . something. It was something.

*If I can work my hand free . . .* I send.

*Listen, can you fall over? Tip the chair?*

*Maybe. It's hard to feel my feet. But I might be able to shift my weight enough. Probably. Why?*

*If they make me stand or lift me up, you fall over, right? They know I can fly. They know we're different, and they're gonna question you about where we come from. The woman—*

*She's a bugfuck, right?*

*Yeah. Not a strong one, but maybe strong enough to get in*

*your head . . .* Jack sends.

*What are you saying? I'm weak?*

Jack gives a silent, mental sigh and rolls his eyes. *Tap, she stopped you, remember? Don't know what she was doing, but she stopped you from running.*

I don't say anything. He's right. Maybe.

*She's gonna try to do that again. If they lift me up I can blast them, but you've got to be on the floor. Low as you can. Shreve and I have done this before.*

The high and mighty Shreve. Giver of gifts. The taker of takes. But where is he now to save us? Right, unconscious back with the girls. I don't say any of that. Or send it telepathically. No point, really. But I can fall over. My right leg is tied more loosely than my left, and I think I can tip the chair up and over with my right foot with some leverage and rocking.

*Yes. I can fall over.*

*Great. You see me get picked up or stand, do it. Because shortly after—*

*Boom.*

*That's right. Boom.*

■■■

The praying goes on for a long time. I can't see anything except Jack and the section of the office that has the bookshelf and desk. We must be in a church, and the worship area is behind me.

The biblical chanting and quoting drones on, and like when my mom would make me sit through church, I find my attention drifting. The ropes at my wrists chafe and cut off my circulation. I can't seem to concentrate on the religious blather but, goddamn, it's just gobbledygook. At some point there's some nonsense sounds, like people saying, "oh conshalla non falla dalla was it talling conshalla" over and over again, and I hear yelps and strange vocalizations. But then everything quiets and the woman says, "Go, go from here, to your homes. To your children. Rejoin flesh of your flesh and blood of your blood and rejoice that soon you will be gathered to a greater flock. You will become one with the All-Seeing God and visit the fields and plains of the vaults of Heaven. You will know happiness. You will know being one with your maker. All praise the Panopticon!"

In chorus, the worshippers respond, "Praise the Panopticon," and there's some serious brainwash fervor going on in their voices.

Then silence except for shuffling. The sound of a push-handle on a door. Then footfalls echoing in a larger space, coming closer. Then silence.

Someone else is in the room. You can feel the change now, like you know when someone—your sister or brother—is behind you. Jack's eyes go to something behind me, and then a woman comes into view and stands, looking at us.

She's not an ugly woman. She's not pretty either. She's sweating some now, and her hair is wet at the temples and she's got it pulled back, away from her face. With the fruitiness of her voice, I thought she might be fat but I don't know why I thought that. She looks like she's very fit but not muscular. She wears frumpy mom-jeans and a turtleneck sweater. Hiking boots. No makeup and no jewelry. She looks like she's just returned from a strenuous hike.

"My name is Ruth Gulch," she says, moving to half sit on the edge of the desk. "And you two are different." She lets that sink in some before continuing. She crosses her arms. Stares at us.

"How did you destroy the wall of the library?" she says, her voice suddenly powerful, a whipcrack. It's like I *need* to answer her. But Jack says in my head, **Shut up, idiot.** And I don't.

She looks at me, then over at Jack, and purses her lips. "Why are you in McCall? Why are you here, skulking about in our library?"

She begins tapping her fingers on her arm, and I notice a strange little scar on her pinkie, silver and puckered.

**Check her hands, Jack. Looks like she's chopped off her extra fingers.**

Jack's gaze moves toward her hands, registering the scar, and then back to her face.

"To get warm," Jack says.

"Where did you come from?"

"Devil's Throne. A lodge there."

"And how did you get here? Horseback?"

A pause. "We walked."

"You're lying." She looks at the man standing behind me. "Massey, get Bildings to fetch some firewood and shut the door, if you would, please. Now that our congregation has gone, the temperature is seriously dropping. We could use the heat." The big, bearded man with the shotgun grunts in assent.

Gulch moves behind her desk to sit in the big leather swivel chair there and then rolls it over to the small fireplace grate. The interior of the office looks like what I'd think of for some Irish priest's office, cozy, lined in dark stained wood and leather-bound books, a picture window looking out on firs and frozen windswept lake. Real Old World shit. On the walls I can see the less-weathered places on the wood where pictures used to hang.

And there, the shadow where a crucifix once was pinned.

I'm not looking forward to finding out how far the crazy goes.

Gulch rustles behind her desk, face in the fireplace grate. I can hear the sound of small blocks of wood. She's fiddling with kindling. The heavy footfalls of Massey and Bildings sound, and eventually they come into view bearing armfuls of icy wood that they delicately place near the fireplace. Massey—or is it Bildings—grunts and squats on his hams, ducking out of sight beyond the desk, but I hear the telltale sounds of fire making—the hollow clatter of kindling, the mess of wrinkled newsprint, the hollow *thock*s of logs being placed. Then there's yellow-orange light flickering in the dark room. Wouldn't mind if they burned their goddamned eyebrows off.

It's silent for a long while except for the crackling of tinder and paper, and the air fills with the aroma of woodsmoke. Jack, his face like raw meat, looks like a sausage held over a fire until the angry juices spit and hiss. I hope he doesn't blow before I'm on the floor.

Finally the temperature in the room rises—though not before Gulch bitches at Massey. "Keep that door shut, and draw the blinds! I can feel the cold pouring off the windows!" They brew some tea with a stovetop teapot they shove into the coals. It's so very comfy cozy here, three freaks with their teen prisoners. The ropes have probably turned my hands purple.

Gulch, after she's had some tea and snacked on a granola bar, returns her focus to us. This has all been a show. She crosses her arms like a principal dealing with miscreant youths—which we are, I guess, but *fuck* her—and Bildings and

Massey flank her like a godfather's bruisers, ready to deliver the beatdowns.

"All right, now that it's warm enough in here for higher thought and conversations, I'll ask again: Why are you here?"

Jack's gaze flickers over to me and back to her. "We're looking for a doctor for our friend."

"Your friend? Who is your friend?"

"Does it matter? He's been hurt, and he needs a doctor."

I can see the thought churning behind her plain features. The scary thing about this Gulch woman is that she doesn't look *scary*. Quincrux, that creepy dude Norman that ran with the Red Team, even Shreve—they're scary sometimes. She looks like anyone you might meet anywhere. At the grocery store. At the mall. At the soccer field. At church. Plain Jane, but crazy as shit.

She looks at Massey and Bildings and says, "Would you two excuse us for a moment?" When they're slow to respond, Gulch says, "I need to ask them some delicate questions, and maybe the sight of those two shotguns is tying their tongues."

Massey glances at Bildings, and the larger, bearded one gives a barely perceptible shrug like *Who gives a shit? She's the boss,* and they tromp out—though they're careful to open the door quickly and shut it behind them just as fast. Still, the temperature drops considerably after they leave.

Gulch stands, moves to put her ass to the flames, warming her hands behind her back. "It's getting late, and I have lots to do tomorrow."

"I bet the crazies take a lot of your energy, huh," I offer. She looks at me, eyes narrowed.

She ignores that, but it has irritated her.

"Now that Massey and Billings have left, let's be honest." She looks at Jack. "You, I can't pierce. And Billings says he saw you flying before he shot you. And there's the wall to the library you blew out. Clearly, you aren't normal." She moves to stand behind the desk, placing her hands on the desktop, her face an intense study. "*You're like me.* Are you part of the Panopticon?"

"The Panopticon? You mean the Conform—" I begin, but Jack gives a telepathic shout of *No!*

Gulch's lips purse. "You are in communication. I can't hear what you're saying, but I know something's being said." She leans back, letting her plain, blunt hands fall to her sides. "I didn't want to do this—because, as you two probably know, it's painful for all of us involved, but I'm going to have to *take* the information I need."

"No, you—" Jack says.

"Time for talking is over, whoever-you-are. As I said, I can't read you." She inclines her head toward me. "But him, I can. And I'm going to get the whole story, one way or another."

Once, when I was first recruited by the Director to join the Society, and they brought me onto the plane, they introduced me to him—he was so damn polite—and he sat there chatting with me, smoking (on the plane!), and there was this overwhelming sense of dislocation and otherness. Maybe I was outraged but it's hard to remember. It was only later, when I met some other bugfucks and could feel them scurrying around in my head, that I realized what was going on. Maybe that's why Shreve bugs the shit out of me. I don't know.

But it's pretty obvious what she's talking about.

"Wait. At least tell us why. Why are you doing all this?" Jack's voice is raw.

She looks surprised. "You mean the church? The parishioners? The All-Seeing God?"

"Yes. And questioning us. Holding us."

"These are the end times, and I need to know what I'm supposed to do. To be pleasing in the sight of God. So that I may join with Him. And you have come here to tempt me. Us. To lead us astray."

Jack shakes his head. "No. We don't care. But that thing . . . it's no second coming—"

"Do *not* blaspheme!" For a moment her face is contorted with fury. "You are abominations. There'll be no blaspheming in my presence."

This woman seriously needs to get punted with a size-twelve steel-toe boot.

"We're sorry," Jack says. "We're just trying to understand."

"These are the end days. And the Godhead moves above us, collecting the Saved into His embrace. The Rapture."

Jack's getting desperate. "But why the 'Panopticon'?"

Gulch draws her hand to her mouth and stills, almost as if she's seen something terrifying. For a moment she's vulnerable. Almost sympathetic. She says in a quiet voice, "It watches me when I sleep. I have dreams." She looks at Jack, and her eyes widen until the pupils are totally visible, ringed in white. "It watches me and watches me. I can feel it." Her voice drops even lower. "Behind my eyes. It sees all."

"And you want it to come here?"

Her expression becomes neutral once more. "When the faithful are joined with the Godhead, all will be revealed."

"I'll tell you what you want to know," Jack says. "None of this is what you think."

Her expression remains neutral as she steps forward, drawing back her fist. She's economical in her movements. Drawing back the small fist, pausing just a second, and then lashing out, crushing Jack's nose against his face, rocking his head back. "There'll be no *blasphemy* here."

It's a while before Jack can speak, the blood flows too heavy from his nose, down over his lips. His head lolls to the side, his eyes go unfocused, bleary. After a moment, he rights his head and says, "I'll tell you what you need to know."

"That's interesting. But you could still be lying. I'll need to check."

"Look at my hands! Look at them!"

For a long while, Gulch sits there, chewing her lip as if evaluating the possibility of some treachery. Then she carefully walks behind Jack's chair and looks at his hands.

When she returns, her face is immobile as a mask. "You have the Devil's mark on you."

Jack begins to give a weak, burbling laugh through the blood. "We make a nice pair, then."

This time, when she draws back her fist, it's less composed. Less mechanical. She's getting into it. Her fist connects right below Jack's eye and rocks his head back.

I feel helpless, watching her tenderize the guy like that. He's not my favorite person in the world but . . . *goddamn*, this bitch has got some issues.

"So, who chopped off your extra bits, lady?" I ask.

Her head swivels around to look at me as if it was on some oiled turret. The intensity of her stare makes my stomach loosen in my belly. There's intelligence behind those eyes, along with some ugly promises.

"Shut your mouth."

"Hey, I can do some mind-reading too. Let me guess. Your daddy didn't like your extra fingers, right? Didn't like you poking around in his head?" Strange how someone's face can remain so still while getting so red. "So maybe he took you out to the woodshed where he kept the hatchet? Maybe he put your hand on the chopping block?"

The fury on her face is more frightening because her face itself is so placid. But the emotion pours off her like radio waves fanning out from a tower. She stands, knuckles bloody, watching me.

"This conversation is over." Her voice is cold. "May the Panopticon guide me. And by guiding me, lead me toward salvation."

She puts her index fingers to her temple and her eyes grow large, like diving into pools, and suddenly I've joined Jack in a bloody, burbling nose and it feels like I'm being swallowed whole. All I see are her eyes and then there's the pressure, like that time when I leaped from the top stair all the way to the bottom and my ankle twisted and then grew fat and tight with blood, but now it's just in my mind, like it's swelling. Distending. A wrenched ankle filling with someone else's blood. There's nothing I can do to stop it.

She's in me and I'm paralyzed; I can only observe what she's doing in my head. It's like lying on an operating table and trying to figure out what the surgeons are doing in your body cavity with scalpels, bloody and searching. Images of fire. Of Jack, huddled over the trash can, surprised. Of wind and flying. Snow and cold. The feel of Jack's voice speaking in my mind. The elation and pure joy of flight, whooping and sweeping in the frigid currents of air. The musty scent of the lodge. Shreve lying on his pallet, unconscious. She focuses on Shreve for a long while, chasing memories of the Li'l Devil far back. The feel of him. His sheer mental power. His flight. The unity of our minds in answer to the Conformity. Falling and a great wrenching. Backward through our memory until the physical glommed-together mass of the Conformity swells like a star growing in our joined minds and she gives a psychic yawp of greed, of victory. She's got what she wants.

Now she digs deeper. Back and back to the campus and all the extranaturals there, the dorms, the faces of the bugfucks and jocks and the Red Team. Everything.

In the end, she has everything. And then the pressure stops. Gulch looks up, alarmed. Her mouth open in surprise.

Massey and Billings walk into the office, followed by the woman from the medical clinic. She's holding the rifle on them.

"Don't make a move. I *will* shoot you," she says.

## TWENTY-THREE

—a simple game, that's all it is, just a game. We run into the woods, a gang of us, the black kids, the white kids, the mix-up kids that live in that racial world of halves and degrees of color, each of us with a ribbon or scrap of bright fabric hanging from our belts. We run screaming into the woods behind Holly Pines, into the trees, into the woods, separating into teams, shirts and skins, and for hours hunt each other, racing, juking, dodging, doing whatever it takes to keep the others from snatching our flags. And I am fast! I am fearless and move so like thought. Jay-Jay and Willis, I nab their flags and send them to the skins' prison, a circle drawn in dirt, with an Arkansas Razorback flag as the ultimate prize. But after a moment, I realize I've lost sight of Vig who'd last been screaming near the hobo camp by the train tracks, and abandoning all pretense of game, I tear through the woods, racing toward the shirts' territory, calling his name, drawing the shirts to me. Something about my demeanor is wild and the boys coming near me stop, maybe sensing my rising panic, and I catch flashes of their faces as I barrel past them, yelling, "Vig, VIG! Goddamn it, Vig," terrified that something's happened, something terrible—

## CASEY

The sunlight's only a brief respite. Slate-gray storm clouds spill across the sky, and the wind picks up so that it moans and groans in the eaves of the old lodge as the day progresses while Ember and Negata put together a bundle of rice and flour hard biscuits they baked in the oven and an old plastic water container fished from the trash bin. It becomes obvious she's going nowhere today, and she settles down for a long sulk, intermittently glaring at me, Negata, and Shreve's unconscious form.

Eventually, she shakes a smoke from a wrinkled pack, I give her a coal to light it, and she puffs away, furious that she can't leave as the snow begins dumping on top of us and the lodge shudders with wind.

Later, we slurp salty chicken noodle soup from coffee cups and stare at the windows. The light outside dims, and Negata places the last of the firewood in the hearth. From here out, it's furniture-burning time. In the silence, I think about all the items in the lodge—the dressers, the chairs, the credenzas— that we can break apart and burn to keep us unfrozen.

I find a spot near Shreve and lie down, pressing my body close to keep him warm. I can see my breath in the low light of the room. At some point, I fall asleep hoping I don't dream of towering masses of people or ghosts of the dead.

■ ■ ■

In the middle of the night I wake, heart racing. Certain that the war has come home to us.

People are dying out there, in the cold and dark. People are becoming one with . . . *it*. And we're stuck here. After a long while, I sit up and go and look at Shreve, staring at his face. Thinking about our invisible war.

Eventually, I can keep my eyes open no longer, and I lean back against the wall and sleep.

■ ■ ■

I wake to bitter cold and the sound of splintering wood. The fire is growing, and in the dark I can make out the lean figure of Negata as he tosses what looks like the component parts of a wooden chair onto the fire.

"How did it get so cold so fast?" I ask.

Negata gives his smile-not-smile and says, "I imagine it was when Ember opened the door and left."

It takes only a moment to sit up and begin to understand what's happened. Of course she left without telling us. She's not going to go search for the Liar until she's found out what's going on with Jack.

*Ember! What are you doing?*

Nothing. Radio silence.

Everything's going to shit, and I can't do anything about it.

I look at Shreve—I'm always looking at Shreve, it seems like, I know his angular face better than I know my own—and realize his eyes are open.

...

It's a long while before he speaks, but I guess that's because I've kissed him, his mouth, his eyes, his forehead and cheeks. I press myself against him; I want his closeness, and I want him to *know* I'm close.

"Hey, you," he says. He must be tired and still hurt, because the I-know-something-you-don't-know grin he usually wears isn't plastered across his face. It's not there at all. He looks at me and simply smiles, happy to see me. And that's when I lose it.

No tears. No sobbing. But I'm lost. I love him. And the way he grips my ghosthand, I know he loves me too. Our secret bond. It's that simple. I can just look at him and know it. I don't need a song or poem or some sappy pronouncement. That smile—the one he gives me without hurt or self-mockery or loathing. And the pressure of his hand on an arm that isn't there anymore. That is all I need.

"Shreve. We've been so worried."

He shuts his eyes for a moment, and as they close I can see how ineffably tired he must be, dark circles around his sunken eyes, his cracked lips, the harsh lines of hunger and fatigue. He hasn't eaten in days, and by now his body is cannibalizing itself. He has good color and seems to be breathing fine, but he's dehydrated and wasted. He didn't have enough meat on his bones before the fall. Now it's like he's almost half cranium. I can see the vein at his temple pulsing. The throb of life in the hollow of his throat.

Negata is already moving, bringing Shreve a cup of water. He hands it to me and lets me place it at Shreve's lips. Shreve takes a sip, coughs, and then takes another.

"Do you want food? Are you hungry?"

He smiles at me again, a real smile, and shakes his head. "Let me sit up." It's then that he notices Negata kneeling nearby. "Hello, Mr. Negata," Shreve says. "*Hello.*"

Negata bows his head.

"I see you," Shreve says, tapping the throbbing vein at his temple. "I see you now." There's a sense of wonder there, in the way he says it.

"I always knew you would eventually," Negata replies. "Though I hoped you wouldn't."

"Wait, what's going on?" I ask.

Shreve glances at me and shakes his head, just slightly.

"I understand a lot of things now that I didn't before," he

says. And in his voice, there's this alarming calmness I've never heard there. He's changed.

"Ember said you were awake. Like dreaming, or something," I say, and then a thought occurs to me. "And the ghosts! You sent Danielle and Bernard back."

Shreve pushes off the pallet into a hunched-over sitting position and takes another painful sip of water and hands me the cup.

"I had some housekeeping to do," he says. "I had too many guests and needed . . ."

"Yes?" I realize I'm kind of pawing at him, my flesh hand on his chest and my ghosthand on his back.

"I had grown too large," he says, and looks from me to Negata. "Inside. At all times there was . . . a congress in my head. And I needed to lock it all away. So that the Conformity can't see me."

For an instant, there's a flash—one of those disjointed images we get from sharing minds, being one with each other—I see a hall, an infinite hall stretching away into the distance, but it's not a hall, it's a cellblock with many doors, each one with bars, and Shreve leading thousands of people into individual cells and locking them away. It's just a single moment and then it's gone and I'm not even sure I experienced it in the first place.

Shreve pats my knee. "It's hard to explain. But now I'm just me for the first time in a long time. And I have to stay that way. Otherwise . . ."

Negata, his voice soft, says, "The entity will come for you. It's drawn to power. But it's more drawn to the collective, isn't it? The joining of minds is a challenge, yes?"

Shreve looks at him. His eyes are as clear as I've ever seen them. "Yes. I have to stay just me and nothing else. If I do, it won't be able to see me." He grins. "As long as I'm incarcerado here—" He taps his chest with an index finger. "It won't know where I am."

He's too quiet. He looks to the dark window and then to the ceiling and then into the fire, smoldering.

"Until it's too late," he adds finally. Then: "It's time to go."

## TWENTY-FOUR

## JACK

"Don't move. I *will* shoot you," the voice says.

The woman from the clinic—we never even got her name—

I feel a hand nesting in my hair, jerking my head up and back and wrenching my neck horribly. The Gulch woman's straddling me, with some sort of long knife—or a letter opener?—in her already bloodied fist.

"I don't think so, Madelyn. Unless you want me to poke some holes in this *abomination*." Her voice, fruity and rapturous, blows in my face. Her breath smells like mint tea. I can feel the hard tip of the knife at my throat. My throbbing face, my eye, my broken nose, the agony of ropes cutting into my flesh, the ache in my muscles from the wheeling fall—all of those sensations dim and disappear, and all I can focus on is the sensation of that metal point on my throat and her minty, wholesome breath.

Madelyn clucks a little, like she's seen a kid fall and scrape his knee on her front walk. It's a sympathetic sound.

I wish I could see her. But Gulch fills my senses.

"Let these boys go. You have your church. You have your god now. Let them go."

Gulch blinks and says, "No. They have a use. We shall call

the All-Seeing here, to us." It takes a moment for what she's saying to sink in. "And then—"

*She got in, Jack,* Tap says. There's no attitude in his voice. No snark. Just pain and shame. *She got in and took what she wanted.*

"And then we shall ascend."

"Well, I've always known you were a loon, Miss Emily Ruth Gulch. You hid in your grandmother's house and had your prayer meetings with whoever'd listen to your nonsense, and that was just fine. But I'm taking those boys with me."

I can feel the knife dig into my flesh. It's outrageous, the feeling of metal entering the body. Like the pain isn't enough. There has to be a violation too. For a moment I think about the Witch, Ilsa Moteff. Her in my mind. I'll choose the knife any day. But still, I cringe away from it. It makes me want. Want my mother I never knew. Want warmth and to be back at the campus. It makes me want Shreve.

God, I'm scared. And this woman will kill me. I can feel it in the strength of her fingers, the way she bludgeoned me. Her grip is like death.

I'm scared.

"No, Madelyn." A smile crosses Gulch's features. It expands slowly until it stretches across her face like a pool of oil spreading. "We allowed you your clinic because I could find no use in killing you or dealing with the animals you harbor there. The All-Seeing God cares nothing about the dull beasts of the earth. But now—"

"Bullshit. You left me alone because I shot Simon through his torch-carrying hand when you all came to rout me out. You left me alone," she says, fury in her voice, "because I fought back against your collective madness."

"Madness?" Gulch actually sounds tickled. "The Godhead is proof that this is *no madness!* You saw it, did you not, before the electricity went away. It was on every station! The Godhead is real! The All-Seeing is real!"

"That is no god, woman. It's just something . . . something unexplainable."

"Blasphemy." Gulch shifts her weight, getting ready to plunge the metal into my neck. "I believe we're in a stalemate, then," Gulch says. "Because I will kill this boy. And if you allow me one moment . . ." She closes her eyes, and I can see her eyeballs scanning in their sockets like someone deep in REM sleep.

*Jack, I can hear her!* Tap sends. ***She's calling her . . .***

***What? You can hear her?*** I send back.

***She's calling her "faithful"!***

Gulch, whose face is so close to mine, snaps open her eyes once more.

"My Saved. Those who shall be gathered into the flesh of the Panopticon." She chuckles. The smell of the woman on top of me is overpowering. "They are on their way."

## TWENTY-FIVE

## EMBER

Ghosts or no ghosts, they've got to be out of their goddamned minds to think that I'm going to go flying off to find that little liar who fucked with my head in the testing before I discover what's happened to Jack. Casey can whine about it all she wants, but I'm the super-duper in the sky and she's just the sap with the invisible arm.

Should have nabbed more blankets before taking off because it's cold here and it only takes moments before all of my body is numb. The only warm part of me is my mouth, chuffing moist air into the stale fabric of my improvised mask only to have it freeze moments later.

Eyes water and tear with the force of the wind and my speed. The land passes below me in dark, green-black waves like a sea, undulating.

Brought some armament, unlike Jack and Tap. Can feel the M14's strap cutting into my shoulder as I arc through the wintry sky. We might have got comfy-cozy sexy-wexy back at the lodge there for a while, but I never misplaced my rifle. It is my rifle. There are many like it but this one is mine. Or so Gramps used to say when he wasn't quoting the Bible at me.

From this great height there are a few fires visible in the

overwhelming darkness below, and I'm tempted to fly down to them, just long enough to warm up, but more than likely that would end in gunfire or a witch hunt. The world's likely to get medieval pretty quick. Girls who can fly are going to be the first bitches the local yokels throw on the fire.

Maybe.

Boys with twelve fingers are probably fucked too.

Even in the darkness, I can see the wide expanse of the frozen lake—just like the map back at the lodge indicated—and I follow it south to McCall, where Jack and Tap said they were going. If they're anywhere, they'll be there.

*Jack!* Yelling with your mind is like whispering as loud as you can.

*Jack, are you there?*

*Yes.* It's faint. So very faint. ***Shit, Ember. We're in trouble. Come quick.***

***On my way.*** Pause only long enough to unsling the M14, shuck a round into the chamber. ***Locked and loaded.***

Airspeed is brutal. Feel like my nipples are going to freeze and shatter, along with my toes and fingers and nose and ears. All my pointy, sensitive parts. Never flown faster than I do now. The lake whips by below me. In the dim distance I see a shoreline growing in my sight. Some buildings.

***They're holding us captive,*** Jack sends, his voice stronger now.

***Who is?*** I ask.

***Religious fanatics.***

Oh, shit. Exactly what I was afraid of. Whenever things go south, the religious nuts go into overdrive. It's like they're taking notes from the Conformity. As it swells its numbers, gathering people into itself, so do the nutjobs. Maybe they've always been that way. Grandma could cook a mean apple pie, but when she got wind of my abilities, she was goddamned quick to call it the devil's work.

The town of McCall is below me now, trees whipping past, not very far below my feet. The squat, rectangular dark houses passing silently by.

*They're holding us in a church. So look for a steeple or something like that.*

*I've found you,* I send.

*What? How can you know? There's probably two or three churches in this town.*

When I smile, my skin creaks and it actually hurts a little. The moisture of my breath has frozen on my skin. I raise the M14 and sight the ground below. *I'm pretty sure the church they've got you in is the one I'm looking at. The one surrounded by a mob holding torches.*

## TWENTY-SIX

## TAP

The Gulch woman's on top of Jack doing a twenty-dollar lap-dance when Jack suddenly sends, *Ember's here!* The relief is palpable.

*That's right, bitches,* Ember says in my mind. *I'm here to pull your asses out of the fire. Should I take these crazies out?*

*No!* Jack sends, powerfully. *Don't kill her followers. When I give the signal, shoot the windows.*

*All of them?*

*Unless you know which room we're in,* Jack responds.

*There's only a couple of choices, really,* she says. *In position.*

Gulch says, "Massey. Come here and cut this boy's ropes." She tenses, and Jack moans a little. It looks like the knife she has is a good quarter inch in the meat of his neck. If it's not in the carotid already, it's a single push away from it. "Don't be stupid, Madelyn. I'm absolutely prepared to sacrifice the boy." Another moan from Jack. "Hear that? He agrees with me."

Madelyn doesn't say anything, and I don't either because I'm not quite up to the level of banter around here. Shreve would jump right in.

"We never really knew each other, did we, Ruth?"

The crazy woman says nothing in response.

"While you were inspecting the sanctity of your hymen or whatever you were doing in those prayer meetings at your grandmother's house, you know what I was doing?"

Gulch says, "They're almost here. My Saved. And then this will be over. Because I know how to call the Godhead of the Panopticon now."

Massey quickly cuts Jack's feet and hands free. Gulch pulls him up into a half-standing position and wrenches his arm up behind his back, removing the knife from its place at Jack's neck only long enough for her to twist his body around to face Madelyn and the rifle.

"Move over toward the desk or I'll kill the boy. Massey!" She barks the name, and her voice is like the cracking of thunder. I don't know if that's her bugfuckery in action or she's just a natural commander, but even I feel like jumping to attention.

Madelyn, who I gotta say is growing on me, says, "Remember your manners, Ruth. You interrupted me." Her voice is casual. Tinged with disappointment. "While you were praying, I was down at the target range."

The sound of the rifle in the small room is eardrum-shattering. There's a flash and a fleeting afterimage of a bright point of fire and then Massey falls. His eye is vacant and bloody and the back of his head, even in the low light of the room, is a mess, slowly pumping blood onto the rug.

The bore of the rifle is unwavering. "Call off your people and let the boys come with me, and I'll let you go."

"Too late," Gulch says, and her eyes roll back in her head. Her feet leave the floor. Rising. Jack's rising with her, in her arms, and now I see that his eyes have rolled back too, showing only whites. "The All-Seeing comes . . ."

## TWENTY-SEVEN

## EMBER

Hanging in the air near the boughs of a taller fir. *When the bough breaks, the cradle will fall* . . .

Even in darkness the training kicks in. Biggest weakness of being a flyer: there's no cover once you're in the air. Any of the pitchforks down there sees me and has a gun, well, it's aerial acrobatics and pure speed until I'm out of range. Or out of sight. Best to stay near the cover of the trees.

*Jack, what's going on?* I send. *They're almost all in the church.*

Track the torchbearers in my sights. It would be so easy just to slip my finger onto the cold metal of the trigger and . . . *squeeze.*

And I'll do it. I will. And not give one damn.

Tap sends, *Something's happening! Oh shit!* Catch a panicked image from his mind of a woman, arms wrapped around Jack, her head turned upward toward the ceiling. Eyes rolled back in her skull. And Jack, his mouth open in a painful O of surprise or alarm. His eyes white.

Can feel an invisible wind tugging at me, pulling me down toward the church. The air, so cold, has become electric, full of energy, and when I blink I get tracers and afterimages of lightning in the darkness of my eyelid cinema. It's as if there's an electrical storm emanating from the center of the church.

***Tap, what's going on?*** Screaming now, silently, and I can feel that I've bitten the inside of my mouth. I realize my nose streams with blood—*again?*—and I feel a strong pull on my body, tugging on my pelvis, my gut. My center of gravity.

Like the earth has gained mass, becoming denser. Shrinking. A collapsing star. More gravity. *Pulling me.*

A massive *CRACK* and something's happening with the structure of the church. The roof hitches with a great groaning of timbers and avalanches of snow falling away, revealing the roofing tiles that now flutter and rip as if the building itself was pregnant with a tornado.

There's another *crack* and a *boom*. Knocked back by the percussive wave, losing my grip on the M14 and wheeling head over heels away, away from the tree and the church and the howling and screams I now hear from the pitchfork- and torch-bearing villagers below.

Right myself in the air. The roof opens wide like the maw of some creature, jagged wood splinters for teeth, and bodies rise up, into my line of vision, and I can see that it's Jack and the woman, locked in a painful embrace. But then there's Tap and a larger man floating up to join them. The specks of people let the pitchforks and torches fall, and they're rising as well.

The Conformity. It's here and calling us to join it.

I can't resist the pull.

## TWENTY-EIGHT

## JACK

I am one with it. The darkness and the light.

When I was little and my foster parents would take me swimming at the community pool, I'd dive to the bottom of the deep end, my breath expanding within me, and sit there as long as I could, beneath the water, until I had to rise or die. And I'd feel an expansion, then. I feel it now.

I begin to see with many eyes, breathe through many mouths. I am nothing. We are all.

And behind the tectonic movements of our joined bodies, beyond the stressing of our minds, the entity comes like ink in water. It infests my mind. It controls my body.

*More. Gather more*, it whispers, and our mouths move in time with the words.

We search, eyes roving. Our separate flesh joining as one. Moving.

Such a puny thing below us. There. On the earth, looking up. It doesn't have the spark. It doesn't have the flame burning within and means nothing to us. It offers no power. But it moves. It may try to thwart us.

*More. Gather more to our flesh*, the darkness whispers.

There's a little of the boy that is me left. The part of me

that hides at the bottom of pools and never wants to rise. That part of me sees Madelyn below, looking up, holding her rifle. Sighting, peering into the scope. And the other part of me, the part joined with Gulch and the others and the horrible *thing*, recognizes the danger. She's sighting down Gulch. Our tether. Our leash to whatever lies in Maryland. All of our mouths bellow "*NO!*" in a chorus, as if we were still in the church.

And then there's a small sound, so very small, like the cracking of a twig, and the small flash of light and a puff of gun smoke and we're tumbling—*I am tumbling.*

...

When I come to, the woman named Madelyn stands in front of me in the snow, holding her rifle, the wreckage of the church behind her. She's bleeding from her scalp, and the blood makes long, weeping tracks on her weathered face. Something has caught on fire, and it's spreading quickly through the ruins of the building. The light hurts my eyes. But there's warmth.

She lifts her weapon, gesturing in the deep drift of snow. "That was a tricky shot, boy, but I managed it. Good thing you didn't hit the church on your way down."

I'm sore but well enough to stand. When I do, I can see the moaning tracks of the fallen, some still prone, some sitting upright, some standing, stunned, and toddling about like refugees from some war-torn country. Which they are.

We are.

The woman smiles, a sad smile but warm enough, slings her rifle over her shoulder by the strap, and tugs off her gloves. She brushes my hair from my face and pulls back my eyelid and peers at me. Turns my head back and forth like I'm some dog she's inspecting. Then she pats my cheek. "I'm just a veterinarian, but you'll be fine. Help me with the others. And after . . ." she says slowly, "you can take me to your friend."

■■■

We're lucky only two people died. The Gulch woman and Massey, both with perfect head shots. Massey's body burned up with the fire, but Gulch's fell with all of ours. Some of the locals drag it away in the snow. For burial maybe. Looks like their fervor has died with Gulch. They have a hard time meeting my gaze. Or Madelyn's.

Ember is here. She twisted her ankle pretty good in the fall but can walk well enough. Tap looks unharmed other than some scratches and contusions. "Hit every goddamn branch in that tree on the way down," he says, but his grin spans most of his face as he says it. He looks at Madelyn, who's kneeling by one of Gulch's Saved, and says, "You're a regular Annie Oakley, ma'am. Thanks."

"Annie Oakley?" she says, and looks at me. "Tell this one to keep his mouth shut. I don't like the looks of him."

Tap's jaw unhinges and drops. Maybe he's met his match.

■■■

Ember tugs me away when we get a chance. The church roars with flames and the sky in the east lightens, but the clouds are thick and snow fills the air, lashing down, hissing as it comes close to the church fire.

She grabs my coat and tugs me into her body.

"The cavalry requires a kiss," she says, eyes bright with mirth. Happiness is a relief. A pressure valve.

Her lips are warm, and I lose myself in her for a while. This is a joining I can get into.

●●●

The townspeople of McCall come out of their houses and help with the injured and stand around to watch the church burn. We stand with them for a while, mute, enjoying the warmth and watching the building collapse in on itself with great discharges of sparks and cinders curling and twisting in the frigid air. Then Madelyn sets us to work with the injured. After rigging stretchers from bedsheets and hastily gathered lawn implements—rakes, hoes, brooms—we move those who have no one else to take care of them into one of the nearby houses, and again Tap and I are set to gathering firewood. I'm guessing that before the world had electricity, most of humanity's time was spent looking for firewood, chopping firewood, or wishing they had firewood.

Madelyn shows us how to clean and bandage the wounded while she takes care of the larger injuries, setting bones, removing glass and splinters, doing what she can for burns. It begins to snow again, and the candlelight grows inside the still air of the stranger's home we've invaded. A mousy man in lumberjack clothes, he tries to make everyone comfortable, wringing hands, gathering blankets and extra clothes. His name is Herman, I think, and this is the most people he's ever had in his house. He actually seems pretty stoked about it. Like it's a dinner party. He keeps offering us his homemade limoncello, which is sweet but leaves a burning in my stomach.

It's long after dark before we're through, and Ember, looking exhausted, tugs me away to find a soft place to lie down and share the warmth of our bodies.

...

In the morning, one man has a high fever so Madelyn, being the only medical person on hand, tends him, forcing him to drink water and pumping him full of ibuprofen until the fever drops. He's one of the ones who fell and didn't quite miss the shattered corpse of the church building. He lost a sizable amount of blood— more than I thought the human body could hold—and now he doesn't look so good. I've seen people die—more than I ever need to again—and it freaks me out. The duality of the human body. On the one hand, it's so damned tough, it can take so much abuse and pain heaped upon it, falling from a height, extremes of heat and cold, being pushed to its limits. But on the other hand, the human body is weak. Every sharp thing wants to poke holes in it.

But soon the man is sleeping soundly. Looks like Madelyn knows how to deal with a broken body, whether it's an animal's or a human's.

No one notices when Madelyn pulls on my arm and says, "Come on. I need to get some more supplies before I can help your friend."

We follow her through the snow. It only takes a few minutes to reach the clinic. Madelyn takes a large key ring from her bulky jacket and unlocks one of the doors and leads us inside. It's a pediatrician's office. We stand in the cold room, somewhat dazed. Ember presses against me, soft and hard all at once, and Tap notices and his face gives a little bitter twist, but then it goes numb and expressionless. Maybe he's dealing with his jealousy now. Maybe he's growing up.

Maybe we all are.

Soon Madelyn returns with an overstuffed backpack. "It's no hospital, but most clinics keep things on hand in case of emergency. I grabbed what I think I'll need. And I don't think Dr. Willamette will mind." She looks at us all huddled together, our breath frosting in the air. "And he's a pediatrician, right? You're kids."

Silence.

"Well, you're young, then."

"Let me ask you something," Tap says, and strangely, his voice isn't challenging or bitter or mocking. Just curious. "Why did you help us?"

She looks at him, emotions churning under the calm exterior of her face. Then she says, "Because you can fly. By yourself." She swallows. "Not a big ball of you in that thing—"

"The Conformity."

"That's what you're calling it, and I guess that sounds about right." She shakes her head. "But you flew. I thought I was losing my mind. But then I saw Gulch's followers escorting her to the library. And I knew she'd do something terrible if she found out what I knew." She's quiet for a little while, thinking. "And she did, didn't she? I *had* to kill her. And her man."

"She called the Conformity," I say. "If you hadn't—"

Madelyn laughs. "Don't try to comfort me. I don't feel one bit of guilt about plugging her in the eye. Hell, I wanted to shoot that self-righteous bitch *before* the shit hit the fan. The world was kind enough to provide me a reason to do it."

It feels good to laugh. But eventually, it sinks in that we're laughing about death and our laughter fades. Madelyn shrugs, trudges to the door, and opens it, and we all file out into the snow-wreathed parking lot in the gray half-light of an overcast, snowy day. Our earlier tracks have already become soft and indistinguishable from everything else.

"So, how's this gonna work? I don't know how to fly."

"It's not something you learn, really. It's something you *are*," Ember says.

"Well, I ain't it. So?"

"I guess I'll have to carry you. Piggyback," I say.

Madelyn looks dubious. "You can't weigh but a buck fifty. The chubby one can carry me," she says, and chucks her head at Tap.

"My name's *Tap*, lady. Tee, ay, pee. Got it? And I'm not chubby."

"Who gives their kid a verb for a name?"

Tap points. "His name's Jack!"

"Touché, kid. Touché. I think we'll get along just fine. But someone better strap me to the boy. I'm not gonna just hold on to him for dear life. We've got some leashes and ropes in my clinic."

After we've literally tied her to Tap's back, he says, "I'm gonna have to get used to this. There's a big weight differential here."

"Watch it, chubs," she responds.

Tap looks at me, then Ember, then spits. "You fuckin' guys."

Then he leaps into the air and rises, halting at first, then faster.

Faintly, I hear laughter. Madelyn peals, "And *away we go!*"

## TWENTY-NINE

## CASEY

"We've got to go," Shreve says, pushing himself up and standing. For the past hour he's taken in sips of water and cold, freshly untinned tomato soup and not much else. The fire has died so low.

I need to understand. It's hard to just turn the reins over to him without even questioning why. Yes, we wouldn't be alive now but for Shreve, but I can't, I won't, follow blindly.

"Why, Shreve? Why can't we wait at least until Jack and the rest of them come back?"

"It's coming. The Conformity. It can't sense us yet—it can't sense *me* yet—but it will soon. Even if I'm running silent."

Shreve moves his arms and cracks his back like an old man waking, trying to stretch out the kinks. With the water, he's lost the hard angles in his face but he's still weak.

"What about the others?" I ask. "Jack and Tap. Ember. The ghosts, Dani and Kicks—"

Shreve perks up. "I didn't dream that?"

"You mean you didn't send them?"

His face clouds, and he thinks for a long while, standing there like he's lost something, his keys or his phone, and he's trying to puzzle out where he might have put them. Everything's become strange now, after the Conformity, and there's a disconnect between the urgency of our situation and the everyday normalcy of our bodies' habits: it's almost as if we should act more desperate than we truly are. The world is in jeopardy, yet Shreve looks simply like he's forgotten his keys.

"I thought they were a dream. And I thought of Reese. We'll need him before the end. But we can't wait here for them to find us. They could be dead and *will be dead* if I try to contact them. Or anyone else." He shakes his head. Holds his open hands before his face.

"Won't the Conformity target them if it can't sense you?" I ask.

"If it gets near enough to sense them, sure." Then he shakes his head. "If it's not nearby, I don't think so. But it can see me from far away. It's always been tied with Quincrux, and I've been marked by him. It's like . . ." He pauses here, thinking. "It's like I'm a beacon."

"You're a challenge," I say, thinking about Shreve. "You draw people to you the same way it draws people in."

The look on his face is disturbed, brow furrowed. "Like I'm a Conformity, myself?"

"Yes," I say, taking his hand with my invisible one. "You joined us, all of our minds."

"It wasn't to create some kind of . . . of . . . collective."

"I know," I say.

He's quiet for a long while. "It's been so long since I've just been *me*, me solely. But I know this." He turns to stare at me, his face so intense I feel like something in him is about to break. "We've got to go. Now."

Negata says, "I found a stable yesterday. Enough horses for

us to ride. But where do we go?"

"To where it all began," says Shreve. "We go east."

...

The snow's stopped falling, and the world stands hushed as we make our way down the mountainside, following Negata. Shreve's too weak to carry anything, so the pack-mule duties fall to Negata and me. We've rigged hobo bindles out of the slats from beds and bedsheets. Not a lot of food, but we have enough of the canned stuff from the lodge's larder to keep us for a while. A single small pan to melt snow. Matches. A small can of lighter fluid we found under the sink.

Before we leave I rummage through the last of the armaments from our hasty flight from the campus—two M9 pistols, multiple grenades on bandoliers, and an M14 with three full magazines. I offer Negata the M14, and he just shakes his head. Negata's a strange one. Shreve stands looking at me and then shrugs. "I'd carry it, but I never managed to get to any weapons training." He grins and looks sheepish. "Quincrux and Ruark weren't really keen on the idea of me with a gun. I was looking forward to shooting stuff."

"It's not that great, really," I say and hand him one of the M9s. "Don't stick it in your pants or you might shoot your dick off." I grin. "We wouldn't want that."

Surprise on Shreve's face is a wonderful thing, it happens so rarely. "No, we wouldn't want that."

Negata's a fine guide, taking us through the firs and pines, on and off roads, his slight figure moving silently through the trees. The snow makes some of the walking hard, and my feet are so cold it hurts to think.

All the world is hushed except for Shreve's labored breathing. After two hours of steady walking except for small breaks, we come upon a level pasture ringed in barbed wire and snowdrifts, some of them up to our thighs. The ground here is churned and brown, and fifteen or twenty horses stand steaming in the paddock, their winter coats furry. Beyond them is an open field with cattle and maybe goats walking on brown paths through the snow. It's dreamlike, this little farm nestled in a mountain pasture.

I took riding lessons when I was a girl and had both my arms. Now the sense memory of all that comes rushing back—Mom and Dad's smiling faces watching me, the smell of hay and manure, and the heat of sun on my arms. The creak of leather and the ache in my legs from posting.

I hope Mom and Dad are okay. And Jayson. Everything happened so fast, and I haven't even had time to think much about my family. But now it all comes crashing back in on me at the sight of the horses steaming in the cold, the red-brown barn at the far end of the paddock. The dreamlike pasture beyond. Everyone I love could be dead. They could all be part of the Conformity. When it's not right in your face, it's so easy to forget your own personal stake out there. Your loved ones could be lost.

"Hey," Shreve says, putting his hand on my shoulder, right above the stump. "You okay?"

So many people think tears are a weakness or an annoyance. But if you can weep without fear, you find they're a strength. I let the tears stand on my cheeks and say, "Just remembering the world before all this."

Shreve grows still. His breath plumes in the air, and he

says, "We'll get it back. Maybe not exactly. But we're going to get something worth having back."

Negata holds two strands of barbed wires apart and quickly slips through. Then he turns and holds them for us.

"I hope you're right," I say, and follow.

■■■

As we get near the barn, squishing and squelching through the half-frozen mud of the horse paddock, a man exits the shadows of the building and walks forward to meet us with a pitchfork in his meaty hand. He's been spreading hay, maybe. He's thick, blocky. With his head uncovered, it's easy to see he's bald with the barest hint of a neck—one of those guys who, due to their baldness, you think's older than he really is. He could crush boulders in those hands.

"Can I help you?" he asks. His tone is open and genial, and now that we're closer, I can see that he's got bright eyes and laugh lines.

"I don't know," Shreve says, shaking his head. "We need your horses."

The man puts his hands on his hips and looks at us closely. "Is that so? You're a motley crew to be coming onto my land, bold as love, and asking for horses. A boy, an unarmed man, and a one-armed girl with an assault rifle slung over her shoulder. This a robbery?"

Shreve puts out his hands, gesturing for everyone to be cool. "Of course not. No. But we need them. We're . . . " He stops, thinking. Since he's awoken, some of what made Shreve Shreve has gone. He's less assertive. Kinder, really. Vulnerable.

"You're what?" The man smiles, and I realize he's enjoying the conversation. He's probably not seen anyone since the Conformity arose. Close to the land, the fields. The end of everything might not have affected him much.

"We're on a mission," I say, moving forward to stand near Shreve.

"Oh, ho! A mission? That sounds important."

"We're going to stop what's happening. We're going to save the people caught up in the . . ."

"The aliens?"

Funny, but when he says it like that it startles me. Aliens?

"It's not aliens," Shreve says. "But *it* is alien, if you get me. And we're going to stop it."

The man chuckles. "I don't get you. Way I figure it, big balls of . . . whatever . . . floating over all the major cities, destroying everything. Sounds like aliens to me."

He's got a point. And to him, it's probably easier to understand the workings of the entity and the state of the world by slapping a label on it. There's a comfort to labels. There's false but satisfying comprehension.

"Whatever," Shreve says, waving a hand to brush away his misunderstanding. "The point is, we're going to stop it, but we need faster transportation."

"Where you going to?" the man asks, genuinely interested.

"Maryland."

The man whistles in response. "Ah. Where the first one appeared. That's a far piece to travel. You'll never make it on horseback. Hell, with this snow, you'll never even make it to Montana." He sucks his teeth and thinks. "I'd be hard-pressed to give you one horse, let alone the six or seven you'll need, just to get them killed." He thinks for a moment. "Not even considering the nutjobs out there or the aliens, it's gonna take you two or three months to get where you're going."

The surprising thing is that he's already calculated what it will take for us to make the journey. Which means there's a possibility.

He looks at us in turn and shakes his head slowly, shifting his grip on the pitchfork. "World's all jiggered up, that's for sure. And you folks seem in earnest, but I'm sorry, I just can't give away my ponies to anyone who asks for them. But let me share with you some of my breakfast, if you would, and we can part as friends."

I look at Shreve and can see his jaw working. Something hard is setting in him. His eyes take on that intense, wolfish cast, and I'm worried he's going to use his power.

But he doesn't. He points to me and says, "You called her one-armed. But she isn't. Are you, Casey?"

I understand now. I shake my head and say, "No, I'm not. I have two arms. One is very special."

I look around the yard for something—anything—to manipulate, but this farmer keeps a very tidy farm. There's a bench, with a bucket nearby, and a curry comb. But none of those have the dramatic element I need. So I settle on the farmer himself.

"I'm not going to hurt you, do you understand?"

A smile curls his lips. His eyes are merry. "That's good news," he says.

"Stay calm, okay?"

He nods again, grinning fully now. "I've had some coffee but not too much."

I take a large breath and reach out with the ghosthand, expanding it in my mind to encompass the whole of the farmer's big, blocky body, and grasp him in my hand. His smile fails and his eyes widen as I set my feet and hoist him up high. His pitchfork falls to the sodden earth, and I lift him up near the apex of the barn roof, right where the classic rooster weather vane sits. It's a strain—I'm reminded of how light Shreve was when I lifted him to the top of the water tower—but I can manage it. I'll be hungry later. Very hungry.

He hangs in midair for a good long while but doesn't struggle or thrash, and I'm careful not to crush him.

"Okay, miss," he calls from above. "That's one doozy of an arm. You can set me down now, if you're of a mind."

For a split second I'm tempted to call out, "So you'll give us the horses?" before releasing him, but that would seem too much like extortion. So I set him down.

He bows his head, scratches his pate. Looks at me again closely. "Don't know what to think of that. It was . . ." He clears his throat. "Unexpected. Didn't think I could be surprised anymore . . ." He gestures with his thick hands feebly. He looks pained. "Come on to the house and break bread with me, and we'll figure out the best route for you to take."

"You mean you're giving us the horses?" I ask.

He smiles, but it's more pained now. "I don't understand how all of that works,"—he gestures at the weather vane—"but since it *is* beyond my understanding, I figure you'll have a chance at stopping the aliens, since *they're* beyond my understanding too. Like to like and like versus like, the missus always said."

Like to like and like versus like. It feels almost prophetic.

"After all, what's a few ponies for the war effort?"

...

After a breakfast of eggs and cured pork, the farmer—he tells us his name is Nelson—takes us out and chooses the six hardiest ponies for us. He drills Shreve and Negata on riding basics for a long while. Eventually, they get it to Nelson's satisfaction and we spend another hour or so rigging our "luggage," as the farmer calls it. We're riding western saddles, and all the long leather straps and things that seemed so foreign to me as an English saddle rider make more sense now—straps and ties for saddlebags and bedrolls and even a holster for a long carbine. The M14 fits poorly inside it, but it'll do.

"It seems like a lot, but believe me, miss," Nelson says, tying down a bag of oats on one of the ponies along with a couple jugs of water, a pan, and a bag of pinto beans. "You're going out there in a pitiful state. I wish I had more to give you."

...

At breakfast we discuss our route. Nelson retrieves a relatively new atlas, opens the book to Idaho, and jabs his finger at the map. "You're here, and you're gonna want to follow highways. Might be more dangerous that way—I'm sure there'll be more and more nutjobs the closer you get to cities—but there's no way you'll make it cross-country. So . . ." He rubs the stubble on his chin and then traces a line north. "I'm gonna lead you out of here, east, to 95. Then your best bet is to go north until you hit Highway 12 and then take it north all the way to Missoula. Once you're there, go east on Interstate 90. That alone will take a couple of weeks, understand? Horses can only travel in this weather around twenty miles a day, and you'll need to switch horses once a day or at least every other day. Horses get tired, they'll put their heads down and start heaving air. They'll stagger about like they're drunk, so keep a lookout. I imagine you'll see it soon enough on our trip to 95." He sucks his teeth. Thinking. "Damn, folks. It's gonna be a long ride. My ponies aren't shod, so keep their hooves clean. Stick to the grassy medians, don't be wearing out their feet on the asphalt." Nelson looks as if he is overwhelmed. He stares at his home, a nice, small farmhouse decorated with photos of him with a lovely woman—strained and thin but lovely—and photos of young men in military uniforms. His sons, I imagine. But none of us ask, and he doesn't offer. "I should go with you, but all my livestock . . . my home."

Negata, who has remained silent in all of our dealings, places his hand on Nelson's shoulder and says, "We will manage. Do not abandon everything you've loved and worked for. It is a long journey, and we cannot see what help we'll find on the way."

"You can't know that. And you're not horse people," he says. "It's a good ninety miles to Missoula. It's thousands of miles to the east coast!"

"We will have to take it slowly. But surely. And we will make it. Do not fear for us."

"It's not you I'm worried about so much," he says, glancing at me. "It's the horses."

"We'll take good care of them, Mr. Nelson," I say. "I promise."

He sits down at the table, the atlas open before him. "I believe you mean that, or I wouldn't be giving them to you. But, again, it's not you. It's everything out there." He waves at the window. "If you're really going up against . . . against the aliens, there'll be danger."

"Of course," says Negata. "As you said outside, this is the war effort. And there will be war."

Nelson glances at one of the pictures of the young men in uniform. He stills.

"Okay. So you got the plan. Once you're on I-90 heading east, at some point you'll start passing rivers. The Missouri. The Mississippi, if you get far enough east. I suggest you trade the ponies for a boat and float downriver when you can. There'll be dams, but you can always portage whatever boat you get or find another on the other side."

It's now that the enormity of what we're setting out to do hits me like a cartoon anvil. I look at Shreve, and he has a sick expression spreading across his face. "We've gone back in time, Casey."

Nelson nods. "That's right. Two hundred years or more. And you'll be backtracking Lewis and Clark, believe it or not."

It is Shreve's turn to whistle. "This is impossible," he says. "I should just face it."

I don't know if Shreve is referring to facing the impossible truth or the Conformity itself.

"Nothing is impossible," Negata says gently. "You and Casey and the rest of the extranaturals are proof of that."

We sit there staring at each other, thinking about what lies before us, until Nelson clears his throat. "We've got to get a move on before the morning's gone. Long way to 95. Got some of my boys' old winter clothes for you all. You're gonna need them."

•••

With the horses packed and tied, us sitting in the saddles while the snow comes down softly all around, everything seems far off and dreamlike. We're in a line, and I can tell—what with the new winter coats and heavy underwear and down pants Nelson has given us—Shreve's having a hard time staying in his saddle. But when I come alongside him, leading my second pony, he gives me such a fierce look that I decide it might be better if I didn't give him any pointers on riding.

Nelson waves a big gloved hand, whistles, and hollers, "Ho!" And he spurs his horse forward, down the road from his farm.

I feel like I'm rising and falling all at once, in slow motion. My heart feels too big for my chest. When I was a girl, I dreamed of riding a horse in the snow, of being on an adventure. Now that it's here, it's such a hard road in front of us, and these few steps are just the beginning.

"The others are out there," Shreve says. "When I was in prison . . ." His face clouds. "When I was unconscious, I had a moment of awareness and I sensed almost everyone I'd ever touched. There are others out there, working to survive. Some even working to fight back." He looks stricken and lost for a moment, his Adam's apple working up and down in his throat, but says nothing. Then, "I'm afraid—"

"You're afraid?" I say, not liking this. "You've never been afraid in your life."

He stares off into the trees and snow and mountains. "I've never *not* been afraid. And never as afraid as I am now."

My pony nickers and chucks its head, blowing white air in a plume.

Shreve turns in his seat, gripping the saddle horn tightly, and looks back at me. He smiles, trying to reassure me that it will be all right. We don't have to be in mind-to-mind connection for me to know that. And then Shreve's pony gives a stagger step, Shreve's face gets this terrified, surprised look, and he's gripping the horse's neck for dear life. The horse seems unfazed.

Barely, just barely, I restrain the laughter.

We disappear down the road, among the snow-covered trees.

## THIRTY

# EMBER

Flying takes effort, any jock will tell you that after a long day at the lower airfield. The energy you expend pulling some extra-natural stunt burns calories just like if you were doing it with your body, because *you are*.

After fifteen minutes of flying, Tap's gasping and losing altitude and we have to land in the middle of a switchback trail, far from any road or home. Deep in the firs and piney woods.

"Get her off me! Get her off!" he yells.

Madelyn looks chagrined as Jack and I begin working on the knots. "I'm getting thicker with age, it's true, but I don't weigh that much. Some Superman you turned out to be."

When the knots come free, Tap falls over to lie faceup in the snow, panting.

When he regains his breath, Tap says, "This isn't a comic book, Grandma!" He pushes himself up on his elbows and then rises, slowly. "You'd think you'd be impressed by the fact that *a fucking human can fly*. But no." He walks over to Jack. "Your turn."

"What?"

"Your turn to carry her. And we've got thirty or forty miles to go to get back to the lodge. Let's get a move on, or this will take all day."

Jack looks at Madelyn like a butcher sizing up a side of beef. "I don't know . . ."

"Share and share alike," Tap grumbles, and then he launches himself into the air, leaving me to tie Madelyn to Jack.

...

Jack manages only five minutes in the air before he has to land. Much like Tap, once he's untethered to Madelyn, he falls to the ground.

"What's the deal?" I ask. "How is it so hard to carry someone?"

"See?" Tap says. "See? She's like an elephant!"

"Hey!" Madelyn says, and I do believe she's actually blushing. "Watch it, kid."

"I guess it's my turn, then," I say. "How far have we come?"

"Not very," Tap responds, looking at the trees around us. "Maybe a couple of miles. Jack was wallowing about up there like a sinking tanker."

"She's *heavy*," Jack says, glancing at Madelyn. "I've got to give a continuous pulse, so fast it's crazy."

"Okay, when you boys are done whining, let's strap her to my back."

Jack hops up almost immediately and approaches me.

"This is getting a little old, hog-tied over and over again," she says. We tie her steady. She takes a big breath. "I'm ready. God, this will be embarrassing if you can't even get off the ground."

When I fly there's a few things happening. It's an

awareness, really, of everything around me, like I'm in a bubble and that space becomes lighter than air and I rise up, ascending, and then it takes only the smallest breath of telekinesis to send me dashing on my aerial way.

With Madelyn, everything is off, slightly. My body rises sluggishly, and I have to concentrate on the lightness of my (our) beings. We rise slowly, but rise we do, and it takes only a few moments to adjust to her being strapped to me. But once we're up, it's not much more effort than normal flight, even if the control of our actual trajectory is a little problematic. It's like a boat wallowing about. Our forward movement is sluggish. *Glacial* might be the better word and just as cold.

Jack and Tap circle us like sharks during the flight, and we go for a good long while—an hour or more—before I need to land.

"Wow, Ember," Jack says once we're back on terra firma. "You were up there forever."

"What, you thought I couldn't carry her because I'm a girl?"

"No," he says quickly, blushing. "It's just . . . just . . ."

"I did," Tap says, staring openly, arms akimbo. A challenge. "You're not as strong a flyer as either Jack or me, yet you were able to keep the anvil up there longer. How's that happen?"

At the word *anvil* Madelyn squawks, but the boys ignore her. Jack looks at Tap and shakes his head, and they're talking mentally but keeping it from me.

"You ever think that brute force doesn't solve everything?" I say.

Tap shakes his head. "Nope, it's pretty much the key that'll unlock any door."

"You're an idiot."

"Screw you. I can fly circles around you, and you know it. How did you keep her up there for so long?"

"God, you're dense," I say. "I *think* different than you."

His eyes bug, and he wants to say something but he knows he's got nothing. Absolutely nothing.

"I think we can all agree you'll be the pack horse from here on out," Jack says, putting his arm around me.

I'm still pissed—at Tap *and* Jack—for doubting I could do it, so I shrug off his arm and ignore the hurt expression on his face.

"We're still going five miles an hour. We could walk faster than this," says Tap. "So you might be able to lift her, but you're not doing us much more fucking good than that."

"Maybe calling her the pack horse was the wrong phrase. Maybe we should call her the wagon," Jack says.

"What?" I say. Madelyn looks puzzled.

Jack says, "Do we have any more leashes or rope?"

"Why?" Tap asks, but I already understand what he means.

"I've got an idea," Jack says.

...

Tap yells over the wind as he and Jack strain against the wind and the tethers. We're going at a pretty good clip now. We've crossed the lake and should get to the lodge before full dark. The two dog leashes are clipped to the boys' belts—we had to turn them around and hook the clip on the buckles—and they draw us through the air like two draft horses hitched to a wagon.

"Some superheroes we are," Tap grumbles to Jack. Normally it would be hard to hear, but they're only at the end of the retractable leashes and well within earshot. "Glorified horses!"

"More like asses," Madelyn says. I can hear the amusement

in her voice. Despite everything—the end of the world, the weird cult and mob rules, the Conformity soldier materializing in the center of her hometown—Madelyn seems pretty chipper to be flying three hundred feet in the air over Idaho wilderness, being pulled by adolescent extranaturals.

"You seem remarkably upbeat," I say. Figure I can concede and make some small talk with the person who's strapped to me. With her pressed to my back, I'm warmer than I've been in a while. It would be weirder if I pretended like she wasn't there.

"We're *flying!*" Madelyn says, and I feel her squirm against my back. "Holy shit. Humans can fly!"

The joy in the declaration is unmistakable. Remember the first time my feet left the ground, in the corn maze outside of Lawrence. It was Halloween, and we'd driven the thirty minutes out to the October Country Pumpkin Patch and Corn Maze, and Grandma, wearing her sun hat and sundress, pointed to the maze and said, "Why don't you go get lost for a bit while I have some sweet tea with Mr. Calander," and I squeed and ran off. Didn't mean to take her literally but got lost anyway and for an hour or more found myself trapped in the maze until desperation took over and some invisible part of me, a phantom organ maybe, spasmed in my chest and I made myself rise and *pull*, moving higher over the earth, until I found myself out floating above the amber fields—in the maze no longer and lighter than air, high up where words could not touch me. Free. Maybe people on the ground mistook me for a balloon or some strange part of the attraction of the October Country and discounted their own eyes. Later, when Grandma scolded me for being late and "gone for gee-deed hours, you miscreant witch-child," her words hurt less than they ever had before because I held that moment of ascent tight within me, a secret joy I could never share. The joy birds must feel when shucking off the chains of the earth.

"Yeah, I know." Sometimes life brings you little things that make the larger, painful ones diminish. For a little while. "Yes. Holy shit, humans can fly."

■ ■ ■

The lodge is empty when we return. Find a note on the pallet where Shreve, up until very recently, lay unconscious. It's written in small, crabbed, capital letters like some troll shouting on the Internet.

JACK—
HAD TO GO, MAN. FELT THE CONFORM TRY TO MANIFEST. DON'T KNOW WHAT HAPPENED THERE, BUT I SUSPECT A CLOSE CALL. DON'T TRY TO FIND ME. IF I USE THE JUICY-JUICE, THE THING IN MARYLAND WILL KNOW AND COME FOR ME. FOR US.

I NEED YOU AND E TO FIND THE LIAR. HE'S GOT A PART TO PLAY—EVEN IF I DON'T KNOW WHAT IT IS YET. SORRY I SOUND LIKE I'M WEARING A WIZARD ROBE AND HAT, I'M NOT. START LOOKING FOR HIM AT THE CAMPUS, OR WHAT'S LEFT OF IT.

YOU WILL KNOW WHEN TO FIND ME. I PROMISE.

LATRO ALLIGATRO—
SHREVE

Jack takes the note, reads it silently, his face still, and hands it to Tap, who then reads it aloud as if we're all morons. Madelyn watches him, her arms crossed over her chest.

"Jesus H., he acts like I don't even exist," Tap says. He shifts his weight and drops the note to the floor. "We don't look for him?"

"Reading comprehension problems?" I say.

"Yeah, whatever. I don't do everything Shreve tells me."

"Then you're even a bigger idiot than we all suspected," I say.

"So, we're on our own," Tap responds. The guy just isn't getting it.

"We've got each other," I say as Jack bends over to pick up the note and tuck it away in one of his pockets. "And the doc over here."

Madelyn looks surprised. "I have my animals to attend to," she says, and she chews her lip. "And I'm dead weight to you. But you know where to find me, if you need something." She pauses and looks at each of us in turn. "It's too late now, but you'll have to take me back in the morning." She looks weary now, lines etched in her face. The elation from our flight is gone, and what's left is stress, exhaustion.

Wonder if I'll look like that when I'm her age.

Who am I kidding? I'll never make it to her age.

• • •

The lodge is cold in the morning. Spent the night huddled together, Jack and I, in the remaining blankets. Madelyn and Tap slept separately, though I could swear I saw him glance longingly at her slumbering form. But he's too weak to admit he needs the warmth.

Outside, the sky's still gray but the snow has become flurries and the wind is not as brutal. After a few moments of tethering, we rise up in the wagon formation and head back to McCall. It's quicker going, and before most of the day is through we're gliding above the frozen lake and settling in the clinic's parking lot. The church still smolders, sending a small granite line of smoke into the sky.

On the ground, we untether Madelyn and the boys, and when she's free she touches my shoulder and looks at me closely, considering. Her eyes are watery blue. Once they were probably electric, but now time has leeched the color from them.

"I can't begin to understand the burden that's been placed on you kids," she says, squeezing my bicep. My first instinct is to pull away. Issues of physical contact, *I* like to be the initiator. It's better to touch than get touched. But I don't. Madelyn isn't so bad, and I don't feel any burning need to put the beatdown on her. Rather she not touch me whenever the hell she feels like it, though.

Maybe she picks up the vibes I'm putting out, because she removes her hand. But she continues talking.

"What you kids have shown me has been . . ." She pauses, trying to find the right word. "It's been *wondrous*. Incredible. You know? I feel like I'm a girl again in some ways and Peter Pan has pulled me from my window out into the sky. Does that make any sense?"

Sure it makes sense. Don't understand why she's monologuing now.

"But there's a flip side to wondrous," Madelyn says, shaking her head. She looks at Tap when she says, "Peter Pan can fly, but he's got the Lost Boys. It has a darker side, like many fairy

tales, and what waits in the shadows are things that usually—"
She stops, thinking again, her face clouded. The parking lot is
a study in windswept snowdrifts curled and etched into soft,
white shapes. The firs lining the street beyond stand dark and
silent. There's only us four in a hushed, frozen world.

"Usually what?" Jack asks, his voice low.

She shifts her gaze from Tap to Jack. She stays quiet for a
long while—longer than any dramatic pause should be. "They
eat your youth," she says, voice flat. "Maybe they already have.
You three are jaded, and you're just kids. Maybe it's because this
is a war, maybe because of your abilities. I don't know."

"So?" Tap says. He's trying to be aggressive—as always,
fronting—but the way he says it, that one word has none of the
force of anger or bitterness behind it. It makes him sound like a
little boy.

"So," Madelyn says, "when this is over, I hope you all can
reclaim what's been taken from you. If not your innocence,
then at least a respite from the weight of the world. Freedom
from this crushing responsibility. I don't understand everything
that's going on . . . this Shreve kid and his message . . . but no
child should feel like they're responsible for the whole world."

She turns and walks over to the clinic doors, leaving us
standing there, looking after her.

"You three ever need anything, a roof, an ear, a meal, a
place to crash. Someone to talk to. Anything. Come to me. I
will take care of it. You understand?"

Not sure I do. This dumpy old woman says things that
make me feel angry and confused all at once, like I've been
pushed in the pool and don't know which way is up.

Jack, who's watching her intently, nods slowly, his jaw

locked and the fine muscles in his cheek standing out in relief. He really is a good-looking guy. His awkwardness due to his height has fallen away. Maybe because of the sex, maybe because of some fractional growth—*filling out*, Grandma used to say when discussing my breasts with anyone who cared to hear—but Jack looks more like a man now and less like a boy. Or maybe because of what the old lady has said. We've skipped right over adolescence into adulthood. Hell, maybe Jack even skipped over childhood.

There's a lump in my throat, and no amount of clearing it will make it go away.

"You kids be safe. Protect each other. Be kind," she says as she pulls out her key and unlocks the door. "I'll be here when you're through. Come see me." She stops, gives a small, gloved wave, and says, "Bye, now." The door shuts slowly and she's gone.

"Bye," Tap says, wiping at his nose with his sleeve.

...

No need to hang around this town anymore. There's a break in the clouds and a column of pale winter sunlight passes over us, for a moment transforming the parking lot into a brilliant, crystalline dream. It's been so long since we've seen the sun, the sight of it makes my heart throb in my chest.

Jack looks at me, his expression calm. Quiet.

*Time to go,* he sends. It echoes in my mind.

We rise up on the wind, into the breach in the clouds, perfect for our passing.

## THIRTY-ONE

## CASEY

The old loggers' cabin is hard to make out in the thick, snow-heavy woods. But throughout the day Nelson has been a steady guide—even those times when Shreve lost control of his horse, dropping the reins, and began frantically, helplessly beating at the air. Nelson remained calm and collected, turning his horse and collecting Shreve's before he could fall.

"If you hadn't pointed it out," I say, nodding at the low-slung wooden structure, "I never would've seen it."

"This is why you need to stay on the highways," Nelson says, giving a soft smile. "Even old hands like me have a tough time making out in the winter." Nelson dismounts and pushes his way through the knee-high drifts to the cabin's vacant door-frame and leads his pony past the door into the darkness of the interior.

"We're taking the horses inside?" Shreve asks, incredulous.

"It appears so," Negata answers, sitting placidly on his little skewbald. He swings his leg over the pommel easily and hops down. Negata says he's never ridden a horse before, but it's hard to believe. I'm loath to admit it, but he's a better rider than I am, even with all the lessons I had. I've never seen a man more centered in his body.

I dismount, and Shreve haltingly follows suit.

Inside the cabin, the horses press together, breathing heavily. In the other half of the cabin there's an open space, a stone fireplace that looks like it was cobbled together when the world was young and there was no concept of right angles. Nelson strikes a match, a bright blossom of light in the gathering gloom, and in moments has an ancient oil lantern burning and hanging from one of the low-hanging rafters.

With Nelson leading, we gather firewood. It takes a few moments to realize that he's teaching us how to find dry wood under snowdrifts, his easygoing instruction style is so subtle. A natural teacher, I think.

When we've piled the wood back in the cabin, Nelson sets to work starting the fire. Negata and Shreve watch him closely.

Nelson strips the bark from one of the older, dryer logs and then uses a knife to whittle long, thin strips of wood from the smoother, exposed wood.

"Why're you doing that?" Shreve asks.

"Kindling. Starting fires is hard work and usually done at the end of the day, when you're tired, right?" Nelson says. Before long he's got a pile of long, thin pieces of wood. He splits the pile in half and says, "Put aside some, because you never know when you might need it." With the remainder he makes a small, misshapen pile in the hearth. Taking one of the longer pieces, he lights it from the lantern and then returns to ignite the pile. Then he continues to feed the fire with increasingly larger pieces of wood until it's burning merrily.

Later, we gather snow for water and set beans to cooking. Everyone is silent. The constant static motion of the fire has a hypnotic quality, and I find it more entrancing than a television.

Shreve makes a pallet and studiously does not look at me. If I stand in front of him, he looks elsewhere. It's only when I place my blankets by his that he glances at me. And then blushes.

"Oh, for crying out loud, Shreve," I whisper in his ear. "Don't be so silly."

We're silent for a long while until the beans are done. At the farm, Nelson seemed somewhat gregarious and good-humored, but now he's quiet, and there's never been much dialogue from Negata. We eat the beans in steaming tin cups with cheap spoons—all provided by Nelson—and listen as the fire cracks and pops. Exhaustion washes over me. It's been so long since I've ridden hours upon hours, and I can feel the burning in my thighs and calves and ass. I can't even begin to think of how Shreve feels.

I arrange the blanket over us. Watching the fire, we push our bodies together against the cold. And sleep.

...

It's late, and the fire's been banked but is still giving off enough light to make out the rough shape of Nelson, lightly snoring in the corner nearest the horses, and the silhouettes of Negata and Shreve sitting near each other. The air smells of woodsmoke and horse, manure and piss. It's a swampy, moist smell that's strong but not totally unpleasant.

"It's not enough that you consider solely yourself," Negata is saying in a hushed voice. "You can become infatuated with the flesh—and this is a good thing, I think, a *right thing* for a boy your age. The act of negation is much like meditation. It is a lessening of all desires. Stripping away of wants. Stripping away of needs until all that is left is the naked blade—"

"The match flame," Shreve says. He's got a piece of wood in his hands, and he's slowly whittling off long, curling slices for tinder. There's some emotion there, behind his words, but like the fire, it's banked.

"If that is how you view it, then yes. I consider it a blade because—" Negata pauses here. His stillness is remarkable, and the space between words makes it seem like he's decided to stop talking altogether midstride. "A blade represents action. All paths will lead to that alone."

Shreve bows his head, his hands still. He shifts and pulls the blanket that's draped over his shoulders—his cape—tighter. "Flames spread."

Negata thinks on that for a moment. "That is so."

"I don't know. I've spent so much time living so many other lives," Shreve says, huddling in on himself. He holds up the knife to the fire and looks at it. "It's hard to . . . diminish. Is that the word?"

"I do not know."

I don't either, truthfully. I'm having trouble following the conversation.

"It's a big burden," Shreve says. He shifts slightly. "You know, I don't even know your first name."

"It is Nobu."

"Nobu Negata? So you are Japanese?"

"Of course. I thought this was obvious."

"Not really. You don't talk much. And you don't really have an accent. Up until the moment I woke, you were invisible."

"Yes." Negata's voice is faintly tinted with amusement. "You once called me a 'meatghost,' I believe. Which is amusing, because that is what we all are."

"I meant you had no . . . no shibboleth. You had no . . ."

"Soul?"

"Maybe. I don't know."

It's quiet now except for the crackle of the fire and Nelson's soft snores. Negata leans forward, picks up a small branch, and places it on the fire. After a moment, it catches and the interior of the cabin brightens and the shadows shift and flicker on the moldering timber walls and ceiling.

"How did you get involved with Quincrux and the Society of Extranaturals?"

"This is a large question. Larger than we have time for," Negata says.

"Right, we've got that appointment in the morning with the governor." Shreve draws the blade down the length of the wood, curling away a slice for the fire.

Negata raises his hand in a halting gesture. "I see your point. But we do have an appointment with some horses, and it is late now."

"You don't want to say?" Shreve's voice pitches up. "At one time, I would have just snatched it right out of your head."

Negata says somewhat sadly, "Ah, but that time has come to an end, has it not?"

"Yes. All that's over." Shreve glances at me. My eyes are lidded, and I hope he doesn't realize I've been listening to his conversation. I want to reach out, to touch him with my hands. To touch him mind-to-mind. Anything.

But I don't. I wait. And listen.

"I am what is considered *nisei*, which means second generation. My father was *issei*, first generation. He was born in Kyushu, but eventually he made his way to Argentina, where

I was born. My first language was Japanese. My second was Spanish. And then English."

"You don't have an accent. Which is kinda weird."

"Yes. I've been told I have no accent in Portuguese as well. A natural. Very much about me is, as you would put it, weird," Negata says. "My father was *tasai*, or gifted. He was, as you call it, a bugfuck."

Shreve snorts. It's loud in the stillness of the cabin. Nelson's snores stop, and he shifts and rolls over in his sleeping bag. And then begins snoring lightly once more.

"He always told me he left Kyushu because of the flooding there before I was born, but as I got older, I learned it was due to the *mó fa*, the Chinese version of the Society. Above all things, Father hated the Chinese."

"Why?"

"War. Always war. Japan was a very warlike nation then. And, consequently, many young men died."

"Seems like that is the way of it," Shreve says, his hands working steadily on the wood, knife moving. "Wars are declared by the old and fought by the young."

"This is undeniable. The *mó fa* had approached Father and tried to recruit him, and much like you and your friend Jack, he fled. When he stopped fleeing—with my mother in tow—they found themselves in Argentina and made a life in Buenos Aires. Father was a card player. My mother, a seamstress."

"A card player? Ha! Why didn't I think of that?"

"You were probably too busy running, and most card players don't like to play with children," Negata says, and there's real warmth in his voice. I don't know if it's him talking about his family or Shreve letting his guard down, but it's like I'm watching two people become fast friends right before my eyes. It's a strange sensation: I feel jealous and not a little abandoned.

"When I was born, I was a problem for my father because, as I grew older, I could not be read. This was unspoken yet obvious. My father fretted and fought, but I was to him as water is in a hot pan. By the time I was ten, I was totally invisible to him both in psychic terms and in parenting." He looks at me. "I am your companion, Shreve, and I will safeguard you, but I am not trying to fill your father's shoes. Bear that in mind with what I say next."

"I don't have a father. But, okay." The knife stills on the wood.

"People like you . . . these *bugfucks* . . . they are racked with needs and desires they cannot control due to the loneliness and isolation their abilities bring. Is this not true?"

After a long while, Shreve simply says, "Yes."

"My father picked the most obvious of vices. Alcohol."

Shreve goes back to whittling. I know from what he's told me about his mother that she's a sauce.

"I understand," Shreve says.

"You must guard yourself against addiction, Shreve."

"Yes. That's old news. I've—" He stops. Swallows hard. "My mother was the same. And I'm like her, except—"

"Except what?"

"I'm a thief. I—" Shreve looks at the wood and knife in his hands as if he can find an answer there. "I've stolen memories. The good ones. Drank the emotional content from them like a drunk cracking a can of beer."

Negata leans back. Watches the fire. "And you still do this?"

"No. Not in a long while. But I know the urge. Weird thing is, I used to look down on Moms because I had to raise Vig, my little dude, myself. And she was such a lush. I was doing *her* job. But then I *became* her." The knife begins moving once more. "I wouldn't want it on my highlight reel."

"Nor would I."

"And since then . . . shit, I've killed thousands. I didn't *mean to*. I try to help . . ." Shreve throws the wood block he's been carving into the fire, and when it lands on the coals there, they brighten and flame. He folds his pocketknife. "Every monster I've had to face, I've had to *become them* to survive."

Negata stands and moves over to his sleeping bag silently. Once he's inside, he says, "I have nothing to say to help ease this pain except this: Children have the luxury of looking at the world simply, in terms of black and white. Good and evil. But adults must make compromises."

That sounds about right. Negata stills, closes his eyes.

Shreve sits there a bit longer, staring at the banked fire.

"There will come a time, Shreve," Negata says softly from his bedroll. "You will have to go to face this evil that has fallen upon us all. I have done what I can to protect you, but when you must go, you must go. I do not know what gods decided that this is a war that must be fought by children, but I fear it is so. You must leave me behind and go to the fight, when the time is here."

"You can come with us. All you have to do is open your mind to me—"

"No," Negata says sadly. "I've spent all my life becoming nothing. I cannot become more than I am now."

"But . . ." Shreve trails off.

Negata says no more, just remains still, and then his breath deepens and he's asleep.

Shreve returns to our nest of blankets and slips in beside me. The length of him presses against me, and I feel him press his lips to my forehead. I put my arms around him and share his warmth.

The frozen world beyond these walls requires compromise. It requires us to fall. But here, with his arms around me and his face soft and quiet in the low light, his eyes closed and no sign of the wolf about him, we need make no compromise. We can be pure.

## THIRTY-TWO

## JACK

We land in the open space of the dorm, and Tap pulls back his hood, pulls off his gloves, and stares at the remains of our room. He looks like someone's gut-punched him. He steps over a frozen corpse, walks over to Shreve's old bed. The wind from the great opening in the wall blows his hair as he sits down on the thin mattress.

It's taken us a week to reach the campus. We had to search for our old home as if we were geese or carrier pigeons. It was only when we spied a road sign pointing to Bozeman that were we able to trace the dead, empty trails of white highways below us and then thread our way back to the campus.

The campus itself is in ruins. Some structures still stand, but it looks as though the Conformity had a tantrum after we escaped, if you can call *that* an escape. Buildings are crumpled and shattered, massive spills of red and gray brick, jagged snarls of shattered timber, partially cloaked in white. The canteen and admissions are rubble, along with the research and development housing. The Army barracks has been squashed flat, as well as the girls' dorm. On the heights, the water tower lies where it fell. I'm thankful the field of human bodies below it has had a blanket of snow drawn across it, with only a few mangled limbs poking through the crust here and there. I wish I could do something for them all, but it would take months of work to get them buried. The bears and mountain lions will be well fed this winter.

The boys' dorm still stands, but half of our room is sheared away; the floor is jagged and buckled, the rest open to the sky. It's a brilliant winter's day, bright and bitter cold, throwing the whole world in sharp relief. There are three frozen corpses splattered about what's left of the room—two men and a little girl, probably sloughed off from the soldier as it struck the building.

"We knew it was never going to be permanent," Ember says, inclining her head toward the ruinous view before us. "You knew, eventually, we'd go on assignment or move on."

"Speak for yourself," Tap says. "I never would've come here if I'd thought that. I would've stayed with my family, even though *this*—" He sweeps his arm to take in me, Ember, the remains of the campus, the corpses, the existence of extranaturals in general. "—would've put them at risk. *I love my family, goddamn it. I wouldn't have left!*"

Tap's shaking. He covers his face with his hands. Yeah, he's still a dick. But now I can see what motivates him, and it's not that different from what drives me. Strange to say, Ember—my girlfriend . . . no, we've gone beyond that. Ember, my *lover*—is more opaque to me now than Tap.

There's not much I can say to Tap's outburst. So I switch subjects. "They evacced out of the south pass," I say, looking down the valley—a wide view now that the whole of our dorm room has been ventilated. It's like King Kong just ripped half of the dorm building away. "They were in Jeeps and troop transports. How long did the Conformity chase us before it—"

"Turned off the electricity?" Ember asks. "Seemed like only minutes."

Tap stands, wipes his eyes. I'm very careful not to notice his tears. "Nah, it was way longer, we were just terrified. That made it feel like things were happening faster than they were."

"So they could've gotten quite a ways. We were on the switchbacks, but when you go that way," I say, pointing to the south, "Highway 10 is right there. Once they got on the pavement, they'd be moving fast."

"Let's go, then," Tap says, pulling his hood back over his head. "The quicker we find the Liar, the quicker we can—" He stops.

We can what? Find Shreve? Confront the Conformity? And then? Will we be dead? Will we become part of the great pulsing mass? Be consumed?

Everything waits in ruin.

■■■

Ember wants to sift through the rubble of the girls' dorm to look for some of her things. Mementos. A necklace. A picture of her grandmother.

I don't tell her it's pointless.

Maybe the point is to realize it's all gone.

From on high, Tap and I scout the area for any signs of life. Not surprisingly, the only signs are of wildlife. The forest and animals have already reclaimed some of what once was our home. Game trails lead to piles of rubble that possibly have dens in them now. There's big-cat shit—probably mountain lion—in the boys' dormitory atrium, right outside Roderigo's little office.

*Let's check the bunkers,* Tap sends in the face of wind. *I could stock up on ammunition. And I'm hungry.*

*I'm hungry too.*

The entrance to Bunker H is no more; the Conformity battered it to oblivion. But on the far side of the mountain, at the end of the switchback, the motor pool door stands open and we're able to gain entrance there.

We trudge down the long hall, into the guts of the mountain where there's absolutely no light; we have to resort to the matches and candles we took from the lodge to see our way back to the underground armory and cache. There's still some MREs and weapons and ammunition, so we both stock up, taking another M14 and pistols for each of us. Tap slings a bandolier of rounds for the grenade launcher over his shoulder.

Looking at him, I laugh.

"What?" he asks, not far from outrage.

"You look like a bandito. You got the bandolier, and you're still wearing that old wool blanket cape. All you need is a cowboy hat and cigar."

He looks at me, the corners of his mouth curling up in an involuntary smile. "You're not so bad, Jack."

"Thanks."

"Let's not start sucking each other's dicks just yet. Help me with this bag."

"You gonna be able to carry all that?"

"Don't start, man. The doc was *heavy.*"

We lug the nylon bag full of ammo and MREs back out. Tap threads his arms through the handles, making an improvised backpack, and we lift off, heading back over the mountain, back to campus. At the apex, as we're passing over the snow-wreathed peak, the valley beyond seems strangely washed out. The firs seem dark, not green. The sunshine is bright yet brings none of the buttery color. The sky, normally blue, seems just gray. The colors are there, but only the barest hint.

*What the hell?* Tap sends. In flight, it's easier to speak mind-to-mind. *Who put on the black-and-white movie?*

We make it back to where Ember waits for us in the aerie of the ruined dorm room. Tap unslings the bag, and we divvy up the ammunition and food.

"You notice anything different?" I ask Ember, moving next to her. Sometimes I just want to ditch Tap, find some little abandoned house with a stocked kitchen and a thick woodpile, and hide away from all of this with Ember. We'd spend the rest of our lives in bed. But thinking about it makes me uncomfortable. And she'd never go for it, and I couldn't live with myself if she did.

"You guys look like zombies."

I glance at Tap and then back to her. She's right. "It's like the color has been leeched out of everything."

Ember shrugs. "It's the Conformity."

"How do you know that?" Tap says. "You don't know that."

"No," she responds. "You're right, I don't." She takes out an MRE labeled MEATLOAF WITH GRAVY, rips the top part off, and dumps the contents out on the bed. She snatches up a packet and, with her teeth, tears the top open. From her jacket breast pocket she removes a metal spoon—over the last days, we've taken to carrying everything we need on our persons at all times—and digs in. Around a mouthful of meatloaf she says, "The Conformity turned off the juice, right? We agree on that much."

Tap nods, reluctantly.

"Then what's to say the fucking thing hasn't washed the color away? It feeds on misery and can alter the fundamental aspects of the universe." She digs her spoon into the meal packet, stirring. "More people it takes over, the more power it has. Maybe soon it'll be able to black out the sun or . . . shit, I don't know . . . eliminate gravity. Alter quantum physics. Feed on our emotions, maybe." She takes another bite.

"You don't know what you're talking about. You're just speculating."

"That's right, dude. There's only one way to know for sure, and I'm not going to trot right up to one of those shitballs and ask. But whatever the case, the world's had the color sucked right out of it. I'd say the Conformity is the prime suspect."

There's nothing I can say to argue with her. There's no way to prove she's right or wrong, but what she says *feels* right.

Ember looks into the opening of her meal packet, glances at the frozen corpse of the girl in the corner, and purses her lips. She cleans her spoon off with her mouth and tucks it back in her pocket. "This tastes like shit," she says, and chucks the meal into the void. "Let's get out of here."

*You okay?* I say to her alone.

*The fucking thing has sucked the color out, Jack. There's a dead girl in the corner. How do you think I am?*

Before I can say anything, she takes three quick steps toward the jagged opening in the wall of the dorm and leaps into the air.

"Come on, man," I say to Tap. "Let's go."

## THIRTY-THREE

## CASEY

"This is where I leave you," Nelson says when we emerge from the tree line and the horses find their footing on the pavement of the highway. All is silent, and there's a hush in the trees and on the mountain.

"Come with us," Shreve says. "What we're doing is important. Possibly the most important thing—"

"No," Nelson says, his face clouding. "I've got my horses to think about. And—" He looks at our back-trail, a large furrow in the snow. And then his gaze goes to the pass we just came from, beyond. "My whole world is there, and I can't leave it."

"But, you're alone—" I begin.

"Here's the thing, kids." He looks back at us, an expression of sadness on his face. "It might not seem like it, but you've got a million paths in front of you. You're young, and life is full of possibility. But me? I've used up all of my possibilities." He shrugs. "There's but a single path in front of me," he says, looking at Shreve. "And it goes back. To home."

Shreve says nothing, a strange look on his face. Negata manages to bring his horse alongside Nelson's and offers a hand. They shake.

"Thank you," I say, simply. Nelson nods at me and turns his horse around and follows the trail back. Very quickly, he's hidden by tree line.

We follow the highway north. Shreve huddles in on himself, silent.

"What's wrong?" I ask and then realize the ridiculousness of that question.

He shakes his head. Says, "Nothing."

■■■

We're on 93 outside of a little town called Lolo when the big burly man steps out from behind one of the firs lining the highway, holding a rifle.

"Dismount! Drop all your weapons!" he bellows, walking forward quickly. He's got a bead on Negata, the closest rider to him. "I will blow your face off, man!"

Negata slips off the horse like water off a duck's back and steps away from the animal, a little to the side, a little forward so that the man's rifle moves away from us.

"Mister," Shreve says, pitching his voice to be heard. "You're making a big mistake."

"That right?" the man says. "How do you figure? I got two compadres behind trees with their guns on you." He glances at Shreve. "So why don't you get off the fucking horse, kid, before I lay your friend out." He takes another pace forward, his eye to the sights. The cant of his shoulders and tension of his whole body is palpable. A big guy, he looks hungry and desperate.

"We can't do that," Shreve responds.

The man whistles, and two more men step out from the side of the highway. One's got a pistol, and the other's holding what appears to be something metal.

"Does that guy have a sword?" I ask.

The men glance at me, probably surprised to hear a female voice. It's been a long time since the specter of rape has passed by, ever since I gained the ghosthand, but these guys don't know what I can do.

Shreve does, though. He looks at me and nods. I know what to do.

All I have to do is slip my ghosthand into his chest and give his heart a small squeeze, and his face drains of color and he pitches over into the snow, rifle and all.

Negata leaps forward, kicks the gun away into the snow, and begins to feel for a pulse. The other two men, at the sight of their fallen comrade, yelp in alarm. But I've already yanked the pistol out of the second man's hand and floated it over to Shreve, who catches it out of the air, checks the load.

"Empty. These jokers are toothless," he says, though he keeps an eye on the fellow with the sword. He's a younger man with stringy blond hair, dressed in a motley assortment of ski clothes and winter wear. Eyes bugging.

"You're part of it!" the sword-bearer yells, shaking his head. "You're one of them!"

Shreve tosses the empty gun back to the man I snatched it from. "We're not gonna hurt you guys." He darts a glance at the man on the ground. Negata has begun administering CPR. "Or, we're not gonna hurt you guys any more than we already have," he says, holding up a gloved hand. "We just want to know about the road ahead."

The young man with the sword walks forward, holding the blade up like he's Conan or something. I can snatch it right out of his mitts if I need to, but why not let the guy keep it for a while? He's terrified already. On the other hand, terror is just one step away from hysteria, and hysteria is dangerous.

With his approach, I can see that the sword looks like a prop from a fantasy movie. Maybe he's one of those people who dress up in armor on the weekend and talk with *thee*s and *thou*s. Who knows? I'm not going to let him get any closer. It's a big sword.

I stretch out the ghosthand and place an invisible palm on his chest, halting his forward movement. He staggers a bit, looking around himself, as if to discover the wall or fence he's run into.

"Let's not make a mess of this, buddy," Shreve says. "Are there soldiers ahead?" He pauses, reevaluating his wording. "You know, big towers made of people. Grabbing folks. Moaning and dripping and yelling weird stuff. You know."

The sword-bearer shakes his head. It's a little frantic. The guy is frazzled, that's for sure. He's probably hungry. Maybe they wanted the horses for food as much as transportation.

"One appeared two weeks ago, right after the electricity went out," he says, voice hoarse. His knuckles are white on the pommel of the sword. "Took a lot people from Missoula, maybe a fifth. Or more. Then it . . ." He sobs once and then looks surprised that the sound came out of his own mouth. "Then it divided. Holy Christ, the thing *split in two!*"

Shreve nods, somberly. "Did both the soldiers go the same way?"

The man lowers the tip of the sword. "Soldiers? Why do you call them soldiers?"

Shreve waves his question away. "Doesn't matter. Which way did they go?"

"One went northwest. The other followed the interstate east."

Negata stands, looks at the man with the sword. "You may collect your friend now. He's breathing on his own, but he'll need to be watched." He returns to his pony and leaps upon its back—graceful despite the heavy winter clothing—and takes up the reins again.

"Thanks for the info, dude," Shreve says. "I'd suggest you guys give up on being highwaymen. It's not working out too well for you."

Negata kicks his horse forward, and Shreve follows. I bring up the rear, watching the men. They look at us with hungry faces as we ride past.

"But you've got more horses than you need!" the sword guy says. "You're just leaving us to die!"

Negata doesn't react, but I can see Shreve's shoulders hitch, like he's waiting on a blow.

We ride past, leading the ponies, leaving the would-be robbers behind us in the snow. A flight of ravens erupts from the tree line with loud caws, banks and wheels above us, and disappears.

···

The next day, we've skirted Missoula and begun riding east on the interstate median. From horseback, 95 is covered in snow and doesn't so much look like a road as a never-ending field, stretching off into infinity, the white mounds of abandoned cars and the highway signs and mile markers the only things marring the illusion.

"It's only after everything stopped that I realized how much of life," Shreve says, lifting his hand to indicate the snow-covered road, "of *human* life, was dedicated to holding back . . . disorder."

"Chaos," I say. "Someone would have plowed this road."

Negata sniffs and says, "An unplowed road is hardly chaotic. It is merely inconvenient."

Now that we're moving—slowly, very slowly—Negata's opened up. The little man seems to want to share with us now. Maybe because time's running out. For everyone. When we realized the color has been leeched from the world, maybe that was the stone that cracked his icy surface.

"What I find interesting," Negata says, drawing his horse in line with ours, "is how *little* chaos the Conformity has caused. Some small devastation, but not as much as one would think. The world has simply gone into a state of decay. People gone. Absence."

I think I get what he's saying. In most wars—and if we have to compare this to something, it might as well be a war—there are explosions, buildings in flames, people dying slowly and in pieces. But that's not what's happening here. America is like an empty house now, slowly falling apart.

Negata turns in his saddle to look at us closely and continues to think out loud. "Maybe this is due to the nature of the Conformity—it gathers people unto itself. It has its own internal order. Whatever its goals—the absolute harvesting and subjugation of humanity, the reshaping of the universe—it isn't here for destruction's sake." He looks around us at the derelict cars. "Otherwise, I think this planet would be in cinders."

As Negata speaks, my flesh—even in the cold—breaks out in gooseflesh. "You know," I say, "that's almost the worst thing . . . the most terrible thing I've ever heard."

"Yeah," Shreve says. "The idea that it's got its own idea of *order*—oh, man. Where does that leave us?"

"In the end," Negata says, "we are merely fuel. We are its flesh. This entity—this consciousness from beyond the stars—has found a way to fashion a body for itself. And that body is the human race. Or the part of humanity that is best suited to it."

"The extranaturals," I say. "Us."

Shreve says nothing. He's not chewing his lip; he's not railing against our fate. I'm riding close enough to see his face under the hood. It's placid, if uncomfortable. He's decided on something. He's made up his mind. I don't know what it is, but I can tell by the way his jaw is locked that he's going to act.

When he does, I'll be there to catch him.

## THIRTY-FOUR

## EMBER

Can't let the boys see how upset I am—not because I need to be all tough, but because the panic and desperation are catching. Saw Tap's tears, and if he's so broken that he'll cry in front of us . . . we're in bad shape. Tap's like Shreve, to a certain extent. They'll never let you see their weakness.

Like me, I guess, too.

Feel lost. Desolate. Not just because the campus lies in ruins, or because our cozy little life has been wiped away. There are so many dead. So many frozen bodies littered about as if they were candy-bar wrappers, just wadded up and thrown away. We mean so little to the Conformity in the end. Each life is just an infinitesimal spark, worthless in the larger scheme of things.

The little girl in the dorm room. White-eyed and half covered in snow.

Dani, Bernard, I wish I could have done something for you.

There's nothing there, inside me. Was terrified at first when the ghosts came. Felt as though I was losing control of myself. But then there was a comfort knowing that Dani and Bernard were in me, somewhere at least.

After sex, when both Jack and I fade to black, I have dreams that are not my own. Wake to strange rhythms, pulsing and pounding in my head, and images of people I love that I've never seen or met before but that remind me of Dani and Bernard. And the strange thing is, we were never close in life. Weren't buds. Were just kids who went to the same school—thrown together by chance. But now, they live inside of me. Don't know what I'd do if I could be rid of them. Would that mean they'd be dead forever? Is any part of them alive even now?

Jack and Tap follow closely in the howling currents of air, and that's fine because they can't see my tears up here, and if they did, I could blame them on the wind.

■■■

The first day's a bust—we must have taken the wrong route on Highway 10. We bunk down in an abandoned motel, all sharing the same room. I wanted to be with Jack, alone, but he insisted. Worried for Tap, he said—he shouldn't be by himself. I gave in but didn't like it. Because the sex is like a drug. *Sex is like a drug, uh huh uh huh, baby.* Know that's been sung so many times before in a bajillion different ways, but that's because it's true. Not just the physical sensation, the hushed breath and taste of his lips and him moving under me, or above me. It blots out higher thought, and all that's left is the urgency of my body, the urgency of his, and the rest of the world is gone away, remote. There's nothing that can dethrone me from that mindless seat of heaven.

But last night, we all bunked together and there was none of the mindless release. We piled under blankets and sleeping bags—with Tap on the other bed—with nothing to do but think about how fucked up our situation is. Pretended to watch television on the dead idiot box. Talked about the old shows we used to love back when electricity existed. Thought about our families. Jack was very quiet then.

Finally fell asleep, kept imagining a frozen little dead girl in the corner, holding a silky blanket and staring at me with white eyes.

...

Backtracking our route this morning, keeping the highway below our feet as we fly, and making our way east and then south.

*They'll stay together, I think,* Jack says as we circle a small town that consists of a gas station, a weathered post office, a bar, and a trailer park.

*Why do you think that?* I ask. *Why won't they just head off to wherever the hell they want to go?*

*They're members of the Society. They'll want to continue to be around people like themselves, right?* Jack says.

Tap's not scornful, but there is doubt in his mental tone. *There were Army and lab coats in the evacuees. They'll want to go home.*

*Well, sure,* I say, *but if they're all split up, it'll be because they're scared of the Conformity. If I was traveling in a large group, I'd worry that a soldier would be drawn to us.*

*I guess so,* Jack concedes. *But whatever. We need to find the Army vehicles and from there we can find Reese.*

Maybe seventy miles south I spot the line of dull gray Jeeps and troop transports lolling on the side of the highway. We land long enough to determine that the vehicles are stripped of belongings and there's no one hanging around. At the next exit there's some indication that the evacuees came this way. Behind the Town Pump truck stop there's a huge steel building, the bay garage doors standing open but deserted. We land in a gravel parking lot, weapons ready. The parking lot sits surrounded by reclaimed lumber and the rusting hulks of thousands of cars, neatly stacked.

"Two big campfires over here," I say. "Looks like they burned half a building."

"And here's where they spent the first night. This would've been a bit over a week or so ago," Jack says, pushing back the garage door all the way. It's a warehouse-like garage, concrete-floored and easily over five thousand square feet. There are wooden pallets arranged in a grid, one of which still has a tent on it.

"Looks like they made their own little campsite inside," I say.

"They're close, then," says Tap. "With no vehicles, they couldn't have gone far."

"Some of the Red Team were with them," I add. "The jocks like us, they probably would have flown the coop."

"Yeah, I wouldn't have stuck around," Tap says.

"I don't know," Jack says slowly.

"What do you mean, 'I don't know'?"

"Reese is with them. And the Bomb."

"So?" Tap's natural surliness is returning.

"They're not gonna let themselves go unprotected, you know? In the testing—" Jack thinks for a little bit. "Did either of you go up against Reese in the Testing? Or the Bomb?"

"The Bomb did her stuff on me," Tap says, and then whistles. "Ooof. Hurts so good. I don't think my boner went away for a month." He shakes his head, shifts the weight of his M14 to his left hand, and adjusts his bandolier. "But I didn't get the Liar."

"I got the Liar," I say. "He made me think my hair was on fire. That my grandma was dead."

"Then you both got off lucky. I was on the receiving end of both of them. Here's the deal—if there are two extranaturals to watch out for, it's those two. The only person who could probably withstand their power is the one person we can't talk to right now." He looks around, walks over to the dead campfire, and kicks at a piece of lumber. "More than likely, the Liar will have taken control, unless the Bomb got to him first. We'll have to be super careful."

"Why?" Tap asks.

"Because the Liar can convince us to do *anything* by just saying one sentence. He could tell us that he's the messiah, and we'd believe him," Jack says.

"That's some serious bugfuckery, man." Tap looks up at the sky. "We've got lots of daylight left. Let's do this."

"Shouldn't we wait? We should scout out the situation first," I say.

"Yeah, that's a good idea . . ." Jack says, rubbing his chin. "Once we spot them, maybe just one of us will go in, right? They might bugfuck one of us, but they can't bugfuck all of us."

"Okay," Tap agrees. "Who's it gonna be?"

"It should be me," Jack says. "They know I'm . . ." He stops here. Rubs his chin again. He doesn't know how to describe his relationship with Shreve because boys aren't self-aware enough to be honest and just say *Shreve's my brother*. "Close to Shreve. And I can speak for him."

"It should be Tap," I say. Tap wheels on me, spluttering. "Or me."

"Why?" Tap asks.

"Jack, you're the only big gun we have here. If Tap or I go in and don't come back, you can go in blasting."

"I'm not going to attack other members of the Society."

"Why not? If the Liar uses his ability on me, he's *attacking* us. There's no difference."

"No difference? You don't *die* when he uses his ability on you. No, it has to be me. If I don't come back with him, you find Shreve."

"How?" I say.

"Scream your head off." He looks grim. "You're the strongest of us, Ember. You're a bugfuck yourself. If you scream into the—" He searches for the right phrase, but I already know what he's talking about. "The space between all of us. The Irregulars."

"The ether."

"You scream there, Shreve will hear," Jack says.

He's right. And that makes me afraid. Because if Shreve can hear, what else will be listening?

## THIRTY-FIVE

# JACK

Smoke passes into the sky in a gray diagonal from a cluster of houses by a small river, choked with ice floe. I can see figures moving among the houses, chopping wood. Carrying things.

*I'll investigate,* I say, waving Tap and Ember away. *You two hang back. I'll holler if I'm in trouble.*

I land in the drive of the largest house. It's much bigger than it looked from the air—a rich person's getaway home on a trout stream in the Rockies. Probably well stocked.

A guard yelps when he sees me standing there, looking up at the massive front of the home. He's sitting in a folding chair on an upper gallery of the house, one of those built-in patios that you see in ski lodges and rich folks' homes. There's more plate glass in this building than on a skyscraper. Good view of the mountains and valley. Didn't see me coming, though.

"Halt!" the guard hollers, lifting his rifle.

"I'm a member of the Society," I say, raising my hands. I don't recognize the man pointing the gun at me. He seems familiar, but I can't remember anything about him. "I was part of the team that led the Conformity soldier away. Who's in charge here?"

"Doctor Hemming. Stay there. I'll get him." He backs up to

the sliding glass door behind him and slides it open, disappearing inside. Within moments three more gunmen are on the gallery, dressed in fatigues. Army guys. One I recognize from the campus. They've got me covered. From the corner of my eye I notice a bit more movement at the corners of the house.

I raise my hands high. "I'm unarmed!"

"I know who you are, Jack," a voice says from the gallery. A small, mousy woman moves to the railing of the gallery and looks down at me. Tanzer.

"Did you want something?" she asks. "I'm sorry, but we can't offer you anything—we are trying to conserve food and ammunition."

"I don't need anything from you," I say, craning my neck to get a better look at her. "Just some information."

"You can ask. I'll do my best to answer."

"Can you get your guys to lower their weapons?"

Tanzer smiles, but it's brittle and insincere. "Jack, I know what you can do. I ran your testing, though you may not have known that. And to my knowledge, your abilities don't allow you to stop—or dodge—bullets. So, I'm sorry, no. We can't let down our guard."

"Uh, did something happen? You know me. I'm not violent."

She laughs. "I doubt I've ever met anyone with *more* capacity for violence than you."

Well, that's not the nicest thing anyone's ever said to me. I can feel my back tighten, and before I know it my hands are balled into fists.

She says in a quieter voice, "I don't mean to taunt you, Jack. I'm sorry, but things have gotten . . . difficult."

"How so?"

"When the extranaturals took control—"

"Who?" I say. It's rude to interrupt, I know. But this is important. "The Liar?"

"Yes. He took control of what's left of the Red and Green Teams and told us we'd be better off waiting here. Of course, he was right."

"You sure he wasn't, uh, lying to you?"

"No, I can't be sure. But I don't *think* he was. He just explained that they'd be able to move faster without the Army or research personnel."

"What about you?"

"I'm just an administrator. A tech, really, with low-level telekinesis. I can lift a few pounds and float it around. There are a few other folks like that here. Non-flyers. Non-bugfucks. Low-watt bulbs, you know?"

Right. I know the type. Extranaturals whose abilities wouldn't be good for much more than parlor tricks. *Or being subsumed by the Conformity.*

"You know which way the Liar went when he left you?"

"No."

"You mean you didn't see which way?"

"No, I have no idea. I can remember them leaving but . . ." Her face clouds and her forehead scrunches up. "I'm sorry, I can't remember."

"Okay," I say. Reese got to her. "Listen, we're working on the Conformity."

"Working on it?"

"Working to defeat it."

She looks incredulous. "You have a plan?"

For a moment everything stills and I can feel my heart hammering in my chest. I can feel the surge of blood in my veins. I've got nothing.

We've got nothing.

Our plan is to get the Liar and bring him to Shreve. That's it. What kind of plan is that?

"Okay," says Tanzer simply, after I've been silent a few seconds. "Do me a favor, will you?"

"Uh, okay."

"Make sure you're far away from here when you try to kill yourself."

...

*What's wrong?* Ember asks when I rejoin them in the sky.

*We're idiots. That's what's wrong,* I say.

I get varying degrees of mental alarm from them. There's a wide field below us with a small barn, so I descend and go inside, pulling an MRE from my backpack. I don't want to make a fire, so I just sit down on a bale of hay and open the MRE and begin to eat, not even paying attention to the flavor. It's salty and meaty. That's all I know.

Tap and Ember follow me inside.

"What's the deal, hoss?" Tap asks.

I quickly unspool the memory of my conversation with Tanzer right into their minds.

"So you didn't tell her anything," Ember says when she and Tap have absorbed the flashback.

"What's there *to* tell? We're getting the Liar and bringing him to Shreve. That's our immediate plan. But what happens after that?"

Tap walks over and takes my gum. He tears open a piece and shoves it in his mouth.

"So what?" he says. "Why are you getting so jumpy?"

"Because we're running all over creation, but we have no idea why."

"So?" Tap says.

"So, we don't know if Shreve knows what he's doing. *How are we going to deal with the Conformity?*"

Ember laughs. "That's what you're worried about?" She shrugs and sits down beside me, puts her hand on my thigh. "Put your mind at ease, then, lover. I can promise you Shreve has an idea what he's doing. He's got some kind of angle. We're talking about Shreve, here." She laughs. "That kid has always got some kind of angle. Never met anyone with more agendas than Shreve, except maybe Quincrux."

She rubs my leg. I can feel my back unkink. The anger ebbing.

"Or Priest," I say. "And look what happened to him."

"Forget all that for the moment. If we start to despair now, before we've even done anything, we're all going to die." Her hand feels good. She's warm, and her warmth is seeping into me through her contact. "Just remember. Priest had a plan—"

"Fat lot of good it did him."

"But it *did* save us—most of us—and the rest of the Society. Crazy to think about it, but Shreve's as close as we've got to Priest," Ember says, and leans in.

"That's what's worrying me."

"No." She bows her head for a moment and then snatches my spoon and takes a bite from the MRE packet. "Dani and Bernard seemed to believe in their message. And they're dead."

She blinks. "Or kinda dead. All the clutter and confusion of living swept away. So that's saying something."

"Saying what?" I ask.

"Something," she says.

"It's saying," Tap interjects, "that they trusted him enough to do one last thing for him."

"You know Shreve," Ember says. "What do you think?"

"He's got a plan," I say. "But it definitely won't work out like he thinks it will."

■■■

I understand how the Native Americans always knew where the settlers were: where there's fire, there's smoke. It's the oldest giveaway in the book.

They've set up their homestead in a lodge, way back in the aspens, so we have to make two close passes before we can see anything. Funny how their hidey-hole mirrors ours on Devil's Throne, except that ours sucked pretty hard and theirs looks like a mansion. Who knew there were so many rich people in Montana?

"He's here," Ember says. "I can feel it."

She doesn't have to say more than that. I don't know how she does it. I don't know how Shreve does it. They just do. Bugfucks. Maybe that's why I was so eager at first to follow along with the "plan." Because in the end, I don't really comprehend the nature of being a telepath. All I know is what I can do. I can fly. I can move things: air, water, rock, earth. Walls. Myself.

So. Get the Liar. Bring him to Shreve. That's what I'm going to do.

But the Liar, he can just say one thing and it'll all go to hell.

He could be like the Conformity itself just by saying, "You will do everything I command," and he'd have an army behind him. He could tell me I can't fly and I'd believe him. The pressure of that realization becomes unbearable.

Not much conversation's needed, and I'm in no state to talk anyway. Tap, Ember, and I keep a tight formation on our circuit and then drop out of sight of the lodge.

"Back in an hour, or you start screaming, right?" I say.

"Right. But how will we know?" Ember says.

"Know what?"

"When an hour's up." She lifts her arm and pulls back the sleeve, showing bare skin. "No watches."

"Your best guess, then."

Ember's face is taut and pale, and I can see she's worried. But there's nothing for it except to buckle up and fly on in.

...

It's only a small hop over the aspens and onto the back deck of the cabin.

Blackwell and Galine are posted as guards, and they perk up at my approach, raising rifles—one a hunting rifle—and taking shooting stances.

"Jack," Blackwell says. "We thought you were dead." He doesn't lower the rifle.

Galine scans the skies. "Who else is with you?"

"Just me," I say. They look unconvinced. "Though there are people waiting for me. Just so you know. They'll be . . ." I'm not prepared for this cloak-and-dagger stuff, and I feel myself resorting to dialogue from all the movies I've seen. "They'll be *alarmed* if I'm not back very soon."

"Alarmed?"

"And agitated. So, let's do this quickly, shall we?"

"Do what?"

"The Liar. I need to talk with him. Alone."

Blackwell doesn't say anything, just chucks his head at the French doors, indicating to Galine to go inside.

"What happened with your team?" I ask. "After the soldiers took the campus?"

His need to talk about himself wins out over his personal distaste for me.

"Rode hell-bent for leather, as fast as we could." He looks about. "Made it a ways before all the cars died. After that, it was obvious that wrangling the pencil-necks and normies was a no-win situation, so the rest of the Red Team, and Reese, we decided to move on our own, since being shepherds wasn't really in the game plan—"

"'We decided,' or Reese told you what was going to happen?" I ask.

"We decided, man."

"And you made it here. That was your game plan?"

"The game plan is always first and foremost to stay alive."

I think about that. "So you set up shop here?"

"Yeah. We got one wounded—friendly fire—but once she's better, we're going even more remote. The way we figure it, the more people around, the more likely that evil asshole thing will come for us. You should keep that in mind."

After a moment or two, the doors open again and Galine motions me inside.

The cabin isn't what you'd think of as a cabin. The ceiling's forty feet above us and crowned by a massive chandelier made of antlers. A *lot* of animals died to make that chandelier. There's an upright bear in the corner of the great room. A moose head glares down at me from above the fireplace. One girl—her name's Cat, I think I remember—lolls in an over-stuffed chair near the fire with a copy of *People* in her hands. In the oversized stone hearth a fire burns, the wood popping and cracking. There are a couple of extranaturals sitting at the dining table—the house is set up in a wide, open layout, the kitchen connecting to the great room—with books open in front of them. They look me up and down as I enter and then return their attention to their reading material. Not worried about my presence.

Cameron Reese stands at the foot of a large stairway lead-ing up to what I assume are bedrooms. He's dressed in a Misfits T-shirt and ratty jeans. His Mohawk's grown out since I last saw him during the testing, and he's got a little blond vandyke and a nose ring. Multiple earrings. Lots of metal on his hands. Dressed for the occasion, I guess. Nice to feel important.

Looking at him, I'm instantly wary. They call him the Liar, and I wouldn't trust him as far as I could throw him. Although I could probably throw him a mile or two, if I was angry enough.

"Jack, right? Hey, man, how you doin'?" Reese smiles. "Galine here," he says, gesturing to her standing behind him on the stairs, "tells me you've got something to talk to me about. Come on. We'll go in here."

Reese turns and pads down a hallway. None of his cohorts follow, though Galine and the girl from the overstuffed chair wait at the end of the hall, watching.

"Not taking any chances, are you?"

Reese doesn't laugh. He puts his ringed hand on a door-knob, twists, and pushes the door open, revealing a private theater with two rows of plush, almost-recliner seats. Entering, Reese says, "Man, you know how it is out there. Everything's crazy. People are desperate." He walks over to the wall and twists a rod, opening the blinds. Thin, watery light pours into the room. "Shit's getting seriously weird. No electricity. Like, it doesn't work. This house has a generator, full of gas too." He sits down in one of the seats. "And now everything's gone black and white, like some crazy old movie. What's next?"

"I don't know what's next, but we do have an idea of what's happening."

"Really?" Reese's eyes light up. "Tell me what's going on."

I don't really know where to start, but Reese takes my hesi-tation as distrust. He says, "Listen, man. You're wary. I know that. You know what I can do, and you know the nickname they gave me." Reese mouth twists in distaste. "I didn't ask for any of this, and I don't want it. I just want to get back to where I was before."

"The campus is destroyed. There's nothing—"

"The campus? I don't want to go back there. I was a prisoner. Quincrux was gonna force me to become his own little espionage unit. He—" His voice thickens and he flexes his hands into fists, realizes he's doing it, and releases. "He had my mom. My sister. He was holding them hostage so I'd do what he wanted."

Of all the possible scenarios I'd imagined involving the Liar, they never involved him starting to cry. The tears well up in his eyes and run down his cheeks.

"What I want is to go back to life before all this. Before everything became so fucked up." He looks helplessly around the theater. "I just want to go home."

"Okay," I say slowly. "Can I ask a question?"

He nods, wiping away the tears.

"What happened to everyone? We found Tanzer and all the lab coats. Some of the Army guys. What happened to the rest of them? The Bomb?"

He looks uncomfortable. "After the vehicles stopped working, things got tense pretty fast. Some guy made a play for the Bomb, and her guards shot him. They went off with her on their own. No idea what happened to them."

"What about Tanzer and her group?"

He looks sheepish. "Yeah, I did my thing on them," he says defensively. "It made sense to split up, man! There wasn't going to be enough food, real soon. And with fewer folks, we could travel faster."

"So you just set yourself up here as a little king?"

He snorts. "Really? That what you think?" He jerks his thumb at the windows. "You think I'm in charge here? You gotta be kidding me. I'm the golden goose to these assholes."

"What?"

"There's one girl here, Cat, I can't work my stuff on. She's not much of a bugfuck, but the lies don't take. So, she makes sure that everyone knows when I'm doing my thing."

That's surprising. "Why don't you just have them . . . I don't know. Stop her?"

"Yeah. How do you suggest I do that? Kill her?"

"I don't know."

"See, this is where nicknames really suck, man. They saddle you with a name like the Liar, and everyone thinks you're totally amoral."

"So, what? They're holding you hostage just like Quincrux did?"

"I don't know about that. But they're not making it easy for me to leave. No food, no guns, no protection if I leave."

It's a lot to take in. When I think about how we worried that the Liar was some sort of mastermind . . .

"You want to tell me what's going on out there," Reese says. He's right, I do.

I start at the point we left the campus, leading the soldiers away. The telling is quick, and I don't skip over much—only the joining of minds, our telepathic conformity. Reese listens carefully, wants to know how we all didn't die when the plane failed. Instead of explaining our shared abilities, I simply say, "We caught who we could as they fell. Bernard and Dani died. The pilot. Davies."

His face clouds, and I guess he isn't too far removed from humanity to know when death has weight. "Okay. Tell it to me again," he says. "You just remembered your condition. A heart problem. This time, if you leave anything out, your heart will stop. You understand?"

Suddenly, sweat's prickling all over my body. I stand there rigid, barely able to move for fear that my heart will stop beating. I run through the story again. I tell him everything. Falling. The joining of the Irregulars' minds with Shreve as the hub. Our miniature Conformity. Before I'm through, Blackwell and Galine stand in the doorway with weapons.

"Holy shit," Blackwell says. "Things have gone way off the deep end."

"And they want me," Reese says. "They don't even have a plan. Jack said it himself. Just to bring me to that kid Shreve."

"Shreve's trouble," Blackwell says. There's no love lost there. "But we can use Jack and Ember. They could be rovers. Scavengers."

Galine nods, eyes bright. "We can't draw any more attention to ourselves." A shiver passes through her, and her face goes still. "I can't face that *thing* again."

"They're calling it the Conformity. You got that, didn't you? They're planning on taking it on," Reese says.

"Holy Christ," Blackwell says. "Count me out."

"Hold on, guys," Reese says, holding up his hands to Blackwell and Galine, shushing them. He turns back to me. "Hey, Jack. You totally trust us. Right? Understand? We're the most trustworthy people in the world. We're your best friends."

Something's wrong with what Reese has said, but I can't figure it out right now because I do like these guys. Always have. There was a time when I was next in line to join Blackwell's Red Team. I always knew they liked me and we'd become best friends.

"How much time do we have, Jack? You know, before you have to be back with Ember and Tap?"

"I don't know. Soon, I guess. None of us have watches."

"Okay. Just give us a minute. You probably want to stay here, Jack, don't you think?"

"Yeah, I do."

They go into the hall, and I can hear mumblings and murmurings. When they return, Reese is smiling.

"So, listen, Jack. We've talked about it and we want you, Ember, and Tap to join our group. You know? We think you'll be a big asset, since we don't have any flyers. You want to join us, too, I think."

Again, something's not right, but nothing he's said isn't true. So I say, "Yeah. Sure, that sounds good."

"So, you want to convince them to come in here to talk to us. You really want to convince them, don't you?"

"Yes," I say. Blackwell's and Galine's faces are masks. They seem neither happy nor upset at the idea of us joining. Something's wrong here, but I can't put my finger on it.

"How do you think you'll be able to convince them?" Reese asks.

I have to think about it. "I'll tell them that you're ready to join Shreve. But you have to get some stuff together."

"Right. You said you carried that woman. The doctor lady."

"Veterinarian. Madelyn. And yes. Ember lifted her, and we pulled Ember."

"Okay, you'll tell them that's the plan with me, too, right? And they'll need to come inside and warm up and have something to eat before we leave. Because we're all friends, right?"

"Yes. We're all friends."

"Okay. Let's go outside, and you can go talk to Tap and Ember," Reese says. "You're gonna love it here, you know?"

"Yeah," I respond. "I think you're right."

"You'll do whatever it takes to get them to come down here for a chat, won't you?"

"Of course."

"My man," Reese says, slapping me on the shoulder. "My man."

...

I land near them in the snowy field, in the lee of a brake of ponderosa pines. The wind's not so bad here. The sun feels good on my face. I pull back my hood when I land by Ember and Tap. They look cold and tense.

"Hey," I say, pulling off my gloves. "He's willing to go with us to Shreve."

"What? That easy?" Ember says. "What did you tell him?"

It takes a moment to get everything organized in my head. I haven't thought this out. Something's wrong and I don't know what it is, but still . . . I need them to come inside to talk with Reese. Everything's going to be better once they do.

"Mostly everything—"

"*What?*" Ember's alarm travels even mind-to-mind. "You told him about us? Our connection?" It's weird that she doesn't worry about me talking about the sex—which I don't think I did—but focuses on our invisible connection to each other.

"No," I say slowly. "Just that Shreve has a plan."

"Did he ask about the plan?"

What should I say here—should I tell her he did and that I answered him? Even though she knows that we don't know what the plan is at all?

"No, he remembers Shreve. Likes him," I say. "He wants us to come inside and have some food and warm up before we go."

"That sounds good," Tap says, rubbing his hands together. "I'm overdue for a visit to the john."

"Who else was there?"

"A few other extranats. Blackwell and Galine?"

"The old Red Team." Ember scowls. "Who else? The Bomb?"

"No, he said she took off with her guards. Some guy tried to grab her or something and got shot."

Ember's face darkens, and I can see the thoughts churning under the surface there. "So, he's just gonna come with us, just like that?"

"Yeah."

"You're lying to me," Ember says, taking two steps away.

"Hey!" I say, reaching out to her. She has to understand! Everything will be better once she goes inside. "It's cool! He's gonna come with us! Let's just—"

Ember launches herself into the air, arcing away across the vault of heaven. I've never seen her fly so fast.

I leap after her with Tap close behind. The force of the wind with our speed is brutal.

*Ember! Come back!*

She's like a bullet crossing the sky. She passes over the valley's lip, racing up the mountainside and into the empty air above the snow-clad peaks, and then she's gone from sight.

But I hear her. I hear her screaming into the space-not-space between us all.

*Shreve! SHREVE! We have him! Come to us!*

And something trembles there, between us, that thin connection, indistinct and wavering. I must catch her before she can ruin everything.

Something shifts inside of me, and Tap gives a cry because even hanging in the air, falling in space like angels on the wing, I feel an eye fixing upon me. I feel a consciousness turning its attention toward me even as I chase after Ember. And I know what's coming. If only she had listened.

If only she had come inside.

# PART THREE:
# STORMING
# HEAVEN

"However I with thee have fixt my Lot,

Certain to undergo like doom, if Death

Consort with thee, Death is to me as Life;

So forcible within my heart I feel

The Bond of Nature draw me to my own,

My own in thee, for what thou art is mine;

Our State cannot be severed, we are one,

One Flesh; to loose thee were to loose my self."

—John Milton, *Paradise Lost*

## THIRTY-SIX

## SHREVE

On the inside, everyone's the same. From the heartbroken to the dumbstruck, the burdened and the carefree. The fathers and mothers, sons and daughters. The innocent and the guilty. They're all grist for the Conformity's mill.

Once, I contained multitudes, waking from dreams of other lives. Once, I was large and could take within me the full expanse of humanity.

But I have become small now, infinitesimal.

Just Shreve.

...

It's a buzzing I feel, insistent and frantic, at the edges of my awareness. The world shifts and sways around me, like I was some drunken sailor, cast off of the sea.

You ride the horse; you ride every day, and still your balls never really get used to the abuse. Your taint gets callouses, and *still* you'll be sore at the end of the day. And then when you dismount, the world shifts and sways around you, like you're still moving.

Casey's riding near me—she stays near, always, because I'm one of the suckiest riders ever to mount a horse—and her smile is genuine and warm. We stayed in the husk of a roadside motel last night. With our own room. The bed was warm and so was she.

All the lives I've lived before didn't prepare me for it. Couldn't prepare me for *her*.

But she smiles at me now. A secret smile. It's not fooling Negata. He's ridden point most of the day. "I will scout ahead, Shreve, and see what I can see," he said, and then he glanced from Casey back to me. "Look for me this afternoon."

When he returns, he is strangely quiet, with nothing to share or report. Casey stays near me. Sometimes I feel her invisible hand on my own. It's not warm, but it is warm in my memory.

Part of me feels as though I'm in a dream. The world is dressed solely in black and white and gray now, preparing for either a funeral or a wedding. It can't make up its mind. We ride through white fields like ghosts, as if we've passed some border into the territories of death or dreams. The trees scrabble at the sky, stark and bare. The horses plume steaming breaths into the quickening air. It's snowing again, and the *shshshsssssssshhhhh* sound of snow falling blankets everything, all other noises.

The world's ending. And I'm happy. I have nothing except myself. Her warm body. I thought I knew the warm territories of flesh, but I didn't. I didn't know. A thousand filched memories, and I didn't know anything.

The buzzing gets louder, and for a moment I'm reminded of the thrumming, surging presence of the Helmholtz. It's an insistent bug, buzzing in my hindbrain. Something's wrong.

"Do you feel that?" I ask Casey.

She sits upright in her saddle, looking around quickly. "No, I don't feel—"

*SHREVE!*

The connection is faint but there. Ember.

Casey's face turns worried; she chews her lip. Grasps my hand with her invisible one.

It seems like forever since I've gone beyond myself. Like some slumbering bear, I have to rouse myself. Expand. Become more than just me. Part of me's sad that it's come to this. That I am not enough. That I must become more. But there it is. A movement driving me all my life. Becoming more. I slip into the ether, up and out of my body. Out and away in the space-not-space where distance is crossed as like a passing thought.

*Ember? What's wrong? Where are you?*

Her mind, touching my own, is familiar as a glove. And for a moment she settles into me. I feel wind howling through her hair and tearing at her clothes. Mountains and forests and streams whip by unimaginably fast beneath her, so that it's almost too hard to focus on anything. Her head jerks around, looking down the length of her body, and there's Jack flying behind, arms outstretched.

*The Liar! He's here!* There's real panic in her, surging. *And Jack—the Liar got to him! You have to come!*

But there's something more there, a hissing presence. Ink in water, growing and blossoming. The pressure of an awareness that's huge. It's coming.

The Conformity.

Fixing Ember in my mind, an invisible tether stretching between us like a filament of gold, I mark her. All the old ghost habits of my mind take over, and it's like I've never left—never stopped being more and diminished into Shreve. I can feel the thousands of minds I've touched popping like kernels of corn in hot oil, growing in the hindbrain of my consciousness. I'm swelling huge, rampant.

It takes a monumental effort to disengage from the ether and go back to my body.

•••

I've fallen from my horse, faceup, half covered in snow. Casey's above me, frantic, pawing at my face with gloved hands, trying to sweep away the frozen stuff. Her beautiful face framed by clouds. Snowflakes growing larger in my vision around her.

"It's time, Casey," I say. The day's grown late and the light's failing now and it's time. Time to act. Time to join. Time to become more than what we are.

Maybe she's already touching me mentally, I don't know. Maybe, entering the ether, I've opened myself up. But she's with me now. She's inside me and I'm inside her and, far off, we're connected with Ember and sharing her panic.

"This is the end," we say, together, as Negata approaches. He's dismounted and his hood is swept aside, snow nestled in the strands of his jet-black hair. He looks grim, and not a little frightened. He appears old now, wizened beyond his years. I can see them stretching away behind him like a comet's tail. So much of the world is visible to me now. I grow larger, expanding.

But Negata is sad, and frightened. So strange. I always thought Negata was beyond such feelings.

"Go," he says, simply enough. He raises his hand, palm forward. "Go. And good-bye, Shreve."

More should be said, but there's no time.

Together, we rise, surging into the arteries of air. Lancing forward like some falling star, burning through the atmosphere. It takes a simple adjustment to cocoon us in a shield and then move, even faster, following the golden filament east and south, so fast that the shield of air begins to glow as molecules super-heat into an oncoming wave front before us. There's a shuddering *boom* and my/our body is rocked with force. Merely a thought and we're traveling faster than sound.

The earth passes below us, too fast to see, flickering shades of blurred gray. We were going to cross all this on the backs of horses, and now it rushes by, below, blurred and dreamlike and forgotten almost as soon as it's passed. What a preposterous plan it was—and yet.

And then Ember is there and we've stopped.

■■■

We've reached density. It's just a small effort to take Jack and Tap within. Jack struggles at first but settles down, and then he's one with us and we're moving back to where we left the Liar. We settle on the earth like a fog, moving as one, all our abilities and knowledge shared.

Everything lost. Everything gained.

When our feet touch ground, I disengage.

## THIRTY-SEVEN

## SHREVE

On the inside, I feel such joy at seeing them all again: Jack, Ember, even Tap. My emotions zip around and teeter like a drunk failing a sobriety test. Once, I might have been embarrassed by my joy. Once, I might have tried to hide it.

I grip him in a fierce hug. I think of falling. I think of Booth.

Jack stands poleaxed, whether at the sight of my mug or at the Liar's control over him, now washed away like the colors from the world—I don't know which. After a moment, he curses aloud and then looks at me closely. He grins. "Hope you had a good nap."

I release him, stretching my arms. "I feel refreshed. How 'bout you guys?"

Ember comes close, slips between Jack and me, and throws her arms over our shoulders, squeezing. She waggles her eyebrows at Casey. "I know what you two have been up to. So naughty—"

Casey looks like she's about to belt Ember, but I hold up my hand, shushing them. The ether is in me now that I'm open to it, as if I'm pregnant with it. And the pressure, the dark, black pressure there before me grows, yawning. Huge.

"No time for shits and giggles. It's coming," I say. "It knows we're here."

A branch drops to the ground with a hard, brittle sound. The aspens surrounding the Liar's dwelling begin to sway and topple. Tap gives a little leap—crossing twenty feet in one bound—and looks at the gray trees lying heaped in the snow. From where we stand, the lodge is in clear view. Roofing tiles begin to slide from the roof. The woodwork surrounding the windows crumbles.

"Something's not right here," Tap says, holding up a branch in his hand. It crumbles into dust.

From where we stand, it's easy to see the Liar, Blackwell, Galine, and the rest of their cadre bursting onto the porch.

"What the hell's going on?" Ember says.

"It's coming. And changing the universe," I say. "Rearranging the world to suit it. Changing the rules of physics. Quantum level."

"It's rotting away," Tap yells, dusting his hands. "It's like it's aged five hundred years in seconds!"

By the lodge, the deck slumps to one side. Part of the lodge's roof caves in. The extranaturals there jump to the earth, rolling. Cursing.

At the far end of the valley, an echoing sound comes. The trumpeting bellow of a foghorn in the mist. The groaning, echoing sound of thousands of pained souls, screaming. .

The Conformity comes. It swells like a waxing moon, a great circle of misery growing in the sky. The breath of a hundred thousand humans wreaths it, trails it like a cowl. As it crosses the landscape, passing over toppling forests and crumbling houses, it resembles a smoldering coal, the freezing water vapor pouring off.

Everything happens so fast. The limp forms of the Liar, Blackwell, Galine, and the rest of them begin rising to join with the Conformity. I feel the inexorable gravity of the entity's psychokinetic grasp tugging at my guts and howling at my mind. We Irregulars, we're connected now, joined together in fear and desperation. Together, we're strong enough to resist the Conformity's pull—strong enough to share some abilities. But to do what I must, I cannot be joined.

The ether shudders and splinters and vibrates at a frequency almost beyond my perception. It feels as poisonous as the strongest Helmholtz field. Behind the static there's pure desire, overwhelming hunger, greed so vast and unimaginable that my brain has to cobble together images to allow me to grasp it: the black, pupil-less eye of a shark rolling in bloodlust, the blank, sucking mouth of a lamprey, the towering indifference of a storm front, calving tornadoes.

The wind picks up, tearing at my face and hair. Casey's screaming, with her mouth or in my mind. I don't know. Or is that Ember? Or Jack? As the Conformity approaches, its horrible gravity deepens. And now I realize there's always been an issue of *proximity*. We're strengthened by our bodies. We're centered by them. Why would the Conformity draw flesh to itself otherwise? It seats itself in the flesh, feeds upon it. Takes strength from it. Maybe this is what it means to be incarcerado.

But there's the ether. The wild blue yonder.

We're rising in the air, all of us. I'm in them and they're in me, but I still have my own awareness—it's not muddled or indistinct. We're so loosely federated that we seem a jumble of limbs, disjointed and clumsy. Jack pinwheels away. Ember rises, screaming. Casey's ghosthand swells and fends, palm out, trying to keep the terrible thing at bay. Tap hangs immobile, a fly trapped in amber.

Jack holds in midair, both hands outstretched, fingers splayed. A torrent of force—terrible bone-crushing force—streams away from him, slamming into the Conformity. It lurches and distends, becoming oblong. Moaning. Bellowing.

People are dying.

I know what I must do.

Jack can't help me. No one can help me.

I slip into the ether.

...

In the non-space between us, it truly is a star. The thousands upon thousands of points of light teeming and swirling. Shuddering. Emanating waves of anguish and pain, yet each point mindless. Subsumed. Eaten whole.

*Shreve . . . JOIN US.*

It knows me. Maybe it's always known me.

*There is space within you for us all. Join us. Serve us. Worship us.*

The motes of stolen light swirl like a maelstrom of sparks in an inferno. At the center of the star—the nexus of psychokinetic power—are two burning points: a tremendously powerful telekinetic and, *suprise!* a bugfuck. From them a golden filament stretches away. East. Ever eastward toward the dawn.

I feel the ether, marking everything. The thick wind of sparks coalescing, each one articulated and singular yet undulating together as a whole; the shiver and howl of the entity driving this machine of conformity; my own awareness like an arrow, lancing.

Once, I was Tased by a guard because I stepped over a line. I became the green fuse that drives the flower. I became the electricity itself.

I will always step over the line.

I've done this a thousand times before. With cashiers and murderers and teachers and inmates. I've inhabited women, men. I've stalked the forests of the night on cat feet. The millions of sparks hold nothing for me. I am interested in the center of things, in the heart. I pass through, entering the bright flesh of the etheric Conformity. Beyond the infinite motes of light, dimming now. It's as though I'm expanding and shrinking all at once. I'm the smallest particle of matter; I'm a cosmic spray of stars. And then the great mental wall of obsidian looms. The satellite mind of the Conformity itself is before me.

I'm inside it. It is unseated—suddenly on the outside looking in—like so many others before it. The tether is broken.

There's a howl of rage, echoing. The entity.

The sparks are me now. I'm the ghost in their attic. The gerbil racing at the wheel. I bloom like some fruiting body in their minds. I'm a drop of blood spreading in water. Thousands and thousands of minds held incarcerado. Thousands and thousands of bodies locked in terrible embrace. I spread myself among them. I settle upon them like a cloud.

I am them, they are me. Should we ever disagree.

One and one and one makes three.

■■■

The hardest part is letting them all go. Their flesh is warm. Inhabiting all of them is comfortable. The power thrumming through us would allow me to reshape the universe to suit me.

But he's not here. Every spark, every damped awareness. I'm part of them all, and he's not here.

Vig.

I spread out the mass of humanity softly, lowering them all to the earth. It's difficult, and the extranatural power required is massive. I cannot release until each is standing on the ground. Only then do I withdraw.

Children. Men and women. Awaking to the cold. Standing naked in the snow. Steaming. Sobbing and cries. Fierce screams of joy and misery. The sound is overwhelming, now that I'm back in my own body.

Shreve and simply Shreve once more.

Jack stands near me. Casey holds me up with her invisible hand. Tap and Ember stand, struck dumb by the sea of humanity before them. The smell and sight of the mass of people is palpable—the stench of shit and urine. Bright crimson blood streaks down torsos, marring the varied hues of flesh.

"They look..." Tap says, hands hanging loosely at his sides. "They look..."

"Beautiful," Ember finishes for him.

"Color," Casey says, and she holds up her hand to look at it. She turns her head to the skies.

We stand among the huddled masses. They've been reborn into the world once more. Many of them stagger and fall into the snow. Many shamble about like zombies.

"We have to find the Liar," I say. "Jack? Ember? Can you find him?"

Ember nods, saying, "He's near. I feel him."

Jack grinds his teeth but says through tight lips, "We'll get him."

They lift off, hovering over the mass of people, and pass out of sight.

"What happened, Shreve?" Casey asks, watching Tap take off his jacket and offer it to a woman whose clothes must have disintegrated when she was subsumed by the Conformity.

"I severed the link with the awareness that created the Conformity," I say. "It's hard to explain. But I did what I always do."

"What you always do?"

"I'm a thief, Casey. I steal things."

She smiles, kisses me softly. "Well, this time," she says, pointing at the thousands of people milling in the valley, "you stole all of them."

Ember and Jack hold the Liar's arms as they approach, floating over the crowd. Jack lets him go, oh, maybe ten feet before he should, and Reese tumbles and hits the ground in front of me with an *ooof.*

"Hey! Goddamn it!" he cries. "Was that necessary?"

Jack, settling next to him, says, "Yeah, I think it was."

"Make sure he doesn't talk," I say to Tap, who seems happy to whip out his pistol and point it at Reese's furry dome.

Reese stares at the gun and then looks at all of us Irregulars in turn. Some of the former members of the Conformity begin to gather around us. The constant noise—murmuring, talking, screaming, moaning, crying—grows louder. Some of the newly released look upset. Desperate. Murderous.

"Listen, Reese. I haven't got much time," I say, squatting on my hams to get a good look at him. "And neither do these people."

A hush ripples away from our group. We're surrounded

now. These poor souls will be freezing soon.

"The Conformity will be back. We haven't stopped it," I say. Reese lets a little exhalation of dismay escape—he, too, joined with the Conformity, if only for a little while. "We've delayed it. But look around!" I wave my arm to take in all of our watchers. "The color is back in the world. And, I'll wager, the juice is back on too."

"Oh, shit," Reese says. "That's good—"

Tap swipes the pistol across Reese's dome, adding a little more red into the world. When Reese is able to right himself, he does so slowly, with shaky arms.

"Tap," I say, frowning. "No need to get that rough. We want him to work *with* us."

"Yeah, dickhead—" Reese begins, but he quickly shuts his mouth as Tap raises the pistol once more.

"Here's the deal," I say, looking at him closely. "Now's *your* time. Do you understand?"

He looks at me blankly, mouth slightly open, tears from the blow Tap dealt him streaming from his eyes.

"There are hundreds of thousands of people here, and they're going to start dying very soon. You can choose to work for the greater good, or you can choose to become nothing." I don't want to threaten, but I need him to understand there'll be no power-grab. "I'm beyond your ability now. But that doesn't mean they are." I knock at the door of his mind, hard, to get his attention.

His nose sprays blood. He shakes. Pisses himself. God knows what. Wiping his nose, Reese looks at me, and comprehension dawns on his face. He's pale now, stunned. His mouth opens and closes without issuing any noise.

"It's just a nickname, man. It doesn't define you. They called me the Li'l Devil. But that's not me."

He seems small now. Childlike. The tears streaming from his eyes are genuine.

"I'm taking away your nickname. You're no longer the Liar," I say. "From now on, when you speak, you will not lie, you will *lead*. You got me? You will turn the lies into truth."

He can say nothing, only look up at me, wide-eyed. I hold out my hand, and he takes it. I lift him up.

"These people need to hear what you have to say. You have to talk with them all. You have to tell them they need to work together quickly to survive."

Reese covers his face in trembling hands. "Oh, God . . . oh. It's too much. Too much to bear."

"It's not too much. I've been inside every person here. They will listen. And if you speak with your *voice*, they will do what you say. And they will survive."

He swallows. It's a huge task I've set before him. The Conformity will regroup, and we have very little time. I have to take the fight to it.

Reese takes a deep breath. He lets out the air slowly.

"I can do it," he says.

"All post-humans work together," murmurs Blackwell, who's pushed through the teeming crowd. Galine, coming up behind him, stares at me, intense. Still furious. Some wrongs can never be righted.

"Then it's time to start, Reese." I gesture toward the waiting multitude. "Use your voice. Lead them."

Reese turns to Jack, Ember. "Lift me up, will you? Pass me over their heads. We have a lot of ground to cover."

Jack and Ember take his arms and rise into the air, hovering above the recently freed.

"Listen to me!" Reese bellows into the frozen air. "You want to remain calm! You want to remain quiet!" The silence spreads. The crowd stills.

Jack says something in Reese's ear.

"You want to form groups of twenty! Press close together! Stay warm! We can do this! You *know* you can do this!"

The crowd begins to move, slowly. There are cries of pain. People fall—the stresses of being merely cogs in a machine have left their mark. Some people topple and do not rise.

"You are strong!" Reese says. "Stronger than this! We will find warmth and shelter! Let's move! You want to find shelter!"

Reese passes out of hearing, floating away, borne on the air. But the multitude moves.

## THIRTY-EIGHT

## SHREVE

On the inside, everything's quiet. The ether thrums with after-echoes of the invisible battle the Conformity and I waged earlier, but I can't sense its approach.

Maybe I am wrong. Maybe it's waiting for me.

It's late at night when Reese is done. We've settled everyone we can in the nearest towns—Bozeman, Four Corners, Belgrade—and now we rest before morning. Montana's become a refugee camp.

Weird how far I've come. Once upon a time, I dealt candy in a prison made for kids in Arkansas. Now I'm squatting in a split-level home in a residential neighborhood in Montana, plotting to overthrow a god.

Jack and Ember bring Reese to the house we've chosen in Bozeman. There are still thousands on the road, marching, following Reese's instructions, searching for shelter and warmth, but the cars are running once more and electricity—in some places—is back.

Some will die. But most will live.

Children look at the world simply, in black and white. But adults must compromise.

Jack and Ember collapse on the carpeted floor of the house,

staying conscious only long enough to drink some water. Reese flops onto the couch with a weary yet exultant look on his face. I sit next to him. The living room is dark around us, and for a moment it's just us two, chatting.

"We got a megaphone for you, and it's been charging ever since the electricity came back on," I say, looking around the den. There's quite a few people—extranaturals and refugees—sleeping in the house, on the floor, in the bathrooms on beddings of towels, in the laundry room. There's very little food, but there is warmth. And rest. Casey moves among them, lightly touching foreheads with her one visible hand. Offering what medicine she can give to those who are injured. Tap's found some enormous wellspring of energy and has spent his day in constant motion, finding blankets and clothes to distribute to the injured, flying back and forth between Bozeman and its outlying townships to usher the refugees into shelter, directing the revived vehicles toward lodging. Tirelessly working. It's as if I've seen him grow up before my very eyes. I'm proud to know him.

But many, so many are injured. It's worse than a war zone.

Yet the world seems hushed now. Waiting.

"You seem different," I say. The weasely skeeviness of Reese's face is gone. Now he looks like a kid—underfed, with a shitty haircut. Just a kid. Happy to be doing something. Doing something right for once.

"Yeah, I guess I am," he says. "Thank you. I came to think of myself as a liar. But that's not what I am."

"No," I answer. "Not always."

He looks miffed that I might spread a little black lining among his silver clouds. "Yeah. The people who've died already.

What I said to them ended up being a lie."

"You do the best you can," I reply, thinking about what Negata said.

"Yeah," he says, but his tone indicates he's not convinced. "I guess so."

I can see the weariness etched into his features. He'll recover, but not anytime soon.

"Listen, man. You're gonna be terribly busy for . . ." I think about it, try to estimate. All those lifetimes of memories, of knowledge, still don't help much when it comes to the logistics of this situation. "For a long while, dude. A long, long while. Soon there will be *millions* of refugees who need your help, if what I plan works. So, I need you to do something for me."

"What's that?"

"I need you to use your *voice* for me."

"On who?"

"Casey. And Jack."

"Do you want me to tell them lies?" He looks sad when he says this. He doesn't want to lie—never did, I suspect—but he will. Such a fallen world we live in.

"No, I don't. If I'm successful, they won't be lies at all. They will be true. They will be . . . *prophetic*."

He closes his eyes and remains silent for so long I think he might have fallen asleep. I'm about to nudge him when he says, very quietly, "Okay. What do I tell them?"

I've thought for weeks about what I'll say next.

"To Casey, say this: everything will be fine if you let Shreve fall."

Reese's eyes open, and he looks at me. "What?"

"You didn't get that?"

"No, I did. It's just—"

"And tell Jack this: find Vig and remember."

Reese continues to look at me for a long while. His gaze searches my face.

"And that's it?"

"That's it. You'll tell them? You'll use your . . ."

"Yes."

"Thank you," I say, the relief washing over me. It's hard enough as it is. I don't need it to get all sticky-icky melodramicky.

"No," Reese says, taking my hand. As a gesture, it's kinda gay, but I guess we're beyond that. "Thank you. You've given me—" He stops. Holding my hand, he pulls me into a bro hug. Like dudes do. "Everything."

When we're done, he rises from the couch and, stepping over a slumbering woman and her child, gingerly walks into the dining room to find Casey.

## THIRTY-NINE

## SHREVE

On the inside, the refugees lie sleeping with Reese, Blackwell, and Galine. More members of the Society have popped up out of nowhere. The multitude of people once part of the Conformity will do well in their hands now, I'm sure.

On the outside, we gather in the snow-clad streets, just the five of us.

"This is it, then," I say, looking at Casey.

"Why don't we stay?" Ember asks, her shoulders hunched against the early morning cold. She's found cigarettes somewhere, and one of them smolders in her lips. "You defeated the one. You can defeat another."

I can't tell them my courage fails me. I can't tell them I'm scared. To death.

"Not like that. We can't hide. It will come again, and this time something will have changed. And look—" I point to the house, sweep my arm down the street. Even now, vehicles move, carrying the injured, while shambling, frozen refugees struggle down the street. There's a boy lying dead, faceup in the snow.

It's too much to bear. I can't take any more. If I tried, I could recall that boy—*I am you and you are me*—and tell them about his happiest memory before being sucked up into the monstrosity. I could describe how he screamed and reached for his mother, but she was rising and screaming too.

Once, when Jack didn't believe me about the Dubrovnik monster, I had to get inside his head and show him. I had to make him face the monster.

I could do that now. I can make them see as easy as joining minds.

Tap says, "No. This has to end. Right *fucking now*." I've never seen him more intense about anything.

I can feel all their gazes on me. Casey slips her hand in mine—her real hand, the one full of warmth. You can forget these things. The press of a hand from someone you love and who loves you. The smell of hair. The bite of tears making their salty path down a cheek.

Jack looks worried. We've come so far. We've spent so much time apart when once we were so close. When things were simple. Three square meals a day, TV privileges on Saturday. Class with Mr. Appleby. Assistant Warden Booth watching over us.

*Parens patriae*, the sign in juvie said. I never found out what that meant. Booth had jabbed a finger at me and said, "When you're in here, *I'm your daddy*."

All that runs in my head, faster than thought.

It's time.

Jack nods and says, "Okay, Shreve." His Adam's apple works up and down painfully in his throat.

Once more, we join ourselves, bridging the space between our bodies. We share sights and sounds. We see from many eyes.

It's nothing to ascend. The sky welcomes us, and we become cocooned in wind.

A star streaking east, burning bright against the morning.

...

The world jars, goes gray and drab. We're moving faster than the speed of sound, and the superheated air around us begins to phosphoresce.

The ether's full of alarm, hissing and spitting. The Conformity knows we've come. Behind us, two great circles follow us, and more behind them. They're joining together; they're marshaling their strength.

Whatever it is, whatever dark thought in God's mind the entity in the east is, it's not above fear. It's not above self-preservation. It's *one thing made from many*, and it wants to survive.

The land flows beneath us like waves on dark seas.

We've come to the end now, the end of the land, the end of all things solid. The laws of physics have changed, and we feel heavier and lighter all at once. Slowing. The color has gone, and now sound is gone too, and heat.

Soon light itself will be gone. But for now it's still here, the sun shining so far away, just a pinprick in the sky. The earth has become featureless, gray. It looks like some three-dimensional topographical rendering: bland, smooth, plastic. Beyond the land, a flat mirror—waveless. The ocean. Only its reflective properties indicate it is liquid. And in the sky, the first Conformity. Static. Still. Crowned in flesh. We float above what was once Maryland.

No sound comes from it because there's no sound anymore, no horrifying stench rippling in miasmatic waves. The avatar of the entity is huge. A small moon hanging in space. It's so large that it bends perception. No longer is the earth *down*. No longer is the sky *up*. *Down* is toward the Conformity, and *up* is away.

*Oh fuck. God. Oh. No.*

I've been so stupid. I can't match this thing. We can't match this thing. I am a mote in this God's eye. I am a single atom against all the fabric of creation.

I thought to swallow this entity whole. I thought I could bend it to myself and make it become *one with us*. There's no making it bend. It will not become part of us.

It's a black hole. It's the death of light.

*We are so completely fucked.*

I can do nothing but separate myself from them. I wrench myself away from Jack, from Ember. I tear my consciousness away from Tap.

And finally from Casey.

*Go!* I scream soundlessly. ***Run! I can't stop it. I was wrong! But I can delay it!***

I get a momentary image of Casey flailing with her ghost-hand, grabbing for me, for anyone. Jack blasting, his fury titanic, making the great surface of the Conformity shudder and ripple.

I am wrong.

I can do nothing as my body falls away.

The world spins, flipping over and over once more.

Everything slows. The earth rises and looms in my vision. The last thing I feel is when my body impacts with the plain, smooth ground. My feet and legs break like glass rods in bright explosions of pain. My pelvis becomes a thousand calcium-sharp shards. My vertebrae pop and explode one by one as my spine hits. My viscera is liquefied, spilling out in wet sprays. My skull hits the earth, flattening into a sack of blood and gore.

Just a small—infinitely small—smudge on the face of the earth.

I am no more.

I am no one.

...

"Hey, boss," Bernard says, snapping his fingers. "We've been waiting for you."

It's the assembly field at the campus. Bernard's there, with Dani standing by him. Everything's covered in snow, and our breath hangs in the air. He's smiling.

"It's happened, finally," Dani says. She's not smiling. But she's not grim either. Just stating the facts, ma'am. "You're dead."

That makes sense. I feel dead. But not dead inside, if that makes sense. I feel like I could eat some pizza, but that's just a thought. The memory of flesh. I can't remember what pizza is. I feel like I'd like to kiss Casey again, or hug Jack, but I can't remember what either of those things would feel like.

"You might be dead, man-child," Bernard says, "but that don't mean you're done." He hums. It's an easy tune to remember.

Here we go, into the wild blue yonder . . .

...

In the ether, above the dark plane.

It's always been about proximity. The nearer you are to something, the easier it is to affect it. It's gravity, really. The power of mass. But my body is gone now, and I have nothing other than love tethering me anymore. I can pass through the silences of stars with a thought. I can see the whole of my history, every life I've ever touched.

295

Incarcerado no more. I am free.

Behind me stretches a long line of dead. They've been loosed from their prisons too. We are all beyond death. We are beyond the Conformity.

I pass into the stasis field amid the great howling rage of the entity. He sees me. He knows I'm coming.

"I sense you passing on those etheric heights," Quincrux said. Says. He's with me here now.

I can feel the entity lash and squirm at my presence. But I am stronger. I have the weight of a million lives behind me.

They called me a punk. They called me a thief. They called me a devil.

That I am. I'm all those things.

■■■

We're born into pain, our constant companion through life.

It's worth mentioning what I cannot remember: the feel of sun on my skin, my mother's breath laced with alcohol, the smell of Booth's aftershave, Jerry's smile. I can't remember what Jack looks like or how Casey kissed when we finally came together. I can't remember the fear I felt for the Witch, the defiance I felt toward Quincrux. I have only the emotions of this moment. I can't remember what it was like to have balls or take a shit, or the taste of candy or the coolness of water on my tongue. I can't remember pain. And maybe that is the final prison: pain. The pain I've held so dear.

All of it's gone.

In the end, it's a titanic contest of wills, the entity and me scratching and grappling with thoughts, bolstered by hate. Buttressed by love. The black thing is old and knows all the wiles of man. But I'm young and, goddamn it, I'm a habitual line-stepper.

I'm the Li'l Devil.

I'll unseat this god from his throne.

Reborn into the world.

## FORTY

## JACK

Screaming. Shreve falls away and there's a moment of panic—I can feel a flutter of his mind—and then he's gone.

Casey's howling now, desolate. Somehow she's remained hanging in the air, and I feel her weight encircling my waist— she's latched on with her ghosthand.

The Conformity shudders and contracts.

There's no sound still, and the massive globe of flesh hangs there, but something is happening inside it, something loosens, and even though I'm no bugfuck I can feel it.

Behind it in the east, the first rosy blush of morning tinges the sky in great radial streaks. The sun shatters on the dark sea into an infinite mosaic of colored light. The sky grows blue, and the earth becomes brown. Green. Gray.

The sound, when it comes, is huge and hard to take in all at once. It's the sound of billions of mouths around the world all exhaling in unison. Almost all the human race.

"Holy shit," the Conformity says. "Do *not* try that at home."

It laughs, and the force of the sound waves pushes me back. It laughs and laughs.

Then the Conformity begins to flatten, becoming oblong. Spreading out and descending. It's losing its cohesion, settling to the ground. Breaking into individuals. Separating back into distinct and perfectly whole human beings. But before it does, the last sound comes, whispering.

"I love you guys," Shreve says through a billion mouths. "I love you."

The words burn me like fire. I can't bear it.

Shreve.

"Later, taters," he says.

And he's gone.

## JACK

It takes me six months to find him, but once the immediate aftermath of the Release is over and people begin taking stock, piecing back together the fabric of civilization, it isn't that hard. After all, his name is Vigor Ferrous Cannon. And I can fly.

The world post-Conformity has righted itself, but it will never be the same. People wake with dreams that are not their own. They remember lives they haven't lived. Millions died. But billions more survived. And they live with an understanding of one another they've never had before.

There's hope.

...

When I dream, I see a yard, the last of the summer sun upon it. A group of boys and girls playing Wiffle ball. A slight kid with a swagger and a mop of dark hair hiding intense, wolfish eyes. He's laughing there in the dream, and everything's all right. We've got money in our pockets. The sun's still up, and there's time—all the time in the world—before our mothers call us to come home.

Weird, I have a mother in the dream.

And a brother.

When I wake it's all gone.

But I remember.

...

He's reading in his room at the foster home in Atlanta when I come in. His eyes get this strange, knowing look that I've seen before so many times.

"Hey, Vig," I say. "I've come a long way to see you. My name's Jack Graves."

I hold out my hand to shake, and Vig cocks his head, looking at my mitt. It's pretty obvious he's counting all the fingers.

"I was friends with your brother," I say lamely. "Best friends."

He looks me up and down, his face still and unmarked by emotion.

"I know," he says, and takes my hand. "I know, Jack."

We walk through the house, hand in hand, until we're outside, in the sun. The grass is green and everything's in bloom now that spring is here.

"Hey, Jack, you wanna play catch?" Vig asks.

"Yeah." He's so small, but still so much like Shreve. "Oh, yeah, I do."

"Okay," he says, beaming. "I've got a killer arm, dude."

Of course he does.

...

Upon the mountain, beneath a brilliant sky strewn with a million stars, the mountain lion pads on silent feet. When it sleeps, it dreams the lives of man.

THE END

## ACKNOWLEDGMENTS

My love and extreme gratitude goes out to my wife, Kendall, who (in addition to helping me proof this book) keeps me on the straight and narrow, relatively sober, fed, in clean clothes, and healthy. And she does so for our children as well (though she doesn't have to worry much about their sobriety). Without her, I would, most likely, be dead, due to my own self-destructive ways. I will, however, pat myself on the back for having the good sense to marry her.

I'd like to thank Andrew Karre, my editor, for his wisdom and guidance. I've never worked with an editor who understands character and story as well as he does and I feel lucky to have been able to work with him on this project. Hopefully there will be many more books in the future.

I could not have hoped for better partners in this endeavor than the team at Lerner Publishing Group—Amy Fitzgerald,

Lindsay Matvick, Katie O'Neel, Laura Rinne, and many more—and I am very thankful for their efforts on my behalf.

As always, huge ups go to my agent, Stacia Decker, for her advice and first draft editing. She, too, is an amazing partner in this bizarre, wonderful business.

Is it weird to thank one of your own characters? Over the last four years, I feel like I learned much about myself through living with Shreve, living *through* him, so much so he no longer felt like one of my creations. He emerged from my psyche, dredged up from the leftover pain of adolescence, grew into his own man, a flawed and wonderful person, and now we are rejoined once more.

## ABOUT THE AUTHOR

John Hornor Jacobs is the author of several novels, including
*The Twelve-Fingered Boy*. He lives with his family in Arkansas.
Visit him online at www.johnhornorjacobs.com.